TAKING
THE FIELD

◆

The Best of
Baseball Fiction

Edited by George Bowering

🐾

Red Deer College Press

"I Guess You Fellows Just Don't Want Me," from *The Last Carousel,* by Nelson Algren. Copyright © 1973 by Nelson Algren. Reprinted by permission of Donadio and Ashworth.

"October 1, 1961," by George Bowering. Copyright © 1990 by George Bowering.

"The Hector Quesadilla Story," from *Greasy Lake & Other Stories,* by T. Coraghessan Boyle. Copyright © 1984 by T. Coraghessan Boyle. Originally published in *The Paris Review.* Reprinted by permission of Viking Penguin, a division of Penguin Books USA, Inc.

"A Cap for Steve," from *Morley Callaghan's Stories,* by Morley Callaghan. Copyright © 1959 by Morley Callaghan. Reprinted by permission of Macmillan of Canada, A Division of Canada Publishing Corporation.

"The Greatest Slump of all Time," from *The Greatest Slump of All Time,* by David Carkeet. Copyright © 1984 by David Carkeet. Reprinted by permission of Harper & Row, Publishers, Inc.

"The Answer," by Fielding Dawson. Copyright © 1985 by Fielding Dawson. Reprinted from *Virginia Dare* with the permission of Black Sparrow Press.

"The Pitcher," from *Finding a Girl in America,* by Andre Dubus. Copyright © 1980 by Andre Dubus. Reprinted by permission of David R. Godine, Publisher.

"Losers," from *My Career with the Leafs,* by Brian Fawcett. Copyright © 1983 by Brian Fawcett. Reprinted by permission of Talon Books Ltd.

"August Nights," from *August Nights,* by Hugh Hood. Reprinted by permission; Copyright © 1985 by Stoddart Publishing Co. Limited.

"The Sand-Lot Umpire," by Masuji Ibuse, translated by Ted Goossen. Translation copyright © 1987 by Ted Goossen. Reprinted by permission of *Descant Magazine.*

"Ronnie on the Mound," by Jack Kerouac. Copyright © Jack Kerouac 1948. Reprinted by permission of Sterling Lord Literistic, Inc.

"The Thrill of the Grass," from *The Thrill of the Grass,* by W.P. Kinsella. Copyright © 1984 by W.P. Kinsella. Reprinted by permission of Penguin Books Canada Limited.

"Ball Two," from *Short Season and Other Stories,* by Jerry Klinkowitz. Copyright © 1988 by Jerry Klinkowitz. Reprinted by permission of The Johns Hopkins University Press, Baltimore/London, 1988, pp. 29–34.

"Alibi Ike," from *The Ring Lardner Reader,* by Ring Lardner, reprinted by permission of Charles Scribner's Sons, an imprint of Macmillan Publishing Company. Copyright © 1915 by The Curtis Publishing Company; renewal copyright © 1943 by Ellis A. Lardner.

"The Centerfielder," from *Stories,* by Sergio Ramírez. English language translation copyright © 1986 by Readers International Inc.

"Playing Ball on Hampstead Heath," from *St. Urbain's Horseman,* by Mordecai Richler. Copyright © 1971 by Mordecai Richler. Used by permission of the Canadian Publishers, McClelland & Stewart, Toronto.

The Publishers
Red Deer College Press
56 Avenue & 32 Street Box 5005
Red Deer Alberta Canada T4N 5H5

Credits
Cover photograph courtesy of UPI/Bettmann Newsphotos.
Cover Design by Jim Brennan.
Text Design by Robert MacDonald, MediaClones Inc.,
Banff Alberta and Toronto Ontario.
Typeset by Boldface Technologies Inc., Edmonton Alberta.
Printed and bound in Canada by Gagné Printing for
Red Deer College Press.

Acknowledgements
The publishers acknowledge the financial assistance of the Alberta
Foundation for the Literary Arts, Alberta Culture and
Multiculturalism, the Canada Council, and Radio 7 CKRD.

Canadian Cataloguing in Publication Data
Main entry under title:
Taking the field
ISBN 0-88995-054-7
1. Baseball stories. I. Bowering, George, 1935-
PN6120.95.B33T3   808.83'9355   C90-091156-5

Contents

Introduction George Bowering

Ring Lardner **Alibi Ike** / 11
Damon Runyon **Baseball Hattie** / 37
James Thurber **The Tree on the Diamond** / 55
Morley Callaghan **A Cap for Steve** / 67
Masuji Ibuse **The Sand-Lot Umpire** / 83
Nelson Algren **I Guess You Fellows Just Don't Want Me** / 99
Jack Kerouac **Ronnie on the Mound** / 107
Richard Wilbur **A Game of Catch** / 117
Sergio Ramírez **The Centerfielder** / 123
Mordecai Richler **Playing Ball on Hampstead Heath** / 131
Andre Dubus **The Pitcher** / 147
David Carkeet **The Greatest Slump of all Time** / 169
Brian Fawcett **Losers** / 193
W.P. Kinsella **The Thrill of the Grass** / 205
T. Coraghessan Boyle **The Hector Quesadilla Story** / 217
Hugh Hood **August Nights** / 235
Fielding Dawson **The Answer** / 257
George Bowering **October 1, 1961** / 269
Jerry Klinkowitz **Ball Two** / 289

Introduction

Have you ever heard hockey fans and basketball fans and auto-racing fans complain that as a game, baseball is too slow? You bet. But have you ever heard a writer complain that baseball is too slow? Not a chance. I once heard a hockey reporter say it, but he isnt really a *writer*. I mean a *writer*.

A large proportion of the writers I know play some sort of baseball, usually softball. Not that stupid desecration called slo-pitch. Maybe medium-pitch. Maybe medium-fast. They carry their personal stats in their heads, and they get a new piece of equipment every season—a batting glove this year, say.

Baseball is slow, sometimes. It is slow when it should be, and suddenly very fast when it should be. It is like thinking and writing. If you are a writer you will recognize and value both the slow and the fast. How long did it take you to write that story, someone will ask, and you will say all your life. But remember how the quick sentences slid out and settled into place. Remember how still Carl Yastrzemski stood at the plate while the pitcher fooled around, and then how swiftly that bat came around, and how slowly he was allowed to run around the bases because the ball was arcing high into the right field stands.

It is not absolutely necessarily true that writers like baseball. For all I know, Emily Dickinson didnt like baseball. It is not even necessarily true that male writers like baseball. But if you look around the ball parks and the bookstores you will see that male writers have more to say about baseball than they do about other sports. Boxing is probably in second place. It appeals to battlers such as Norman Mailer and Joyce Carol Oates.

Over the past few years there have been lots of explanations offered for the connection between writing and the diamond—explanations earnest, fanciful and semiotic. There's your childhood in the gloaming, decades ago in the stubble grass of South Dakota. There's Tim Raines stepping into the batter's box, top of the first, and wiping out the rear chalk line someone has just drawn a moment before. There's that definable odor of fried onions coming from the hotdog in the hand of the kid in front of you. I havent hit on anything exactly right yet, have I?

One warm February day in Puerto Limon, Costa Rica, 1978, I wandered into old concrete Big Boy Stadium, and found myself a wooden seat high up behind home plate. There was an old black guy hitting fungoes to four skinny young black guys in center field. I figured it must be a kind of pre-season rookie camp. Here's what's funny: I was not surprised to recognize the old guy hitting the fungoes, as well as the other old guy loafing on a seat right behind the chicken wire. I remembered them from the ball park in Oliver, B.C., Canada, where I sold Orange Crush and retrieved foul balls for dimes, and later climbed up on the roof to take over my Dad's job as official scorer.

There I was, sitting over a ball game, pen in my hand.

Now a lot of grown-up fellows sit over a page, a ball game in their heads.

Baseball is a funny game. You've heard that. It can be unfunny, too. Ask Red Sox fans about Bill Buckner's grounder. Sometimes baseball can resemble the stupidity and hurt of your life. Sometimes it is 8–0 in the fifth inning, and it's just a June game between San Diego and Atlanta, and you wonder why you're not upstairs grouting the bathtub.

But look. In baseball we dont talk about the long bomb and the safety blitz and sudden death. What do we want to do in the ball game? We want to get home. We have the only big-deal game I know in which the ball is put into play by the defense. Unlike football, soccer, hockey and basketball, our game is not ruled by lines in space or ticks in time. It is not existential. It is a dream come true. If the dream perishes (check out those Red Sox fans) there's another game tomorrow. If it is October, there is spring training after a few months of early darkness and Cavs' games.

When the 63-year-old painter David Siqueiros was sprung from prison so that he could finish the murals in Maximilian's palace in Mexico City in time for the World Cup tournament, the government wanted to release him at noon. There was a big crowd of supporters waiting to take him away in triumph. But Siqueiros played first base for a ball team inside the walls, and he made them all cool their heels till the afternoon's game was over.

Playing the game is the best experience, even if you are sixty. Sitting in the grandstand in Detroit is an activity (yes, activity) to be cherished. Reading baseball fiction is a very good thing to do, during the season or off-season. The present collection of baseball stories by nineteen writers should provide some game situations for your imagination, whether you are enjoying a home stand or enduring a road trip.

George Bowering
Vancouver, British Columbia

ALIBI IKE
Ring Lardner

His right name was Frank X. Farrell, and I guess the X stood for "Excuse me." Because he never pulled a play, good or bad, on or off the field, without apologizin' for it.

"Alibi Ike" was the name Carey wished on him the first day he reported down South. O' course we all cut out the "Alibi" part of it right away for the fear he would overhear it and bust somebody. But we called him "Ike" right to his face and the rest of it was understood by everybody on the club except Ike himself.

He ast me one time, he says:

"What do you all call me Ike for? I ain't no Yid."

"Carey give you the name," I says. "It's his nickname for everybody he takes a likin' to."

"He mustn't have only a few friends then," says Ike. "I never heard him say 'Ike' to nobody else."

But I was goin' to tell you about Carey namin' him. We'd been workin' out two weeks and the pitchers was showin' somethin' when this bird joined us. His first day out he stood up there so good and took such a reef at the old pill that he had everyone lookin'. Then him and Carey was together in left field, catchin' fungoes, and it was after we was through for the day that Carey told me about him.

"What do you think of Alibi Ike?" ast Carey.

"Who's that?" I says.

"This here Farrell in the outfield," says Carey.

"He looks like he could hit," I says.

"Yes," says Carey, "but he can't hit near as good as he can apologize."

Then Carey went on to tell me what Ike had been pullin' out there. He'd dropped the first fly ball that was hit to him and told Carey his glove wasn't broke in good yet, and Carey says the glove could easy of been Kid Gleason's gran'father. He made a whale of a catch out o' the next one and Carey says "Nice work!" or somethin' like that, but Ike says he could of caught the ball with his back turned only he slipped when he started after it and, besides that, the air currents fooled him.

"I thought you done well to get to the ball," says Carey.

"I ought to been settin' under it," says Ike.

"What did you hit last year?" Carey ast him.

"I had malaria most o' the season," says Ike. "I wound up with .356."

"Where would I have to go to get malaria?" says Carey, but Ike didn't wise up.

I and Carey and him set at the same table together for supper. It took him half an hour longer'n us to eat because he had to excuse himself every time he lifted his fork.

"Doctor told me I needed starch," he'd say, and then toss a shovelful o' potatoes into him. Or, "They ain't much meat on one o' these chops," he'd tell us, and grab another one. Or he'd say: "Nothin' like onions for a cold," and then he'd dip into the perfumery.

"Better try that apple sauce," says Carey. "It'll help your malaria."

"Whose malaria?" says Ike. He'd forgot already why he didn't only hit .356 last year.

I and Carey begin to lead him on.

"Whereabouts did you say your home was?" I ast him.

"I live with my folks," he says. "We live in Kansas City—not right down in the business part—outside a ways."

"How's that come?" says Carey. "I should think you'd get rooms in the post office."

But Ike was too busy curin' his cold to get that one.

"Are you married?" I ast him.

"No," he says. "I never run around much with girls, except to shows onct in a wile and parties and dances and roller skatin'."

"Never take 'em to the prize fights, eh?" says Carey.

"We don't have no real good bouts," says Ike. "Just bush stuff. And I never figured a boxin' match was a place for the ladies."

Well, after supper he pulled a cigar out and lit it. I was just goin' to ask him what he done it for, but he beat me to it.

"Kind o' rests a man to smoke after a good work-out," he says. "Kind o' settles a man's supper, too."

"Looks like a pretty good cigar," says Carey.

"Yes," says Ike. "A friend o' mine give it to me—a fella in Kansas City that runs a billiard room."

"Do you play billiards?" I ast him.

"I used to play a fair game," he says. "I'm all out o' practice now—can't hardly make a shot."

We coaxed him into a four-handed battle, him and Carey against Jack Mack and I. Say, he couldn't play billiards as good as Willie Hoppe; not quite. But to hear him tell it, he didn't make a good shot all evenin'. I'd leave him an awful-lookin' layout and he'd gather 'em up in one try and then run a couple o' hundred, and between every carom he'd say he'd put too much stuff on the ball, or the English didn't take, or the table wasn't true, or his stick was crooked, or somethin'. And all the time he had the balls actin' like they was Dutch soldiers and him Kaiser William. We started out to play fifty points, but we had to make it a thousand so as I and Jack and Carey could try the table.

The four of us set round the lobby a wile after we was through playin', and when it got along toward bedtime Carey whispered to me and says:

"Ike'd like to go to bed, but he can't think up no excuse."

Carey hadn't hardly finished whisperin' when Ike got up and pulled it:

"Well, good night, boys," he says. "I ain't sleepy, but I got some gravel in my shoes and it's killin' my feet."

We knowed he hadn't never left the hotel since we'd came in from the grounds and changed our clo'es. So Carey says:

"I should think they'd take them gravel pits out o' the billiard room."

But Ike was already on his way to the elevator, limpin'.

"He's got the world beat," says Carey to Jack and I. "I've knew lots o' guys that had an alibi for every mistake they made; I've heard pitchers say that the ball slipped when somebody cracked one off'n 'em; I've heard infielders complain of a sore arm after heavin' one into the stand, and I've saw outfielders tooken sick with a dizzy spell when they've misjudged a fly ball. But this baby can't even go to bed without apologizin', and I bet he excuses himself to the razor when he gets ready to shave."

"And at that," says Jack, "he's goin' to make us a good man."

"Yes," says Carey, "unless rheumatism keeps his battin' average down to .400."

Well, sir, Ike kept whalin' away at the ball all through the trip till everybody knowed he'd won a job. Cap had him in there regular the last few exhibition games and told the newspaper boys a week before the season opened that he was goin' to start him in Kane's place.

"You're there, kid," says Carey to Ike, the night Cap made the 'nnouncement. "They ain't many boys that wins a big league berth their third year out."

"I'd of been up here a year ago," says Ike, "only I was bent over all season with lumbago."

◆ II ◆

It rained down in Cincinnati one day and somebody organized a little game o' cards. They was shy two men to make six and ast I and Carey to play.

"I'm with you if you get Ike and make it seven-handed," says Carey.

So they got a hold of Ike and we went up to Smitty's room.

"I pretty near forgot how many you deal," says Ike. "It's been a long wile since I played."

I and Carey give each other the wink, and sure enough, he was just as ig'orant about poker as billiards. About the second hand, the pot was opened two or three ahead of him, and they was three in when it come his turn. It cost a buck, and he throwed in two.

"It's raised, boys," somebody says.

"Gosh, that's right, I did raise it," says Ike.

"Take out a buck if you didn't mean to tilt her," says Carey.

"No," says Ike, "I'll leave it go."

Well, it was raised back at him and then he made another mistake and raised again. They was only three left in when the draw come. Smitty'd opened with a pair o' kings and he didn't help 'em. Ike stood pat. The guy that'd raised him back was flushin' and he didn't fill. So Smitty checked and Ike bet and didn't get no call. He tossed his hand away, but I grabbed it and give it a look. He had king, queen, jack and two tens. Alibi Ike he must have seen me peekin', for he leaned over and whispered to me.

"I overlooked my hand," he says. "I thought all the wile it was a straight."

"Yes," I says, "that's why you raised twice by mistake."

They was another pot that he come into with tens and fours. It was tilted a couple o' times and two o' the strong fellas drawed ahead of Ike. They each drawed one. So Ike throwed away his little pair and come out with four tens. And they was four treys against him. Carey'd looked at Ike's discards and then he says:

"This lucky bum busted two pair."

"No, no, I didn't," says Ike.

"Yes, yes, you did," says Carey, and showed us the two fours.

"What do you know about that?" says Ike. "I'd of swore one was a five spot."

Well, we hadn't had no pay day yet, and after a wile everybody except Ike was goin' shy. I could see him gettin' restless and I was wonderin' how he'd make the get-away. He tried two or three times. "I got to buy some collars before supper," he says.

"No hurry," says Smitty. "The stores here keeps open all night in April."

After a minute he opened up again.

"My uncle out in Nebraska ain't expected to live," he says. "I ought to send a telegram."

"Would that save him?" says Carey.

"No, it sure wouldn't," says Ike, "but I ought to leave my old man know where I'm at."

"When did you hear about your uncle?" says Carey.

"Just this mornin'," says Ike.

"Who told you?" ast Carey.

"I got a wire from my old man," says Ike.

"Well," says Carey, "your old man knows you're still here yet this afternoon if you was here this mornin'. Trains leavin' Cincinnati in the middle o' the day don't carry no ball clubs."

"Yes," says Ike, "that's true. But he don't know where I'm goin' to be next week."

"Ain't he got no schedule?" ast Carey.

"I sent him one openin' day," says Ike, "but it takes mail a long time to get to Idaho."

"I thought your old man lived in Kansas City," says Carey.

"He does when he's home," says Ike.

"But now," says Carey, "I s'pose he's went to Idaho so as he can be near your sick uncle in Nebraska."

"He's visitin' my other uncle in Idaho."

"Then how does he keep posted about your sick uncle?" ast Carey.

"He don't," says Ike. "He don't even know my other uncle's sick. That's why I ought to wire and tell him."

"Good night!" says Carey.

"What town in Idaho is your old man at?" I says.

Ike thought it over.

"No town at all," he says. "But he's near a town."

"Near what town?" I says.

"Yuma," says Ike.

Well, by this time he'd lost two or three pots and he was desperate. We was playin' just as fast as we could, because we seen we couldn't hold him much longer. But he was tryin' so hard to frame an escape that he couldn't pay no attention to the cards, and it looked like we'd get his whole pile away from him if we could make him stick.

The telephone saved him. The minute it begun to ring, five of us jumped for it. But Ike was there first.

"Yes," he says, answerin' it. "This is him. I'll come right down."

And he slammed up the receiver and beat it out o' the door without even sayin' good-by.

"Smitty'd ought to locked the door," says Carey.

"What did he win?" ast Carey.

We figured it up—sixty-odd bucks.

"And the next time we ask him to play," says Carey, "his fingers will be so stiff he can't hold the cards."

Well, we set round a wile talkin' it over, and pretty soon the telephone rung again. Smitty answered it. It was a friend of his'n from Hamilton and he wanted to know why Smitty didn't hurry down. He was the one that had called before and Ike had told him he was Smitty.

"Ike'd ought to split with Smitty's friend," says Carey.

"No," I says, "he'll need all he won. It costs money to buy collars and to send telegrams from Cincinnati to your old man in Texas and keep him posted on the health o' your uncle in Cedar Rapids, D.C."

◆ III ◆

And you ought to heard him out there on that field! They wasn't a day when he didn't pull six or seven, and it didn't make no difference whether he was goin' good or bad. If he popped up in the pinch he should of made a base hit and the reason he didn't was so-and-so. And if he cracked one for three bases he ought to had a home run, only the ball wasn't lively, or the wind brought it back, or he tripped on a lump o' dirt, roundin' first base.

They was one afternoon in New York when he beat all records. Big Marquard was workin' against us and he was good.

In the first innin' Ike hit one clear over that right field stand, but it was a few feet foul. Then he got another foul and then the count come to two and two. Then Rube slipped one acrost on him and he was called out.

"What do you know about that!" he says afterward on the bench. "I lost count. I thought it was three and one, and I took a strike."

"You took a strike all right," says Carey. "Even the umps knowed it was a strike."

"Yes," says Ike, "but you can bet I wouldn't of took it if I'd knew it was the third one. The score board had it wrong."

"That score board ain't for you to look at," says Cap.

"It's for you to hit that old pill against."

"Well," says Ike, "I could of hit that one over the score board if I'd knew it was the third."

"Was it a good ball?" I says.

"Well, no, it wasn't," says Ike. "It was inside."

"How far inside?" says Carey.

"Oh, two or three inches or half a foot," says Ike.

"I guess you wouldn't of threatened the score board with it then," says Cap.

"I'd of pulled it down the right foul line if I hadn't thought he'd call it a ball," says Ike.

Well, in New York's part o' the innin' Doyle cracked one and Ike run back a mile and a half and caught it with one hand. We was all sayin' what a whale of a play it was, but he had to apologize just the same as for gettin' struck out.

"That stand's so high," he says, "that a man don't never see a ball till it's right on top o' you."

"Didn't you see that one?" ast Cap.

"Not at first," says Ike; "not till it raised up above the roof o' the stand."

"Then why did you start back as soon as the ball was hit?" says Cap.

"I knowed by the sound that he'd got a good hold of it," says Ike.

"Yes," says Cap, "but how'd you know what direction to run in?"

"Doyle usually hits 'em that way, the way I run," says Ike.

"Why don't you play blindfolded?" says Carey.

"Might as well, with that big high stand to bother a man," says Ike. "If I could of saw the ball all the time I'd of got it in my hip pocket."

Along in the fifth we was one run to the bad and Ike got on with one out. On the first ball throwed to Smitty, Ike went down. The ball was outside and Meyers throwed Ike out by ten feet.

You could see Ike's lips movin' all the way to the bench and when he got there he had his piece learned.

"Why didn't he swing?" he says.

"Why didn't you wait for his sign?" says Cap.

"He give me his sign," says Ike.

"What is his sign with you?" says Cap.

"Pickin' up some dirt with his right hand," says Ike.

"Well, I didn't see him do it," Cap says.

"He done it all right," says Ike.

Well, Smitty went out and they wasn't no more argument till they come in for the next innin'. Then Cap opened it up.

"You fellas better get your signs straight," he says.

"Do you mean me?" says Smitty.

"Yes," Cap says. "What's your sign with Ike?"

"Slidin' my left hand up to the end o' the bat and back," says Smitty.

"Do you hear that, Ike?" ast Cap.

"What of it?" says Ike.

"You says his sign was pickin' up dirt and he says it's slidin' his hand. Which is right?"

"I'm right," says Smitty. "But if you're arguin' about him goin' last innin', I didn't give him no sign."

"You pulled your cap down with your right hand, didn't you?" ast Ike.

"Well, s'pose I did," says Smitty. "That don't mean nothin'. I never told you to take that for a sign, did I?"

"I thought maybe you meant to tell me and forgot," says Ike.

They couldn't none of us answer that and they wouldn't of been no more said if Ike had of shut up. But wile we was settin' there Carey got on with two out and stole second clean.

"There!" says Ike. "That's what I was tryin' to do and I'd of got away with it if Smitty'd swang and bothered the Indian."

"Oh!" says Smitty. "You was tryin' to steal then, was you? I thought you claimed I give you the hit and run."

"I didn't claim no such a thing," says Ike. "I thought maybe you might of gave me a sign, but I was goin' anyway because I thought I had a good start."

Cap prob'ly would of hit him with a bat, only just about that time Doyle booted one on Hayes and Carey come acrost with the run that tied.

Well, we go into the ninth finally, one and one, and Marquard walks McDonald with nobody out.

"Lay it down," says Cap to Ike.

And Ike goes up there with orders to bunt and cracks the first ball into that right-field stand! It was fair this time, and we're two ahead, but I didn't think about that at the time. I was too busy watchin' Cap's face. First he turned pale and then he got red as fire and then he got blue and purple, and finally he just laid back and busted out laughin'. So we wasn't afraid to laugh ourselfs when we seen him doin' it, and when Ike come in everybody on the bench was in hysterics.

But instead o' takin' advantage, Ike had to try and excuse himself. His play was to shut up and he didn't know how to make it.

"Well," he says, "if I hadn't hit quite so quick at that one I bet it'd of cleared the center-field fence."

Cap stopped laughin'.

"It'll cost you plain fifty," he says.

"What for?" says Ike.

"When I say 'bunt' I mean 'bunt,'" says Cap.

"You didn't say 'bunt,'" says Ike.

"I says 'Lay it down,'" says Cap. "If that don't mean 'bunt,' what does it mean?"

"'Lay it down' means 'bunt' all right," says Ike, "but I understood you to say 'Lay on it.'"

"All right," says Cap, "and the little misunderstandin' will cost you fifty."

Ike didn't say nothin' for a few minutes. Then he had another bright idear.

"I was just kiddin' about misunderstandin' you," he says. "I knowed you wanted me to bunt."

"Well, then, why didn't you bunt?" ast Cap.

"I was goin' to on the next ball," says Ike. "But I thought if I took a good wallop I'd have 'em all fooled. So I walloped at the first one to fool 'em, and I didn't have no intention o' hittin' it."

"You tried to miss it, did you?" says Cap.

"Yes," says Ike.

"How'd you happen to hit it?" ast Cap.

"Well," Ike says, "I was lookin' for him to throw me a fast one and I was goin' to swing under it. But he come with a hook and I met it right square where I was swingin' to go under the fast one."

"Great!" says Cap. "Boys," he says, "Ike's learned how to hit Marquard's curve. Pretend a fast one's comin' and then try to miss it. It's a good thing to know and Ike'd ought to be willin' to pay for the lesson. So I'm goin' to make it a hundred instead o' fifty."

The game wound up 3 to 1. The fine didn't go, because Ike hit like a wild man all through that trip and we made pretty near a clean-up. The night we went to Philly I got him cornered in the car and I says to him:

"Forget them alibis for a wile and tell me somethin'. What'd you do that for, swing that time against Marquard when you was told to bunt?"

"I'll tell you," he says. "That ball he throwed me looked just like the one I struck out on in the first innin' and I wanted to show Cap what I could of done to that other one if I'd knew it was the third strike."

"But," I says, "the one you struck out on in the first innin' was a fast ball."

"So was the one I cracked in the ninth," says Ike.

◆ IV ◆

You've saw Cap's wife, o' course. Well, her sister's about twict as good-lookin' as her, and that's goin' some.

Cap took his missus down to St. Louis the second trip and the other one come down from St. Joe to visit her. Her name is Dolly, and some doll is right.

Well, Cap was goin' to take the two sisters to a show and he wanted a beau for Dolly. He left it to her and she picked Ike. He'd hit three on the nose that afternoon—off'n Sallee, too.

They fell for each other that first evenin'. Cap told us how it come off. She begin flatterin' Ike for the star game he'd played and o' course he begin excusin' himself for not doin' better. So she thought he was modest and it went strong with her. And she believed everything he said and that made her solid with him—that and her make-up. They was together every mornin' and evenin' for the five days we was there. In the afternoons Ike played the grandest ball you ever see, hittin' and runnin' the bases like a fool and catchin' everything that stayed in the park.

I told Cap, I says: "You'd ought to keep the doll with us and he'd make Cobb's figures look sick."

But Dolly had to go back to St. Joe and we come home for a long serious.

Well, for the next three weeks Ike had a letter to read every day and he'd set in the clubhouse readin' it till mornin' practice was half over. Cap didn't say nothin' to him, because he was goin' so good. But I and Carey wasted a lot of our time tryin' to get him to own up who the letters was from. Fine chanct!

"What are you readin'?" Carey'd say. "A bill?"

"No," Ike'd say, "not exactly a bill. It's a letter from a fella I used to go to school with."

"High school or college?" I'd ask him.

"College," he'd say.

"What college?" I'd say.

Then he'd stall a wile and then he'd say:

"I didn't go to the college myself, but my friend went there."

"How did it happen you didn't go?" Carey'd ask him.

"Well," he'd say, "they wasn't no colleges near where I lived."

"Didn't you live in Kansas City?" I'd say to him.

One time he'd say he did and another time he didn't. One time he says he lived in Michigan.

"Where at?" says Carey.

"Near Detroit," he says.

"Well," I says, "Detroit's near Ann Arbor and that's where they got the university."

"Yes," says Ike, "they got it there now, but they didn't have it there then."

"I come pretty near goin' to Syracuse," I says, "only they wasn't no railroads runnin' through there in them days."

"Where'd this friend o' yours go to college?" says Carey.

"I forget now," says Ike.

"Was it Carlisle?" ast Carey.

"No," Ike says, "his folks wasn't very well off."

"That's what barred me from Smith," I says.

"I was goin' to tackle Cornell's," says Carey, "but the doctor told me I'd have hay fever if I didn't stay up North."

"Your friend writes long letters," I says.

"Yes," says Ike; "he's tellin' me about a ball player."

"Where does he play?" ast Carey.

"Down in the Texas League—Fort Wayne," says Ike.

"It looks like a girl's writin'," Carey says.

"A girl wrote it," says Ike. "That's my friend's sister writin' for him."

"Didn't they teach writin' at this here college where he went?" says Carey.

"Sure," Ike says, "they taught writin', but he got his hand cut off in a railroad wreck."

"How long ago?" I says.

"Right afer he got out o' college," says Ike.

"Well," I says, "I should think he'd of learned to write with his left hand by this time."

"It's his left hand that was cut off," says Ike; "and he was left-handed."

"You get a letter every day," says Carey. "They're all the same writin'. Is he tellin' you about a different ball player every time he writes?"

"No," says Ike. "It's the same ball player. He just tells me what he does every day."

"From the size o' the letters, they don't play nothin' but double-headers down there," says Carey.

We figured that Ike spent most of his evenin's answerin' the letters from his "friend's sister," so we kept tryin' to date him up for shows and parties to see how he'd duck out of 'em. He was bugs over spaghetti, so we told him one day that they was goin' to be a big feed of it over to Joe's that night and he was invited.

"How long'll it last?" he says.

"Well," we says, "we're goin' right over there after the game and stay till they close up."

"I can't go," he says, "unless they leave me come home at eight bells."

"Nothin' doin'," says Carey. "Joe'd get sore."

"I can't go then," says Ike.

"Why not?" I ast him.

"Well," he says, "my landlady locks up the house at eight and I left my key home."

"You can come and stay with me," says Carey.

"No," he says, "I can't sleep in a strange bed."

"How do you get along when we're on the road?" says I.

"I don't never sleep the first night anywheres," he says. "After that I'm all right."

"You'll have time to chase home and get your key right after the game," I told him.

"The key ain't home," says Ike. "I lent it to one o' the other fellas and he's went out o' town and took it with him."

"Couldn't you borry another key off'n the landlady?" Carey ast him.

"No," he says, "that's the only one they is."

Well, the day before we started East again, Ike come into the clubhouse all smiles.

"Your birthday?" I ast him.

"No," he says.

"What do you feel so good about?" I says.

"Got a letter from my old man," he says. "My uncle's goin' to get well."

"Is that the one in Nebraska?" says I.

"Not right in Nebraska," says Ike. "Near there."

But afterwards we got the right dope from Cap. Dolly'd blew in from Missouri and was goin' to make the trip with her sister.

◆ V ◆

Well, I want to alibi Carey and I for what come off in Boston. If we'd of had any idear what we was doin', we'd never did it. They wasn't nobody outside o' maybe Ike and the dame that felt worse over it than I and Carey.

The first two days we didn't see nothin' of Ike and her except out to the park. The rest o' the time they was sight-seein' over to Cambridge and down to Revere and out to Brook-a-line and all the other places where the rubes go.

But when we come into the beanery after the third game Cap's wife called us over.

"If you want to see somethin' pretty," she says, "look at the third finger on Sis's left hand."

Well, o' course we knowed before we looked that it wasn't goin' to be no hangnail. Nobody was su'prised when Dolly blew into the dinin' room with it—a rock that Ike'd bought off'n Diamond Joe the first trip to New York. Only o' course it'd been set into a lady's-size ring instead o' the automobile tire he'd been wearin'.

Cap and his missus and Ike and Dolly ett supper together, only Ike didn't eat nothin', but just set there blushin' and spillin' things on the tablecloth. I heard him excusin' himself for not havin' no appetite. He says he couldn't never eat when he was clost to the ocean. He'd forgot about them sixty-five oysters he destroyed the first night o' the trip before.

He was goin' to take her to a show, so after supper he went upstairs to change his collar. She had to doll up, too, and o' course Ike was through long before her.

If you remember the hotel in Boston, they's a little parlor where the piano's at and then they's another little parlor openin' off o' that. Well, when Ike come down Smitty was playin' a few chords and I and Carey was harmonizin'. We seen Ike go up to the desk to leave his key and we called him in. He tried to duck away, but we wouldn't stand for it.

We ast him what he was all duded up for and he says he was goin' to the theayter.

"Goin' alone?" says Carey.

"No," he says, "a friend o' mine's goin' with me."

"What do you say if we go along?" says Carey.

"I ain't only got two tickets," he says.

"Well," says Carey, "we can go down there with you and buy our own seats; maybe we can all get together."

"No," says Ike. "They ain't no more seats. They're all sold out."

"We can buy some off'n the scalpers," says Carey.

"I wouldn't if I was you," says Ike. "They say the show's rotten."

"What are you goin' for, then?" I ast.

"I didn't hear about it bein' rotten till I got the tickets," he says.

"Well," I says, "if you don't want to go I'll buy the tickets from you."

"No," says Ike, "I wouldn't want to cheat you. I'm stung and I'll just have to stand for it."

"What are you goin' to do with the girl, leave her here at the hotel?" I says.

"What girl?" says Ike.

"The girl you ett supper with," I says.

"Oh," he says, "we just happened to go into the dinin' room together, that's all. Cap wanted I should set down with 'em."

"I noticed," says Carey, "that she happened to be wearin' that rock you bought off'n Diamond Joe."

"Yes," says Ike, "I lent it to her for a wile."

"Did you lend her the new ring that goes with it?" I says.

"She had that already," says Ike. "She lost the set out of it."

"I wouldn't trust no strange girl with a rock o' mine," says Carey.

"Oh, I guess she's all right," Ike says. "Besides, I was tired o' the stone. When a girl asks you for somethin', what are you goin' to do?"

He started out toward the desk, but we flagged him.

"Wait a minute!" Carey says. "I got a bet with Sam here, and it's up to you to settle it."

"Well," says Ike, "make it snappy. My friend'll be here any minute."

"I bet," says Carey, "that you and that girl was engaged to be married."

"Nothin' to it," says Ike.

"Now look here," says Carey, "this is goin' to cost me real money if I lose. Cut out the alibi stuff and give it to us straight. Cap's wife just as good as told us you was roped."

Ike blushed like a kid.

"Well, boys," he says, "I may as well own up. You win, Carey."

"Yatta boy!" says Carey. "Congratulations!"

"You got a swell girl, Ike," I says.

"She's a peach," says Smitty.

"Well, I guess she's O.K.," says Ike. "I don't know much about girls."

"Didn't you never run round with 'em?" I says.

"Oh, yes, plenty of 'em," says Ike. "But I never seen none I'd fall for."

"That is, till you seen this one," says Carey.

"Well," says Ike, "this one's O.K., but I wasn't thinkin' about gettin' married yet a wile."

"Who done the askin'—her?" says Carey.

"Oh, no," says Ike, "but sometimes a man don't know what he's gettin' into. Take a good-lookin' girl, and a man gen'ally almost always does about what she wants him to."

"They couldn't no girl lasso me unless I wanted to be lassoed," says Smitty.

"Oh, I don't know," says Ike. "When a fella gets to feelin' sorry for one of 'em it's all off."

Well, we left him go after shakin' hands all round. But he didn't take Dolly to no show that night. Some time wile we was talkin' she'd come into that other parlor and she'd stood there and heard us. I don't know how much she heard. But it was enough. Dolly and

Cap's missus took the midnight train for New York. And from there Cap's wife sent her on her way back to Missouri.

She'd left the ring and a note for Ike with the clerk. But we didn't ask Ike if the note was from his friend in Fort Wayne, Texas.

◆ VI ◆

When we'd came to Boston Ike was hittin' plain .397. When we got back home he'd fell off to pretty near nothin'. He hadn't drove one out o' the infield in any o' them other Eastern parks, and he didn't even give no excuse for it.

To show you how bad he was, he struck out three times in Brooklyn one day and never opened his trap when Cap ast him what was the matter. Before, if he'd whiffed oncet in a game he'd of wrote a book tellin' why.

Well, we dropped from first place to fifth in four weeks and we was still goin' down. I and Carey was about the only ones in the club that spoke to each other, and all as we did was remind ourself o' what a boner we'd pulled.

"It's goin' to beat us out o' the big money," says Carey.

"Yes," I says, "I don't want to knock my own ball club, but it looks like a one-man team, and when that one man's dauber's down we couldn't trim our whiskers."

"We ought to knew better," says Carey.

"Yes," I says, "but why should a man pull an alibi for bein' engaged to such a bearcat as she was?"

"He shouldn't," says Carey. "But I and you knowed he would or we'd never started talkin' to him about it. He wasn't no more ashamed o' the girl than I am of a regular base hit. But he just can't come clean on no subjec'."

Cap had the whole story, and I and Carey was as pop'lar with him as an umpire.

"What do you want me to do, Cap?" Carey'd say to him before goin' up to hit.

"Use your own judgment," Cap'd tell him. "We want to lose another game."

But finally, one night in Pittsburgh, Cap had a letter from his missus and he come to us with it.

"You fellas," he says, "is the ones that put us on the bum, and if you're sorry I think they's a chancet for you to make good. The old lady's out to St. Joe and she's been tryin' her hardest to fix things up. She's explained that Ike don't mean nothin' with his talk; I've wrote and explained that to Dolly, too. But the old lady says that Dolly says that she can't believe it. But Dolly's still stuck on this baby, and she's pinin' away just the same as Ike. And the old lady says she thinks if you two fellas would write to the girl and explain how you was always kiddin' with Ike and leadin' him on, and how the ball club was all shot to pieces since Ike quit hittin', and how he acted like he was goin' to kill himself, and this and that, she'd fall for it and maybe soften down. Dolly, the old lady says, would believe you before she'd believe I and the old lady, because she thinks it's her we're sorry for, and not him."

Well, I and Carey was only too glad to try and see what we could do. But it wasn't no snap. We wrote about eight letters before we got one that looked good.

Then we give it to the stenographer and had it wrote out on a typewriter and both of us signed it.

It was Carey's idear that made the letter good. He stuck in somethin' about the world's serious money that our wives wasn't goin' to spend unless she took pity on a "boy who was so shy and modest that he was afraid to come right out and say that he had asked such a beautiful and handsome girl to become his bride."

That's prob'ly what got her, or maybe she couldn't of held out much longer anyway. It was four days after we sent the letter that Cap heard from his missus again. We was in Cincinnati.

"We've won," he says to us. "The old lady says that Dolly says she'll give him another chancet. But the old lady says it won't do no good for Ike to write a letter. He'll have to go out there."

"Send him to-night," says Carey.

"I'll pay half his fare," I says.

"I'll pay the other half," says Carey.

"No," says Cap, "the club'll pay his expenses. I'll send him scoutin'."

"Are you goin' to send him to-night?"

"Sure," says Cap. "But I'm goin' to break the news to him right now. It's time we win a ball game."

So in the clubhouse, just before the game, Cap told him. And I certainly felt sorry for Rube Benton and Red Ames that afternoon! I and Carey was standin' in front o' the hotel that night when Ike come out with his suitcase.

"Sent home?" I says to him.

"No," he says, "I'm goin' scoutin'."

"Where to?" I says. "Fort Wayne?"

"No, not exactly," he says.

"Well," says Carey, "have a good time."

"I ain't lookin' for no good time," says Ike. "I says I was goin' scoutin'."

"Well, then," says Carey, "I hope you see somebody you like."

"And you better have a drink before you go," I says.

"Well," says Ike, "they claim it helps a cold."

BASEBALL HATTIE
Damon Runyon

It comes on springtime, and the little birdies are singing in the trees in Central Park, and the grass is green all around and about, and I am at the Polo Grounds on the opening day of the baseball season, when who do I behold but Baseball Hattie. I am somewhat surprised at this spectacle, as it is years since I see Baseball Hattie, and for all I know she long ago passes to a better and happier world. But there she is, as large as life, and in fact twenty pounds larger, and when I call the attention of Armand Fibleman, the gambler, to her, he gets up and tears right out of the joint as if he sees a ghost, for if there is one thing Armand Fibleman loathes and despises, it is a ghost. I can see that Baseball Hattie is greatly changed, and to tell the truth, I can see that she is getting to be nothing but an old bag. Her hair that is once as black as a yard up a stovepipe is gray, and she is wearing gold-rimmed cheaters, although she seems to be pretty well dressed and looks as if she may be in the money a little bit, at that.

But the greatest change in her is the way she sits there very quiet all afternoon, never once opening her yap, even when many of the customers around her are claiming that Umpire William Klem is Public Enemy No. 1 to 16 inclusive, because they think he calls a close one against the Giants. I am wondering if maybe Baseball Hattie is stricken dumb somewhere back down the years, because I can remember when she is usually making speeches in the grandstand in favor of hanging such characters as Umpire William Klem when they call close ones against the Giants. But Hattie just sits there as if she is in a church while the public clamor goes on about her, and she does not as much as cry out robber, or even you big bum at Umpire William Klem. I see many a baseball bug in my time, male and female, but without doubt the worst bug of them all is Baseball Hattie, and you can say it again. She is most particularly a bug about the Giants, and she never misses a game they play at the Polo Grounds, and in fact she sometimes bobs up watching them play in other cities, which is always very embarrassing to the Giants, as they fear the customers in these cities may get the wrong impression of New York womanhood after listening to Baseball Hattie awhile.

The first time I ever see Baseball Hattie to pay any attention to her is in Philadelphia, a matter of twenty-odd years back, when the Giants are playing a series there, and many citizens of New York, including Armand Fibleman and myself, are present, because the Philadelphia customers are great hands for betting on baseball games in those days, and Armand Fibleman figures he may knock a few of them in the creek. Armand Fibleman is a character who will bet on baseball games from who-laid-the-chunk, and in fact he will bet on anything whatever, because Armand

Fibleman is a gambler by trade and has been such since infancy. Personally, I will not bet you four dollars on a baseball game, because in the first place I am not apt to have four dollars, and in the second place I consider horse races a much sounder investment, but I often go around and about with Armand Fibleman, as he is a friend of mine, and sometimes he gives me a little piece of one of his bets for nothing.

Well, what happens in Philadelphia but the umpire forfeits the game in the seventh inning to the Giants by a score of nine to nothing when the Phillies are really leading by five runs, and the reason the umpire takes this action is because he orders several of the Philadelphia players to leave the field for calling him a scoundrel and a rat and a snake in the grass, and also a baboon, and they refuse to take their departure, as they still have more names to call him. Right away the Philadelphia customers become infuriated in a manner you will scarcely believe, for ordinarily a Philadelphia baseball customer is as quiet as a lamb, no matter what you do to him, and in fact in those days a Philadelphia baseball customer is only considered as somebody to do something to.

But these Philadelphia customers are so infuriated that they not only chase the umpire under the stand, but they wait in the street outside the baseball orchard until the Giants change into their street clothes and come out of the clubhouse. Then the Philadelphia customers begin pegging rocks, and one thing and another, at the Giants, and it is a most exciting and disgraceful scene that is spoken of for years afterwards. Well, the Giants march along toward the North Philly station to catch a train for home, dodging the rocks and one thing and another the best they can, and wondering why the Philadelphia gendarmes do not come to the rescue, until somebody notices several gendarmes among the customers doing some of the throwing themselves, so the Giants realize that this is a most inhospitable community, to be sure.

Finally all of them get inside the North Philly station and are safe, except a big, tall, left-handed pitcher by the name of Haystack Duggeler, who just reports to the club the day before and who finds himself surrounded by quite a posse of these infuriated Philadelphia customers, and who is unable to make them understand that he is nothing but a rookie, because he has a Missouri accent, and besides, he is half paralyzed with fear. One of the infuriated Philadelphia customers is armed with a brickbat and is just moving forward to maim Haystack Duggeler with this instrument, when who steps into the situation but Baseball Hattie, who is also on her way to the station to catch a train, and who is greatly horrified by the assault on the Giants.

She seizes the brickbat from the infuriated Philadelphia customer's grasp, and then tags the customer smack-dab between the eyes with his own weapon, knocking him so unconscious that I afterwards hear he does not recover for two weeks, and that he remains practically an imbecile the rest of his days. Then Baseball Hattie cuts loose on the other infuriated Philadelphia customers with language that they never before hear in those parts, causing them to disperse without further ado, and after the last customer is beyond the sound of her voice, she takes Haystack Duggeler by the pitching arm and personally escorts him to the station.

Now out of this incident is born a wonderful romance between Baseball Hattie and Haystack Duggeler, and in fact it is no doubt love at first sight, and about this period Haystack Duggeler begins burning up the league with his pitching, and at the same time giving Manager Mac plenty of headaches, including the romance with Baseball Hattie, because anybody will tell you that a left-hander is tough enough on a manager without a romance, and especially a romance with Baseball Hattie. It seems that the trouble with Hattie is she is in business up in Harlem, and this business consists of a boarding and rooming house where ladies and gentlemen board and room, and personally I never see anything out of line in the matter, but the rumor somehow gets around, as rumors will do, that in the first place, it is not a boarding and rooming house, and in the second place that the ladies and gentlemen who room and board there are by no means ladies and gentlemen, and especially ladies.

Well, this rumor becomes a terrible knock to Baseball Hattie's social reputation. Furthermore, I hear Manager Mac sends for her and requests her to kindly lay off his ballplayers, and especially off a character who can make a baseball sing high C like Haystack Duggeler. In fact, I hear Manager Mac gives her such a lecture on her civic duty to New York and to the Giants that Baseball Hattie sheds tears, and promises she will never give Haystack another tumble the rest of the season. "You know me, Mac," Baseball Hattie says. "You know I will cut off my nose rather than do anything to hurt your club. I sometimes figure I am in love with this big bloke, but," she says, "maybe it is only gas pushing up around my heart. I will take something for it. To hell with him, Mac!" she says.

So she does not see Haystack Duggeler again, except at a distance, for a long time, and he goes on to win fourteen games in a row, pitching a no-hitter and four two-hitters among them, and hanging up a reputation as a great pitcher, and also as a hundred-per-cent heel.

Haystack Duggeler is maybe twenty-five at this time, and he comes to the big league with more bad habits than anybody in the history of the world is able to acquire in such a short time. He is especially a great rumpot, and after he gets going good in the league, he is just as apt to appear for a game all mulled up as not. He is fond of all forms of gambling, such as playing cards and shooting craps, but after they catch him with a deck of readers in a poker game and a pair of tops in a crap game, none of the Giants will play with him any more, except of course when there is nobody else to play with. He is ignorant about many little things, such as reading and writing and geography and mathematics, as Haystack Duggeler himself admits he never goes to school any more than he can help, but he is so wise when it comes to larceny that I always figure they must have great tutors back in Haystack's old home town of Booneville, Mo.

And no smarter jobbie ever breathes than Haystack when he is out there pitching. He has so much speed that he just naturally throws the ball past a batter before he can get the old musket off his shoulder, and along with his hard one, Haystack has a curve like the letter Q. With two ounces of brains, Haystack Duggeler will be the greatest pitcher that ever lives. Well, as far as Baseball Hattie is concerned, she keeps her word about not seeing Haystack, although sometimes when he is mulled up he goes around to her boarding and rooming house, and tries to break down the door.

On days when Haystack Duggeler is pitching, she is always in her favorite seat back of third, and while she roots hard for the Giants no matter who is pitching, she puts on extra steam when Haystack is bending them over, and it is quite an experience to hear her crying lay them in there, Haystack, old boy, and strike this big tramp out, Haystack, and other exclamations of a similar nature, which please Haystack quite some, but annoy Baseball Hattie's neighbors back of third base, such as Armand Fibleman, if he happens to be betting on the other club.

A month before the close of his first season in the big league, Haystack Duggeler gets so ornery that Manager Mac suspends him, hoping maybe it will cause Haystack to do a little thinking, but naturally Haystack is unable to do this, because he has nothing to think with. About a week later, Manager Mac gets to noticing how he can use a few ball games, so he starts looking for Haystack Duggeler, and he finds him tending bar on Eighth Avenue with his uniform hung up back of the bar as an advertisement. The baseball writers speak of Haystack as eccentric, which is a polite way of saying he is a screwball, but they consider him a most unique character and are always writing humorous stories about him, though any one of them will lay you plenty of nine to five that Haystack winds up an umbay. The chances are they will raise their price a little, as the season closes and Haystack is again under suspension with cold weather coming on and not a dime in his pants pockets.

It is sometime along in the winter that Baseball Hattie hauls off and marries Haystack Duggeler, which is a great surprise to one and all, but not nearly as much of a surprise as when Hattie closes her boarding and rooming house and goes to live in a little apartment with Haystack Duggeler up on Washington Heights.

It seems that she finds Haystack one frosty night sleeping in a hallway, after being around slightly mulled up for several weeks, and she takes him to her home and gets him a bath and a shave and a clean shirt and two boiled eggs and some toast and coffee and a shot or two of rye whisky, all of which is greatly appreciated by Haystack, especially the rye whisky. Then Haystack proposes marriage to her and takes a paralyzed oath that if she becomes his wife he will reform, so what with loving Haystack anyway, and with the fix commencing to request more dough off the boarding-and-rooming-house business than the business will stand, Hattie takes him at his word, and there you are. The baseball writers are wondering what Manager Mac will say when he hears these tidings, but all Mac says is that Haystack cannot possibly be any worse married then he is single-o, and then Mac has the club office send the happy couple a little paper money to carry them over the winter. Well, what happens but a great change comes over Haystack Duggeler. He stops bending his elbow and helps Hattie cook and wash the dishes, and holds her hand when they are in the movies, and speaks of his love for her several times a week, and Hattie is as happy as nine dollars' worth of lettuce. Manager Mac is so delighted at the change in Haystack that he has the club office send over more paper money, because Mac knows that with Haystack in shape he is sure of twenty-five games, and maybe the pennant.

In late February, Haystack reports to the training camp down South still as sober as some judges, and the other ballplayers are so impressed by the change in him that they admit him to their poker game again. But of course it is too much to expect a man to alter his entire course of living all at once, and it is not long before Haystack discovers four nines in his hand on his own deal and breaks up the game.

He brings Baseball Hattie with him to the camp, and this is undoubtedly a slight mistake, as it seems the old rumor about her boarding-and-rooming-house business gets around among the ever-loving wives of the other players, and they put on a large chill for her. In fact, you will think Hattie has the smallpox. Naturally, Baseball Hattie feels the frost, but she never lets on, as it seems she runs into many bigger and better frosts than this in her time. Then Haystack Duggeler notices it, and it seems that it makes him a little peevish toward Baseball Hattie, and in fact it is said that he gives her a slight pasting one night in their room, partly because she has no better social standing and partly because he is commencing to cop a few sneaks on the local corn now and then, and Hattie chides him for same.

Well, about this time it appears that Baseball Hattie discovers that she is going to have a baby, and as soon as she recovers from her astonishment, she decides that it is to be a boy who will be a great baseball player, maybe a pitcher, although Hattie admits she is willing to compromise on a good second baseman. She also decides that his name is to be Derrill Duggeler, after his paw, as it seems Derrill is Haystack's real name, and he is only called Haystack because he claims he once makes a living stacking hay, although the general opinion is that all he ever stacks is cards. It is really quite remarkable what a belt Hattie gets out of the idea of having this baby, though Haystack is not excited about the matter. He is not paying much attention to Baseball Hattie by now, except to give her a slight pasting now and then, but Hattie is so happy about the baby that she does not mind these pastings.

Haystack Duggeler meets up with Armand Fibleman along in midsummer. By this time, Haystack discovers horse racing and is always making bets on the horses, and naturally he is generally broke, and then I commence running into him in different spots with Armand Fibleman, who is now betting higher than a cat's back on baseball games.

It is late August, and the Giants are fighting for the front end of the league, and an important series with Brooklyn is coming up, and everybody knows that Haystack Duggeler will work in anyway two games of the series, as Haystack can generally beat Brooklyn just by throwing his glove on the mound. There is no doubt but what he has the old Indian sign on Brooklyn, and the night before the first game, which he is sure to work, the gamblers along Broadway are making the Giants two-to-one favorites to win the game.

This same night before the game, Baseball Hattie is home in her little apartment on Washington Heights waiting for Haystack to come in and eat a delicious dinner of pigs' knuckles and sauerkraut, which she personally prepares for him. In fact, she hurries home right after the ball game to get this delicacy ready, because Haystack tells her he will surely come home this particular night, although Hattie knows he is never better than even money to keep his word about anything. But sure enough, in he comes while the pigs' knuckles and sauerkraut are still piping hot, and Baseball Hattie is surprised to see Armand Fibleman with him, as she knows Armand backwards and forwards and does not care much for him, at that. However, she can say the same thing about four million other characters in this town, so she makes Armand welcome, and they sit down and put on the pigs' knuckles and sauerkraut together, and a pleasant time is enjoyed by one and all. In fact, Baseball Hattie puts herself out to entertain Armand Fibleman, because he is the first guest Haystack ever brings home.

Well, Armand Fibleman can be very pleasant when he wishes, and he speaks very nicely to Hattie. Naturally, he sees that Hattie is expecting, and in fact he will have to be blind not to see it, and he seems greatly interested in this matter and asks Hattie many questions, and Hattie is delighted to find somebody to talk to about what is coming off with her, as Haystack will never listen to any of her remarks on the subject. So Armand Fibleman gets to hear all about Baseball Hattie's son, and how he is to be a great baseball player, and Armand says is that so, and how nice, and all this and that, until Haystack Duggeler speaks up as follows, and to wit:

"Oh, dag-gone her son!" Haystack says. "It is going to be a girl, anyway, so let us dismiss this topic and get down to business. Hat," he says, "you fan yourself into the kitchen and wash the dishes, while Armand and me talk."

So Hattie goes into the kitchen, leaving Haystack and Armand sitting there talking, and what are they talking about but a proposition for Haystack to let the Brooklyn club beat him the next day so Armand Fibleman can take the odds and clean up a nice little gob of money, which he is to split with Haystack. Hattie can hear every word they say, as the kitchen is next door to the dining room where they are sitting, and at first she thinks they are joking, because at this time nobody ever even as much as thinks of skulduggery in baseball, or anyway, not much. It seems that at first Haystack is not in favor of the idea, but Armand Fibleman keeps mentioning money that Haystack owes him for bets on the horse races, and he asks Haystack how he expects to continue betting on the races without fresh money, and Armand also speaks of the great injustice that is being done Haystack by the Giants in not paying him twice the salary he is getting, and how the loss of one or two games is by no means such a great calamity.

Well, finally Baseball Hattie hears Haystack say all right, but he wishes a thousand dollars then and there as a guarantee, and Armand Fibleman says this is fine, and they will go downtown and he will get the money at once, and now Hattie realizes that maybe they are in earnest, and she pops out of the kitchen and speaks as follows:

"Gentlemen," Hattie says, "you seem to be sober, but I guess you are drunk. If you are not drunk, you must both be daffy to think of such a thing as phenagling around with a baseball game."

"Hattie," Haystack says, "kindly close your trap and go back in the kitchen, or I will give you a bust in the nose."

And with this he gets up and reaches for his hat, and

Armand Fibleman gets up, too, and Hattie says like this:

"Why, Haystack," she says, "you are not really serious in this matter, are you?"

"Of course I am serious," Haystack says. "I am sick and tired of pitching for starvation wages, and besides, I will win a lot of games later on to make up for the one I lose tomorrow. Say," he says, "these Brooklyn bums may get lucky tomorrow and knock me loose from my pants, anyway, no matter what I do, so what difference does it make?"

"Haystack," Baseball Hattie says, "I know you are a liar and a drunkard and a cheat and no account generally, but nobody can tell me you will sink so low as to purposely toss off a ball game. Why, Haystack, baseball is always on the level. It is the most honest game in all this world. I guess you are just ribbing me, because you know how much I love it."

"Dry up!" Haystack says to Hattie. "Furthermore, do not expect me home again tonight. But anyway, dry up."

"Look, Haystack," Hattie says, "I am going to have a son. He is your son and my son, and he is going to be a great ballplayer when he grows up, maybe a greater pitcher than you are, though I hope and trust he is not left-handed. He will have your name. If they find out you toss off a game for money, they will throw you out of baseball and you will be disgraced. My son will be known as the son of a crook, and what chance will he have in baseball? Do you think I am going to allow you to do this to him, and to the game that keeps me from going nutty for marrying you?"

Naturally, Haystack Duggeler is greatly offended by Hattie's crack about her son being maybe a greater pitcher than he is, and he is about to take steps, when Armand Fibleman stops him. Armand Fibleman is commencing to be somewhat alarmed at Baseball Hattie's attitude, and he gets to thinking that he hears that people in her delicate condition are often irresponsible, and he fears that she may blow a whistle on this enterprise without realizing what she is doing. So he undertakes a few soothing remarks to her. "Why, Hattie," Armand Fibleman says, "nobody can possibly find out about this little matter, and Haystack will have enough money to send your son to college, if his markers at the race track do not take it all. Maybe you better lie down and rest awhile," Armand says.

But Baseball Hattie does not as much as look at Armand, though she goes on talking to Haystack. "They always find out thievery, Haystack," she says, "especially when you are dealing with a fink like Fibleman. If you deal with him once, you will have to deal with him again and again, and he will be the first to holler copper on you, because he is a stool pigeon in his heart."

"Haystack," Armand Fibleman says, "I think we better be going."

"Haystack," Hattie says, "you can go out of here and stick up somebody or commit a robbery or a murder, and I will still welcolme you back and stand by you. But if you are going out to steal my son's future, I advise you not to go."

"Dry up!" Haystack says. "I am going."

"All right, Haystack," Hattie says, very calm. "But just step into the kitchen with me and let me say one little word to you by yourself, and then I will say no more." Well, Haystack Duggeler does not care for even just one little word more, but Armand Fibleman wishes to get this disagreeable scene over with, so he tells Haystack to let her have her word, and Haystack goes into the kitchen with Hattie, and Armand cannot hear what is said, as she speaks very low, but he hears Haystack laugh heartily and then Haystack comes out of the kitchen, still laughing, and tells Armand he is ready to go.

As they start for the door, Baseball Hattie outs with a long-nosed .38-caliber Colt's revolver, and goes root-a-toot-toot with it, and the next thing anybody knows, Haystack is on the floor yelling bloody murder, and Armand Fibleman is leaving the premises without bothering to open the door. In fact, the landlord afterwards talks some of suing Haystack Duggeler because of the damage Armand Fibleman does to the door. Armand himself afterwards admits that when he slows down for a breather a couple of miles down Broadway he finds splinters stuck all over him.

Well, the doctors come, and the gendarmes come, and there is great confusion, especially as Baseball Hattie is sobbing so she can scarcely make a statement, and Haystack Duggeler is so sure he is going to die that he cannot think of anything to say except oh-oh-oh, but finally the landlord remembers seeing Armand leave with his door, and everybody starts questioning Hattie about this until she confesses that Armand is there all right, and that he tries to bribe Haystack to toss off a ball game, and that she then suddenly finds herself with a revolver in her hand, and everything goes black before her eyes, and she can remember no more until somebody is sticking a bottle of smelling salts under her nose. Naturally, the newspaper reporters put two and two together, and what they make of it is that Hattie tries to plug Armand Fibleman for his rascally offer, and that she misses Armand and gets Haystack, and right away Baseball Hattie is a great heroine, and Haystack is a great hero, though nobody thinks to ask Haystack how he stands on the bribe proposition, and he never brings it up himself.

And nobody will ever offer Haystack any more bribes, for after the doctors get through with him he is shy a left arm from the shoulder down, and he will never pitch a baseball again, unless he learns to pitch right-handed. The newspapers make quite a lot of Baseball Hattie protecting the fair name of baseball. The National League plays a benefit game for Haystack Duggeler and presents him with a watch and a purse of twenty-five thousand dollars, which Baseball Hattie grabs away from him, saying it is for her son, while Armand Fibleman is in bad with one and all.

Baseball Hattie and Haystack Duggeler move to the Pacific Coast, and this is all there is to the story, except that one day some years ago, and not long before he passes away in Los Angeles, a respectable grocer, I run into Haystack when he is in New York on a business trip, and I say to him like this:

"Haystack," I say, "it is certainly a sin and a shame that Hattie misses Armand Fibleman that night and puts you on the shelf. The chances are that but for this little accident you will hang up one of the greatest pitching records in the history of baseball. Personally," I say, "I never see a better left-handed pitcher."

"Look," Haystack says. "Hattie does not miss Fibleman. It is a great newspaper story and saves my name, but the truth is she hits just where she aims. When she calls me into the kitchen before I start out with Fibleman, she shows me a revolver I never before know she has, and says to me, 'Haystack,' she says, 'if you leave with this weasel on the errand you mention, I am going to fix you so you will never make another wrong move with your pitching arm. I am going to shoot it off for you.'

"I laugh heartily," Haystack says, "I think she is kidding me, but I find out different. By the way," Haystack says, "I afterwards learn that long before I meet her, Hattie works for three years in a shooting gallery at Coney Island. She is really a remarkable broad," Haystack says.

I guess I forget to state that the day Baseball Hattie is at the Polo Grounds she is watching the new kid sensation of the big leagues, Derrill Duggeler, shut out Brooklyn with three hits.

He is a wonderful young left-hander.

THE TREE ON THE DIAMOND
James Thurber

Group civilization, they tell me, has come to the corner of Parsons Avenue and Bryden Road, where my grandfather built his house in the year 1884, well beyond stone's throw of his nearest neighbor, and I suppose the individual has taken on the gray color of the mass. But there were individuals about during the first decade of the century, each possessed of his own bright and separate values.

There was George Craft, the odd-jobs man, who claimed to be eighty, might have been seventy, but worked like a man of fifty when he put his mind and back to it. George always wore a smile and a dark-blue shirt spangled with medals and ribbons that came from curio shops, state fairs, and the attic trunks of his various employers, but George said he had won them all in the Civil War. It seems that he had been a slave and that he had freed himself. Once I asked him, "How did you do that, George?" and he broke into his loud and easy laughter. "'How did you do that, George?' the boy says!" as if the simple question had been a Johnsonian retort. Our uncertainty about George's age was increased by his fondness for birthdays. He had several a year. "Dis is it! Dis is de real one!" he would tell us gleefully. He would knock on the front door of my grandfather's house on those festive days and say to whoever answered, "Ah wants to see Mistuh Fishah's bright face this fine mornin'!" The person who had gone to the door would call out, "It's George's birthday!" and from his study at the top of the stairs my grandfather would call back, "Give him a dime!" When George got the money, he would flash his great grin and cry, "Lawd bless de gentleman o' dis house!" When George's birthday fell in fair weather, and the walking was good, he collected lots of dimes, but he was a religious man and he sometimes punished himself for pagan thoughts or other errors of faith by decreeing an anniversary on a day of wind and rain or heavy snow. "Too bad you were born in January," my Uncle Kirt said to him once. "You won't collect many dimes on a day like this." George laughed and laughed and slapped his leg, as he did at whatever any gentleman said, and then he sobered suddenly. "Ah'm repentin' fo' mah sins, Mistah Kirt," he said. "Ah'm repentin' fo' mah sins."

When George died, he was laid to rest wearing all his medals. One of these, my uncle said, was a genuine decoration for valor, and another was the blue ribbon that had been awarded in 1905 at the Ohio State Fair for the best Rhode Island cock in the poultry exhibit.

Then there was Charlie Potts, my grandfather's stableman, whose get-up on his Sundays off was the envy of us boys. The dark-skinned Charlie had a high stack of black, curly hair, glossy with Macassar oil, or whatever they used in those days. He affected light suits, gay shirts, and flowered yellow ties; a bright bandanna bloomed in his breast pocket, and he swung a bamboo cane. He preferred to keep his Sunday destinations a secret. When we boys wanted to know where he was going, he had an invariable answer, accompanied by a mysterious wink: "If anybody should ask you, tell 'em I left you inquirin'." His room occupied a corner of the barn loft, and its walls were covered with colorful posters presenting scenes from plays of the period—"The Squaw Man," "Strongheart," "The Round Up," "The Great Divide," "The Call of the North," and "Arizona"—and photographs of Faversham, Robert Edeson, and Kyrle Bellew. When the automobile replaced the carriage, putting Charlie Potts out of a job, he took a trip to Europe on his savings. He called on us when he came back, to tell stories of what he kept calling the "rather peculiar circumstances" that attended his travels. In Charlie's idiom, the phrase fitted the commonplace as well as the extraordinary. It still does. He lives in a town in central Ohio now, and I phoned him when I was in Columbus a few years ago. "I haven't seen you for thirty years, Jim," Charlie said, "but I ran into your brother Bill, under rather peculiar circumstances, when I was spending a few weeks in Columbus recently." It turned out that he had run into Bill, as everybody runs into everybody else in Columbus, at the corner of Broad and High.

Nobody I knew in the Bryden Road days stands out quite so clearly for me as Frank James, organizer, manager, captain, and first baseman of the Blind Asylum team, and jealous overseer of the craziest baseball field in the history of the game.

Few of us middle-aged men who knew Frank James as youngsters forty years ago would have recognized him dressed for burial in his full and formal name, Benjamin Franklin James. The Columbus papers revealed that elegant secret in brief obituaries when he died, a few years ago, at the age of seventy-seven. They also acquainted us with the news that Frank was part Cherokee Indian. We should have suspected this from his singularly erect posture and his fine, springy step —he walked as if the ground under him were pneumatic—but kids in central Ohio accepted the brown-skinned man as a Negro and let it go at that. I count it a happy wonder that nobody resented, in those innocent years, his sharp-tongued command of a ball club on which every player except himself was a white man.

The catcher, a man named Lang, threw a ball like a bullet, and he could take the fastest pitch of any hurler barehanded, and he could have broken his captain in two, but he always obeyed orders docilely ("Bunt it, boy, bunt it! You heah me? *Bunt* it!") and the James insults never provoked him ("What kind o' playin' is that for a grown man, Lang? What kind o' playin' is that?").

The baseball team of the School for the Blind—we called it "the Blinky," in the easy and unmalicious parlance of the young—was made up of employees of the institution. I thought Frank James was always in charge of the boiler rooms, but the notices of his death credited him with having been an instructor, and I have since found out that he taught broom-making during his last years there.

Lang was an engineer, I believe, and the rest of the players came from the kitchen, the laundry, the stable, and other corners and corridors of the gloomy institution.

When my grandfather bought a Lozier, he put Maud, the family mare, out to pasture and tore down the brick barn behind the house, leaving a clear vista across the Blind Asylum grounds all the way to Main Street. The place was to become one of the landscapes of my nightmares. Its central structure was a massive crawl of dank stone. Even the architect whose dark genius for the ungainly had created the brooding monster must have realized that it needed a touch of light. He stuck a fountain in front of it, but it turned out to be a sullen cub of the mother building, an ugly cone of rock blubbering water from a length of pipe that jutted out of the top.

We neighborhood kids used to play around the fountain, but we rarely saw the blind children there. They seemed to be in class most of the time, and from my grandfather's house the institution often looked deserted. The shouting and laughing of the ball team behind the main building on Saturday afternoons in summer seemed out of place, like the sound of a child's voice calling down an old, abandoned well. We could hear occasional noises from the building—a tray falling, a sharp voice protesting, a melancholy hand running scales on a piano lost in the wilderness of stone.

The main building sent back two brown wings, or tentacles, which invaded Frank James' outfield, as if they wanted to crush the players and stop the game. The left tentacle crept up to within fifty feet of the second baseman, and the other swung behind the center fielder, forcing him to play in and cramping the range of his action. The blunt end of this wing was separated from the stables by thirty feet of paved courtyard, on which the left fielder had to stand, an easy victim of ricocheting balls, frightened horses, and stablemen with pitchforks. If these were the stony frustrations of a Freudian dream, the gigantic tree between first and second was a hazard out of Lewis Carroll. It had the patriarchal spread of Longfellow's chestnut, and it could drop leaves on the shortstop and, with its large and sinewy roots, trip up runners rounding first. Many a hard-hit ball that should have been good for extra bases would cling and linger in the thick foliage of that ancient tree, and drop finally into Frank James' glove, or the glove of his right fielder, who had plenty of time to jog in from his position on the concrete walk beside the left wing and wait for it to come down. Visiting players screamed and cursed, and now and then they would gather up their bats and gloves, stalk off the Dali diamond, and go home, while Frank James, his hands on his hips, exasperation in his eyes, his mouth open—he was always excited and breathing hard—demanded to know what the hell could possibly be the matter with the yellow-bellies. Sometimes the finicky enemy would quit in disgust, late in the game, after the James Boys had demonstrated a special and practiced skill in bouncing the ball off walls, losing it on roofs, hitting it into the crotch of the tree, or lining it under the lowest bough, so that it would land on the concrete pavement and roll to Parsons Avenue, a hundred and fifty yards away.

The Miracle Men of Parsons Avenue played the post-office team and the city firemen and police, as well as teams made up of employees of other state institutions, and beat them all most of the time. Panting heavily, his sharp, black eyes taking in every play and every player, Frank urged his men on as if each game were the seventh in a World Series. His tongue was never silent, and he always repeated his loud commands to batters at least once: "Lay it down easy, Steffie, lay it down easy!" or "Get me a double, boy, get me a double!" or "Hit it in the tree, keed, hit it in the tree!" It was the same when his team was in the field: "Close in! Close in!" or "Lay back! Lay back!" or "Watch the bunt, boys, watch the bunt!" If a hard-hit grounder took a bad bounce on the uneven terrain, struck one of his infielders on the chest, and bounced high in the air, Frank would scream, "Ovah ya, undah ya, wheah ah ya?" Human fallibility he could not abide. "What's the mattah, keed, can't ya see 'em?" he would bawl if a player muffed a hard chance, or "Use ya brains! Use ya brains!" It is a wonder that nobody ever took a swing at him with fist or bat. If his team was far ahead and sure to win against men confused by walls and branches, Frank's voice softened and his tone grew friendly. He would let his batters use their own judgment. "Your way's mine, Emil, your way's mine," he would say affectionately. Once this same Emil, in the midst of a tight game, stepped to the plate and said to his captain, "I'll get you a home run, Frank." Instead, he popped weakly to the shortstop. "Thanks for the home run, keed!" screamed Frank. "Thanks for the home run!" Nor did his temper and sarcasm wear off. Every time Emil walked to the plate after that, Frank shouted at the opposing outfielders, "Give him room, men, give him room!"

The James Boys lost few games—not more than four or five, I believe, in all the years they played. One reason for this was that Frank could seldom be lured onto the home grounds of any of his opponents. "The boys can't get away from the institution," he explained once to the manager of a club composed of employees of the State Asylum for the Insane. "If the crazy people want to play us, let the crazy people come ovah heah."

"They are not crazy people," snapped their manager.

"You bring 'em ovah heah an' we'll drive 'em crazy," Frank retorted.

The man stared at the outfield walls, and at the tree that made pop flies out of triples and base hits out of pop flies. "I have no doubt of that," he said testily, and went away.

When Frank James' team did drop a game, he revealed himself as the worst loser in the history of baseball, amateur or professional. He had no heart or philosophy for defeat. The best team had lost, and there was no justice in the world. His voice would grow husky from howling that his men should be inmates, not employees, of the School for the Blind, that they couldn't beat the Columbus School for Girls the best day they ever saw, that the whole team should give up baseball for checkers or lotto, that the Lord God had never seen a man so cruelly betrayed as Frank James. One Saturday afternoon, when I was sixteen, I heard Frank fiercely bawling out one of his pitchers for losing a game. "You threw your arm out in practice!" he roared. "I told you not to pitch more than a dozen balls before the game, but you threw your arm out." The man stared at him in astonishment. "The was five years ago, Frank," he said. "Are you still bellyachin' about that old game?" Baseball time stood still in Frank James' head and the sore of defeat never healed. Once he had a close call at the hands of a team organized by Mr. Harvey, proprietor of a drugstore on Main Street, near Parsons. The Harvey Boys were all young men of the neighborhood, familiar with the weird diamond and capable of hitting into or under the big tree. The Harveys led, 2–1, going into the eighth, and Frank heaped abuse on the head of the Harvey pitcher, a slender, quiet youngster named Billy Allaway, who had Emil and the others missing his curves and popping up his fast ones. He struck out Frank James twice, but the raging captain continued to berate his men for going down on strikes.

"Goddam it, Frank," said one of them finally, "he fanned *you* twice."

"That's 'cause you upset me," yelled Frank, "standin' up theah an' swingin' at nothin'!"

Frank went right on belaboring the impassive Allaway—"that little boy out theah"—with quip and insult. In the ninth inning, the James Boys clumsied two runs across with the help of the enormous tree and won the game. For the first time in his life, Frank James praised an opposing player. "You pitched a good game, Billy!" he shouted. "You pitched a good game!"

Three weeks later, the Harveys took on the James Boys again, with Billy Allaway on the mound, and beat them, 3–2, in a tense and noisy game during which Frank shouted himself hoarse and seemed in danger of breaking a blood vessel. When the last pop fly of the home team had sifted through the branches of the tree into a Harvey glove, Frank James rushed up to Allaway shouting huskily, "If a man beats me he's got to play on my team." Billy pointed out that he was not an employee of the Institution for the Blind, and that this made him a ringer. "My team is my team," Frank yelled, "and if they don't want to play me they don't have to. I ain't goin' to say you're a silverware counter in the dining room, I'm gonna say you're my pitcher. If they don't want to play us they can go home. Nobody tells Frank James how to name his line-up or how to run his team." Billy Allaway won a dozen games for his new captain, and the two became great friends. Billy still insists that Frank James was one of America's great all-around athletes, a star in football, basketball, and track, as well as baseball. "He could run a hundred yards in ten seconds flat, wearing ordinary street clothes," Billy wrote me last year. "When he was forty-three he took up tennis and played it as hard, and as well, as he played everything else." Baseball was Frank's great love, though, and he believed until he died that his team, in its best years, could have licked the Columbus Senators of the American Association—on the Blind Asylum grounds, of course. It was a bitter disappointment to him that his challenge, often repeated, was never accepted by the professional club.

I suppose that shocked Nature has long since covered that crazy ball field with grass and, no doubt, crickets sing where Frank James used to stand and shout his insults and commands. Frank would have played on into his sixties, but his eyesight began to fail thirty years ago. He had thought his legs would be the first to go, but we who had heard him bawl the summer afternoons away were sure it would be his lungs and larynx. One story has it that a broken steampipe in the boiler rooms caused an injury that gradually brought on blindness, but, however that may be, he stayed on the job as long as he could see to grope his way around.

Frank James was king of that crazy ball field, but even in his heyday he was not always the center of attention. Since the diamond was the only one for miles around, officials of the institution allowed the boys from nearby Douglas School to meet their rivals there on Saturday mornings—or in the afternoon, if the James club was idle or playing somewhere else. The Avondale Avenue team came from the West Side, bringing with it, around 1908, a youngster of destiny, its captain and center fielder, Billy Southworth, who was later signed by the New York Giants. Hank Gowdy, hero of the 1914 World Series, must have played there, too, in his day, and old-timers distinctly remember Billy Purtell, who went to Chicago fifty years ago to play third base for the White Sox.

In the autumn, the field was turned into a makeshift gridiron, with one goal post, and several famous football stars scrimmaged there as boys: Chic Harley, Ohio State's immortal halfback and three-time All-American; Allen Thurman, whose long, high, spiral punts helped the University of Virginia beat Yale, 10–0, in 1915; his young brother Johnny, All-America tackle at the University of Pennsylvania in 1922; and the celebrated Raymond (Fike) Eichenlaub, plunging fullback of the Notre Dame team of Rockne and Dorais, which dazzled and smashed Army in 1913. I remember young Donald Ogden Stewart showing up one day in a brand-new football uniform and carrying a brand-new football; Bill Burnett, who was to write "Little Caesar;" Carl Randall, who went on to dance in the "Follies;" and now and then little Joel Sayre would toddle over from his home in Rich Street to watch the goings on. Long before their day and mine, George Bellows, from

Monroe Avenue around the corner, practiced on the diamond—he later became, among other things, one of the best shortstops Ohio State ever had.

I like to think that the aged Frank James, nearing the end of his life, remembered and was remembered by these "keeds" of so long ago. Some of them he outlived, of course; most of the others left Columbus or moved away from the neighborhood, but at least one, Billy Allaway, was a constant visitor during Frank's last days at the School for the Blind. They would sit in Frank's small office, which held a desk and two chairs, and recall the battles of former years. "You know, Frank," Allaway told him one day, "you should have put chicken wire up in that tree." Benjamin Franklin James turned his head sharply in the direction of his guest. "Ah'm a sportsman, Billy," he said reproachfully, "an' a sportsman don't take unfair advantage."

A CAP FOR STEVE
Morley Callaghan

Dave Diamond, a poor man, a carpenter's assistant, was a small, wiry, quick-tempered individual who had learned how to make every dollar count in his home. His wife, Anna, had been sick a lot, and his twelve-year-old-son, Steve, had to be kept in school. Steve, a big-eyed, shy kid, ought to have known the value of money as well as Dave did. It had been ground into him.

But the boy was crazy about baseball, and after school, when he could have been been working as a delivery boy or selling papers, he played ball with the kids. His failure to appreciate that the family needed a few extra dollars disgusted Dave. Around the house he wouldn't let Steve talk about baseball, and he scowled when he saw him hurrying off with his glove after dinner.

When the Phillies came to town to play an exhibition game with the home team and Steve pleaded to be taken to the ball park, Dave, of course, was outraged. Steve knew they couldn't afford it. But he had got his mother on his side. Finally Dave made a bargain with them. He said that if Steve came home after school and worked hard helping to make some kitchen shelves he would take him that night to the ball park.

Steve worked hard, but Dave was still resentful. They had to coax him to put on his good suit. When they started out Steve held aloof, feeling guilty, and they walked down the street like strangers; then Dave glanced at Steve's face and, half-ashamed, took his arm more cheerfully.

As the game went on, Dave had to listen to Steve's recitation of the batting average of every Philly that stepped up to the plate; the time the boy must have wasted learning these averages began to appal him. He showed it so plainly that Steve felt guilty again and was silent.

After the game Dave let Steve drag him onto the field to keep him company while he tried to get some autographs from the Philly players, who were being hemmed in by gangs of kids blocking the way to the clubhouse. But Steve, who was shy, let the other kids block him off from the players. Steve would push his way in, get blocked out, and come back to stand mournfully beside Dave. And Dave grew impatient. He was wasting valuable time. He wanted to get home; Steve knew it and was worried.

Then the big, blond Philly outfielder, Eddie Condon, who had been held up by a gang of kids tugging at his arm and thrusting their score cards at him, broke loose and made a run for the clubhouse. He was jostled, and his blue cap with the red peak, tilted far back on his head, fell off. It fell at Steve's feet, and Steve stooped quickly and grabbed it. "Okay, son," the outfielder called, turning back. But Steve, holding the hat in both hands, only stared at him.

"Give him his cap, Steve," Dave said, smiling apologetically at the big outfielder who towered over them.

But Steve drew the hat closer to his chest. In an awed trance he looked up at big Eddie Condon. It was an embarrassing moment. All the other kids were watching. Some shouted. "Give him his cap."

"My cap, son," Eddie Condon said, his hand out.

"Hey, Steve," Dave said, and he gave him a shake. But he had to jerk the cap out of Steve's hands.

"Here you are," he said.

The outfielder, noticing Steve's white, worshipping face and pleading eyes, grinned and then shrugged. "Aw, let him keep it," he said.

"No, Mister Condon, you don't need to do that," Steve protested.

"It's happened before. Forget it," Eddie Condon said, and he trotted away to the clubhouse.

Dave handed the cap to Steve; envious kids circled around them and Steve said, "He said I could keep it, Dad. You heard him, didn't you?"

"Yeah, I heard him," Dave admitted. The wonder in Steve's face made him smile. He took the boy by the arm and they hurried off the field.

On the way home Dave couldn't get him to talk about the game; he couldn't get him to take his eyes off the cap. Steve could hardly believe in his own happiness. "See," he said suddenly, and he showed Dave that Eddie Condon's name was printed on the sweatband. Then he went on dreaming. Finally he put the cap on his head and turned to Dave with a slow, proud smile. The cap was way too big for him; it fell down over his ears. "Never mind," Dave said. "You can get your mother to take a tuck in the back."

When they got home Dave was tired and his wife didn't understand the cap's importance, and they couldn't get Steve to go to bed. He swaggered around wearing the cap and looking in the mirror every ten minutes. He took the cap to bed with him.

Dave and his wife had a cup of coffee in the kitchen, and Dave told her again how they had got the cap. They agreed that their boy must have an attractive quality that showed in his face, and that Eddie Condon must have been drawn to him—why else would he have singled Steve out from all the kids?

But Dave got tired of the fuss Steve made over that cap and of the way he wore it from the time he got up in the morning until the time he went to bed. Some kid was always coming in, wanting to try on the cap. It was childish, Dave said, for Steve to go around assuming that the cap made him important in the neighbour-hood, and to keep telling them how he had become a leader in the park a few blocks away where he played ball in the evenings. And Dave wouldn't stand for Steve's keeping the cap on while he was eating. He was always scolding his wife for accepting Steve's explanation that he'd forgotten he had it on. Just the same, it was remarkable what a little thing like a ball cap could do for a kid, Dave admitted to his wife as he smiled to himself.

One night Steve was late coming home from the park. Dave didn't realize how late it was until he put down his newspaper and watched his wife at the window. Her restlessness got on his nerves. "See what comes from encouraging the boy to hang around with those park loafers," he said. "I don't encourage him," she protested. "You do," he insisted irritably, for he was really worried now. A gang hung around the park until midnight. It was a bad park. It was true that on one side

there was a good district with fine, expensive apartment houses, but the kids from that neighbourhood
left the park to the kids from the poorer homes. When
his wife went out and walked down to the corner it was
his turn to wait and worry and watch at the open
window. Each waiting moment tortured him. At last he
heard his wife's voice and Steve's voice, and he relaxed
and sighed; then he remembered his duty and rushed
angrily to meet them.

"I'll fix you, Steve, once and for all," he said. "I'll
show you you can't start coming into the house at
midnight."

"Hold your horses, Dave," his wife said. "Can't you
see the state he's in?" Steve looked utterly exhausted
and beaten.

"What's the matter?" Dave asked quickly.

"I lost my cap," Steve whispered; he walked past his
father and threw himself on the couch in the living-
room and lay with his face hidden.

"Now, don't scold him, Dave," his wife said.

"Scold him. Who's scolding him?" Dave asked,
indignantly. "It's his cap, not mine. If it's not worth his
while to hang on to it, why should I scold him?" But he
was implying resentfully that he alone recognized the
cap's value.

"So you are scolding him," his wife said. "It's his cap.
Not yours. What happened, Steve?"

Steve told them he had been playing ball and he
found that when he ran the bases the cap fell off; it was
still too big despite the tuck his mother had taken in
the band. So the next time he came to bat he tucked the
cap in his hip pocket. Someone had lifted it, he was
sure.

"And he didn't even know whether it was still in his pocket," Dave said sarcastically.

"I wasn't careless, Dad," Steve said. For the last three hours he had been wandering around to the homes of the kids who had been in the park at the time; he wanted to go on, but he was too tired. Dave knew the boy was apologizing to him, but he didn't know why it made him angry.

"If he didn't hang on to it, it's not worth worrying about now," he said, and he sounded offended.

After that night they knew that Steve didn't go to the park to play ball; he went to look for the cap. It irritated Dave to see him sit around listlessly, or walk in circles, trying to force his memory to find a particular incident which would suddenly recall to him the moment when the cap had been taken. It was no attitude for a growing, healthy boy to take, Dave complained. He told Steve firmly once and for all he didn't want to hear any more about the cap.

One night, two weeks later, Dave was walking home with Steve from the shoemaker's. It was a hot night. When they passed an ice cream parlour Steve slowed down. "I guess I couldn't have a soda, could I?" Steve said. "Nothing doing," Dave said firmly. "Come on now," he added as Steve hung back, looking in the window.

"Dad, look!" Steve cried suddenly, pointing at the window. "My cap! There's my cap! He's coming out!"

A well-dressed boy was leaving the ice cream parlour; he had on a blue ball cap with a red peak, just like Steve's cap. "Hey, you!" Steve cried, and he rushed at the boy, his small face fierce and his eyes wild. Before the boy could back away Steve had snatched the cap from his head. "That's my cap!" he shouted.

"What's this?" the bigger boy said. "Hey, give me my cap or I'll give you a poke on the nose."

Dave was surprised that his own shy boy did not back away. He watched him clutch the cap in his left hand, half crying with excitement as he put his head down and drew back his right fist: he was willing to fight. And Dave was proud of him.

"Wait now," Dave said. "Take it easy, son," he said to the other boy, who refused to back away.

"My boy says it's his cap," Dave said.

"Well, he's crazy. It's my cap."

"I was with him when he got this cap. When the Phillies played here. It's a Philly cap."

"Eddie Condon gave it to me," Steve said. "And you stole it from me, you jerk."

"Don't call me a jerk, you little squirt. I never saw you before in my life."

"Look," Steve said, pointing to the printing on the cap's sweatband. "It's Eddie Condon's cap. See? See, Dad?"

"Yeah. You're right, Son. Ever see this boy before, Steve?"

"No," Steve said reluctantly.

The other boy realized he might lose the cap. "I bought it from a guy," he said. "I paid him. My father knows I paid him." He said he got the cap at the ball park. He groped for some magically impressive words and suddenly found them. "You'll have to speak to my father," he said.

"Sure, I'll speak to your father," Dave said. "What's your name? Where do you live?"

"My name's Hudson. I live about ten minutes away on the other side of the park." The boy appraised Dave, who wasn't any bigger than he was and who wore a faded windbreaker and no tie. "My father is a lawyer," he said boldly. "He wouldn't let me keep the cap if he didn't think I should."

"Is that a fact?" Dave asked belligerently. "Well, we'll see. Come on. Let's go." And he got between the two boys and they walked along the street. They didn't talk to each other. Dave knew the Hudson boy was waiting to get to the protection of his home, and Steve knew it, too, and he looked up apprehensively at Dave. And Dave, reaching for his hand, squeezed it encouragingly and strode along, cocky and belligerent, knowing that Steve relied on him.

The Hudson boy lived in that row of fine apartment houses on the other side of the park. At the entrance to one of these houses Dave tried not to hang back and show he was impressed, because he could feel Steve hanging back. When they got into the small elevator Dave didn't know why he took off his hat. In the carpeted hall on the fourth floor the Hudson boy said, "Just a minute," and entered his own apartment. Dave and Steve were left alone in the corridor, knowing that the other boy was preparing his father for the encounter. Steve looked anxiously at his father, and Dave said, "Don't worry, Son," and he added resolutely, "No one's putting anything over on us."

A tall, balding man in a brown velvet smoking-jacket suddenly opened the door. Dave had never seen a man wearing one of these jackets, although he had seen them in department-store windows. "Good evening," he said, making a deprecatory gesture at the cap Steve still clutched tightly in his left hand. "My boy didn't get your name. My name is Hudson."

"Mine's Diamond."

"Come on in," Mr. Hudson said, putting out his hand and laughing good-naturedly. He led Dave and Steve into his living-room. "What's this about that cap?" he asked. "The way kids can get excited about a cap. Well, it's understandable, isn't it?"

"So it is," Dave said, moving closer to Steve, who was awed by the broadloom rug and the fine furniture. He wanted to show Steve he was at ease himself, and he wished Mr. Hudson wouldn't be so polite. That meant Dave had to be polite and affable, too, and it was hard to manage when he was standing in the middle of the floor with his old windbreaker.

"Sit down, Mr. Diamond," Mr. Hudson said. Dave took Steve's arm and sat him down beside him on the chesterfield. The Hudson boy watched his father. And Dave looked at Steve and saw that he wouldn't face Mr. Hudson or the other boy; he kept looking up at Dave, putting all his faith in him.

"Well, Mr. Diamond, from what I gathered from my boy, you're able to prove this cap belonged to your boy."

"That's a fact," Dave said.

"Mr. Diamond, you'll have to believe my boy bought that cap from some kid in good faith."

"I don't doubt it," Dave said. "But no kid can sell something that doesn't belong to him. You know that's a fact, Mr. Hudson."

"Yes, that's a fact," Mr. Hudson agreed. "But that cap means a lot to my boy, Mr. Diamond."

"It means a lot to my boy, too, Mr. Hudson."

"Sure it does. But supposing we called in a policeman. You know what he'd say? He'd ask you if you were willing to pay my boy what he paid for that cap. That's usually the way it works out," Mr. Hudson said, friendly and smiling, as he eyed Dave shrewdly.

"But that's not right. It's not justice," Dave protested. "Not when it's my boy's cap."

"I know it isn't right. But that's what they do."

"All right. What did you say your boy paid for the cap?" Dave said reluctantly.

"Two dollars."

"Two dollars!" Dave repeated. Mr. Hudson's smile was still kindly, but his eyes were shrewd, and Dave knew the lawyer was counting on his not having the two dollars; Mr. Hudson thought he had Dave sized up; he had looked at him and decided he was broke. Dave's pride was hurt, and he turned to Steve. What he saw in Steve's face was more powerful than the hurt to his pride; it was the memory of how difficult it had been to get an extra nickel, the talk he heard about the cost of food, the worry in his mother's face as she tried to make ends meet, and the bewildered embarrassment that he was here in a rich man's home, forcing his father to confess that he couldn't afford to spend two dollars. Then Dave grew angry and reckless. "I'll give you the two dollars," he said.

Steve looked at the Hudson boy and grinned brightly. The Hudson boy watched his father.

"I suppose that's fair enough," Mr. Hudson said. "A cap like this can be worth a lot to a kid. You know how it is. Your boy might want to sell—I mean be satisfied. Would he take five dollars for it?"

"Five dollars?" Dave repeated, "Is it worth five dollars, Steve?" he asked uncertainly.

Steve shook his head and looked frightened.

"No, thanks, Mr. Hudson," Dave said firmly.

"I'll tell you what I'll do," Mr. Hudson said. "I'll give you ten dollars. The cap has a sentimental value for my boy, a Philly cap, a big-leaguer's cap. It's only worth about a buck and a half really," he added. But Dave shook his head again. Mr. Hudson frowned. He looked at his own boy with indulgent concern, but now he was embarrassed. "I'll tell you what I'll do," he said. "This cap—well, it's worth as much as a day at the circus to my boy. Your boy should be recompensed. I want to be fair. Here's twenty dollars," and he held out two ten-dollar bills to Dave.

That much money for a cap, Dave thought, and his eyes brightened. But he knew what the cap had meant to Steve; to deprive him of it now that it was within his reach would be unbearable. All the things he needed in his life gathered around him; his wife was there, saying he couldn't afford to reject the offer, he had no right to do it; and he turned to Steve to see if Steve thought it wonderful that the cap could bring them twenty dollars.

"What do you say, Steve?" he asked uneasily.

"I don't know," Steve said. He was in a trance. When Dave smiled, Steve smiled too, and Dave believed that Steve was as impressed as he was, only more bewildered, and maybe even more aware that they could not possibly turn away that much money for a ball cap.

"Well, here you are," Mr. Hudson said, and he put the two bills in Steve's hand. "It's a lot of money. But I guess you had a right to expect as much."

With a dazed, fixed smile Steve handed the money slowly to his father, and his face was white.

Laughing jovially, Mr. Hudson led them to the door. His own boy followed a few paces behind.

In the elevator Dave took the bills out of his pocket. "See, Stevie," he whispered eagerly. "That windbreaker you wanted! And ten dollars for your bank! Won't Mother be surprised?"

"Yeah," Steve whispered, the little smile still on his face. But Dave had to turn away quickly so their eyes wouldn't meet, for he saw that it was a scared smile.

Outside, Dave said, "Here, you carry the money home, Steve. You show it to your mother."

"No, you keep it," Steve said, and then there was nothing to say. They walked in silence.

"It's a lot of money," Dave said finally. When Steve didn't answer him, he added angrily, "I turned to you, Steve. I asked you, didn't I?"

"That man knew how much his boy wanted that cap," Steve said.

"Sure. But he recognized how much it was worth to us."

"No, you let him take it away from us," Steve blurted.

"That's unfair," Dave said. "Don't you dare say that to me."

"I don't want to be like you," Steve muttered, and he darted across the road and walked along the other side of the street.

"It's unfair," Dave said angrily, only now he didn't mean that Steve was unfair, he meant that what happened in the prosperous Hudson home was unfair, and he didn't know quite why. He had been trapped, not just by Mr. Hudson, but by his own life. Across the road Steve was hurrying along with his head down, wanting to be alone. They walked most of the way home on opposite sides of the street, until Dave could stand it no longer. "Steve," he called, crossing the street. "It was very unfair. I mean, for you to say…" but Steve started to run. Dave walked as fast as he could and Steve was getting beyond him, and he felt enraged and suddenly he yelled, "Steve!" and he started to chase his son. He wanted to get hold of Steve and pound him, and he didn't know why. He gained on him, he gasped for breath and he almost got him by the shoulder. Turning, Steve saw his father's face in the street light and was terrified; he circled away, got to the house, and rushed in, yelling, "Mother!"

"Son, Son!" she cried, rushing from the kitchen. As soon as she threw her arms around Steve, shielding him, Dave's anger left him and he felt stupid. He walked past them into the kitchen.

"What happened?" she asked anxiously. "Have you both gone crazy? What did you do, Steve?"

"Nothing," he said sullenly.

"What did your father do?"

"We found the boy with my ball cap, and he let the boy's father take it from us."

"No, no," Dave protested. "Nobody pushed us around. The man didn't put anything over us." He felt tired and his face was burning. He told what had happened; then he slowly took the two ten-dollar bills out of his wallet and tossed them on the table and looked up guiltily at his wife.

It hurt him that she didn't pick up the money, and that she didn't rebuke him. "It is a lot of money, Son," she said slowly. "Your father was only trying to do what he knew was right, and it'll work out, and you'll under-stand." She was soothing Steve, but Dave knew she felt that she needed to be gentle with him, too, and he was ashamed.

When she went with Steve to his bedroom, Dave sat by himself. His son had contempt for him, he thought. His son, for the first time, had seen how easy it was for another man to handle him, and he had judged him and had wanted to walk alone on the other side of the street. He looked at the money and he hated the sight of it.

His wife returned to the kitchen, made a cup of tea, talked soothingly, and said it was incredible that he had forced the Hudson man to pay him twenty dollars for the cap, but all Dave could think of was Steve was scared of me.

Finally, he got up and went into Steve's room. The room was in darkness, but he could see the outline of Steve's body on the bed, and he sat down beside him and whispered, "Look, Son, it was a mistake. I know why. People like us—in circumstances where money can scare us. No, no," he said, feeling ashamed and shaking his head apologetically; he was taking the wrong way of showing the boy they were together; he was covering up his own failure. For the failure had been his, and it had come out of being so separated from his son that he had been blind to what was beyond the price in a boy's life. He longed now to show Steve he could be with him from day to day. His hand went out hesitantly to Steve's shoulder. "Steve, look," he said eagerly. "The trouble was I didn't realize how much I enjoyed it that night at the ball park. If I had watched you playing for your own team—the kids around here say you could be a great pitcher. We could take that money and buy a new pitcher's glove for you, and a catcher's mitt. Steve, Steve, are you listening? I could catch you, work with you in the lane. Maybe I could be your coach…watch you become a great pitcher." In the half-darkness he could see the boy's pale face turn to him.

Steve, who had never heard his father talk like this, was shy and wondering. All he knew was that his father, for the first time, wanted to be with him in his hopes and adventures. He said, "I guess you do know how important that cap was." His hand went out to his father's arm. "With that man the cap was—well it was just something he could buy, eh Dad?" Dave gripped his son's hand hard. The wonderful generosity of childhood—the price a boy was willing to pay to be able to count on his father's admiration and approval—made him feel humble, then strangely exalted.

THE SAND-LOT UMPIRE
Masuji Ibuse
Translated by Ted Goossen

One evening in early summer, five years ago, I visited a friend's house in Tokyo's South Aoyama district to watch an amateur stage rehearsal. It was a long drawn-out affair, with so much time wasted batting around just how things should be staged, that, although it began at nine, it didn't break up until nearly dawn. When at last I reached the street, no taxis were in sight, so I decided to set out on foot for the train station at Shinanomachi. There was a direct route, a broad thoroughfare that cut across the big park adjoining the Meiji Shrine from the bus-stop at Aoyama San-Chome, but it was shrouded by trees and bound to be lonely.

I ended up falling in behind a police officer on patrol. Since his pace was slow and leisurely, mine became slow and leisurely too. It was past the time for courting couples—and the rascals that spy on them—to be out, so the park was deserted. Ahead, the Museum of Art's domed roof tinged the twilit sky black. The policeman cast but a single glance back in my direction, but when we had drawn near the playing fields which lay to our left, he suddenly veered off in that direction and hid himself behind a thick tree-trunk. Close by, near the back-screen of the closest of the baseball fields, a shadowy form could be seen moving about.

Wordlessly, the policeman gestured to me to hide myself too.

I crept over to crouch behind him, using his body, which smelled of leather, as a shield. The moment I reached down and touched the ground, the pounding in my heart began to subside.

The moon had already sunk, but we could see by the light which emanated from the direction of the caretaker's office, that the figure was that of a man. He walked over to a bench which had a bicycle leaning against it, turned his face up to the sky, and began to make a motion like swigging something out of a bottle.

"You don't suppose he's a thief, do you?" I whispered to the policeman.

"He could be," he whispered back. "Perhaps he's after lost valuables, or he's one of those guys who steal pieces from the wire netting."

Breaking off the swigging motion, the figure approached the back screen and stopped next to home plate. He was wearing long trousers, white shoes, and a baseball cap. It wasn't clear how old he was. He started to spread his legs, then suddenly threw his hand up in the air and uttered a strange sharp cry which sounded like "chee!" Then he shouted "chaa!" and then again, "po!"

"It's a ruse," the policeman said. He headed straight towards the man, who immediately doffed his cap and bowed as if in greeting. At first I stayed in my hiding place behind the tree, but seeing that the interrogation was starting, I edged over behind the back-stop where I could hear. The policeman had already worked up a full head of steam.

"Just what time do you think it is?" he grilled the suspect. "Why come so early, if, as you say, you don't start umpiring until six AM! What teams would schedule games so early?"

"They're from a candy company," the man replied respectfully, hat in hand. "The A team and the B team. When it gets to be midsummer there'll be games underway at four-thirty in the morning. Company teams play on their way to work, see, and need amateur umpires to handle their games."

"Even in that case, you'd still be an hour too early, wouldn't you?"

"I came here to study!" the man exclaimed passionately, thrusting his hat back on his head. He seemed to be regaining his spirits. "I'll be taking the Central League umpiring examination, so I came early to prepare before the games start. Don't they say people in the old days used to study by the light of fireflies!"

"This is the first I've heard of the Central League giving a hiring exam," the policeman countered, drawing a notebook out of his pocket. "Where is it held? Can you give me the location, and the names of the examiners?"

"Sure I can. The written test is held in the main hall of the Giants' training camp dormitory in Tamagawa. The head examiner is Mr. Shima, the Central League's Umpire-in-Chief. The practical exam takes place on the Giants' practice field."

The sky had turned a little brighter. The tone of the man in the baseball cap was growing more and more passionate.

"An umpire's got to have a good voice. That's why I was gargling just now—to improve my voice. Hey, I know I haven't got much polish—I'm just a common guy off the streets—but I want to umpire until I die. Women and the like don't matter much to me—it's the exam that's important. Right now I'm trying to figure out whose umpiring style to follow, Shima's of the Central League or Henmi's of the Big Six. See, I'm going to wear a Giants' uniform to the exam. If I copy Shima's style, I'll call the strikes like this."

Clenching his right hand into a fist, the man swept it high into the air and gave a piercing shout: "sui-ku!"

"If it's a ball, I'll call 'po!' I won't raise my left hand though—only amateur umpires do that. Shima gets hundreds of yen each time he lifts his arm, I bet, but I'm paid just three-hundred a game. Sometimes the big company teams make that five-hundred, though."

"Say, what's your name anyway?"

"I'm Hiroshi Kitami of Kanda. If you say 'Kitami the sand-lot umpire,' though, anyone from the big company teams I work for will know who you mean."

"Who's your favourite umpire?"

"In the pros, I like the Central League's Shima and the Pacific League's Nidegawa. Nidegawa's strike call is 'tsee!' When Shima calls 'sui-ku!', he sounds just like a grasshopper. Among the college umpires, my real favourite is Henmi of the Big Six. For Ball One, he breaks his call off at the end like this—'pogh!' Both pro leagues use the same gestures, but the Pacific League umpires wear gloves. In the Central League they don't."

"How about you when you umpire—do you wear gloves?"

The policeman's interrogation had taken on a bantering tone, but Hiroshi Kitami's answers remained deadly serious.

"I stand half-way between the two leagues. I wear a glove just on my right hand."

"What first made you decide to be a sand-lot umpire?"

"It was quite by accident. My mom kept telling me I had to go see a game in person, so I went to Korakuen Stadium. The players didn't attract me all that much, but the instant I saw Shima in his protector, I fell in love just like that. Ever since then, umpiring has been my life. If it weren't for baseball, I'd just as soon die."

"I guess even sand-lot umpires can earn quite a bit once a team gets to know them. It just so happens I love baseball myself. Let's say, when teams from bars or cabarets get together, don't they sometimes bet on the outcome?"

"When I'm the umpire there are never any arguments, whoever wins or loses. That's why I doubt any gambling's going on. But those girls who come to cheer for the cabaret teams—they do bother me. I'm pretty naive when it comes to women, and when I hear them squealing in those high-pitched voices, my face starts burning. It's hopeless!"

"Aren't there batters who ask you to call pitches balls even if they're strikes? Don't they whisper that kind of thing to you on the sly?"

"Yes, some try that. They'll sort of sidle up to me before the catcher takes his position and say something like, 'Sorry to ask, but call a few my way, would you?'

But, you know, I always just turn the other way. I guess I really am too naive."

"Haven't you ever taken any other kind of job?"

"Sure. Up until last year I worked in a tiny bar in Tsukiji. I even worked my way up to be manager, but then last summer I chucked it to devote myself to this career. The way I am now, there's no way I could keep my butt in a chair once the season started. I'd end up working sand-lot games for free, or itching to go see a Big Six game. I can work hard in the winter months, but when March comes and it starts to get warm, I can't sit still. Before the bar job, I was a delivery boy in a take-out restaurant, and before that I worked half-a-year as a shipping clerk in a news agency, but they gave up on me once they realized I couldn't fill in as editor or write even a single line of copy. I guess I'm just a man bound to live and die for baseball, eh!"

The policeman glanced down at his watch and then up at the cloudless blue sky.

"Sure is perfect weather for baseball today," he said; then, without another word, he set off in the direction of the road.

Trains could already be heard running in the distance. I pulled out a cigarette only to realize I had no matches.

"Excuse me, but do you have a light?" I called to Umpire Hiroshi Kitami from behind the back-stop.

"Good morning," he answered, fishing a box of matches from his trousers' pocket. "Let me light it for you. I don't smoke myself, but the players often ask me for a match, so I carry them."

He struck one and extended it to me through the screen. I took this opportunity to pick up some tips about the playing fields, an umpire's equipment, and so forth to supplement my pitifully small store of knowledge.

Renting a single field, Umpire Kitami informed me, cost five-hundred yen for two hours, although a rumour was circulating that this would likely be raised to a thousand yen before long. The regulations stipulated that these fees were to be passed up to the park office.

I had him show me the indicator umpires use in their work. It was slightly larger than a match-box and made out of celluloid, with three openings which registered the number of strikes, balls and outs. These figures could be adjusted by rotating the small cogwheels fixed on the side.

"One of these costs a hundred yen," he told me. "Sporting goods stores sell them. They're the single most important tool in the umpiring trade."

Then Umpire Kitami showed me another of his tools—a small whisk-broom.

"This is what we use to dust off home plate. They cost two-hundred yen at the store, but I found this one here at the field."

"You know, I've always rather liked the way umpires look when they sweep home plate. Of course, I've only seen them do it on television."

"Yeah, I've picked up the habit of sweeping home every time the teams change."

"To change the subject, I've heard that in women's baseball there are pitchers who burst into tears when they walk a few batters in a row, but still keep right on pitching. Is that really true?"

"You've got me. I've worked only one women's game as a volunteer for two amateur teams but as it turned out, I couldn't make the calls, not even 'out' or 'safe.' I was struck dumb—my voice just disappeared. I felt like this irresistible force was flooding out from around home plate, like the air around me was changing. Some things are really powerful, aren't they!"

As Umpire Kitami talked, however, it became clear that the presence of female spectators actually spurred him on in his work. Even amateur umpires have their fans, and in Kitami's case there was a sweet young junior high-school girl of about twelve or thirteen who would show up discreetly at his games, watch about two or three innings, and then leave.

I discovered that the sand-lot umpires of Tokyo are organized into clubs, according to district. Umpire Kitami apparently belonged to none of these clubs. Instead, he would just show up at the playing fields, where two or three games were invariably going on, and volunteer to act as umpire. Once a particular team had gotten to know him, they would start phoning him two or three days in advance. On occasion, he would be the one to initiate the arrangement.

This, then, is what I saw and heard one morning in early summer five years ago.

Last month, I had the opportunity to chat with Umpire-in-Chief Shima of the Central League, so I asked him about the qualifying exam five years before and whether or not Kitami, the sand-lot umpire, had passed.

"That fellow Kitami leaves quite an impression, doesn't he," Shima answered. "Even today, I can still picture him clearly. No, he failed. We had a hundred applicants show up that day and two passed. Not one received perfect marks. They all tried their best, though."

"Did Hiroshi Kitami wear a Giants' uniform to the exam? I guess he wouldn't have worn one with a numeral on the back!"

"No, none of the applicants wore uniforms. We instructed them to come in clothes that would let them move freely—we never said 'bring your uniforms.'"

Although I don't know much about the rules of baseball, I was curious what sorts of questions had appeared on the test. I also wanted to know exactly what it was the evaluators were looking for in the practical exam. The following, therefore, are the sorts of things that were asked, all of which, I was told, the average professional umpire could answer in an instant:

QUESTION: What is an 'illegally batted ball'?
ANSWER: One in which the batter's feet are not properly within the lines of the batter's box.

QUESTION: If, in the umpire's judgement, a pitch is headed for the strike zone and the batter moves in a way that suggests he is trying intentionally to be hit by that pitch, what should be done? If, in this situation, the ball does strike the batter and roll away, and the baserunners advance, what should be the umpire's verdict?
ANSWER: In either case, the pitch is called a strike, play is halted, and any baserunners sent back to their original bases.

QUESTION: A batter hits a bouncing ball which strikes in fair ground in the infield but then lands outside the outfield foul line. Is it fair or foul?
ANSWER: If, in the umpire's view, the ball has passed over any part of the base on its way to the outfield, it is a fair ball.

QUESTION: A batter hits a ground ball and runs to first base. The infielder's throw arrives just at the moment his foot hits the bag. Is he safe or out?
ANSWER: He is safe. In the case of a tie, the decision always favours the runner.

QUESTION: What is 'obstruction'?
ANSWER: When a fielder intentionally blocks a baserunner's progress. 'Baserunning Interference' is another term.

To qualify, applicants had to be between twenty-five and thirty years of age, have graduated from middle-school (pre-war system) or high-school (post-war system), and have at least some umpiring experience. As a result, men from a wide variety of backgrounds —school teachers, painters, gym instructors, carpenters, sailors, young green-grocers, restaurant delivery-boys, the unemployed, etc.—showed up to take the exam. When interviewed, each and every one pledged, as if by prior agreement, that they loved baseball more than food, were willing to work without pay, and would even eat rocks if asked.

Umpire-in-Chief Shima went on to describe how those who managed to pass the interview and the written test then went on to take the practical examination at Giants' field, with the Giants' second team acting as 'model players.' The first step in this simulated game was to have the batters run out ground balls to the infield. This allowed the examiners to judge the candidate's positioning at first base and the timing of their calls. Then their judgement on attempted steals at second base was scrutinized, as was their accuracy in judging whether the Giants' hurlers' fastballs were balls or strikes. Besides making the correct calls, one needed a good style, a clear voice, and effective gestures. Gestures had to be pronounced when a play was close, but otherwise they were supposed to be given in an understated but clear manner. A strong voice was an asset. A weak voice could kill a game. Yet an umpire's presence should never overshadow that of the players—his was always a supporting role. His calls had to be clear, but any touch of showmanship could lead to grandstanding.

I expected candidate Hiroshi Kitami had taken the practical exam with great gusto, but Shima told me he'd never reached that point, having failed both the written test and the interview.

Just the other day, the same day that the third and deciding game in the annual rivalry between Waseda and Keio Universities was being played, I went back to my friend's house in South Aoyama to return a collection of photographs of Chekhov's plays. On my return, I was once again cutting through the park on the road that runs from Aoyama San-Chome to Shinanomachi station when I heard the sound of the Waseda-Keio radio broadcast. It was coming from near the playing fields, right around where the policeman and I had hidden in the shadow of the trees that early morning five years before. Recalling everything that had happened then, I began to cast my eyes about to see if I could spot precisely which tree-trunk I had crouched behind.

When I stood by the road-side and faced the playing fields, a grove of Japanese beech trees and Japanese elms lay to my left, and a stand of leafless horse chestnuts to my right. For some reason, trees in this area tended to grow in clumps, with several trunks branching out from each base. Had they been trained to grow in such a fashion? I made a rough guess and decided the tree I had squatted behind five years before was likely one of those beeches with divided trunks. Beyond lay some elms, and beyond them the back-screen of the baseball field.

A game was presently in progress. One team was dressed in cream-coloured uniforms, the other wore white, and they were playing with a sponge ball. A small group of male and female spectators were sitting on the bench, and two men who seemed to be passers-by stood watching behind the screen; one looked like a vagrant, and the other was wearing a suit. I realized that the Waseda-Keio broadcast was issuing from a portable radio slung over the shoulder of the man in the suit. In other words, he was watching one game while reverberating with the sounds of another.

I moved over behind the screen to better hear the Waseda-Keio broadcast. Thus I too was put in the position of watching one game while listening to another. I wasn't rooting for Waseda, but neither was I a Keio fan. At first, Waseda was winning so I pulled for them, but when the lead shifted to Keio, so did my sympathies. In sumo wrestling and Japanese chess as well, I invariably supported the winning side. I knew this made me a faithless fan, but since that's what I felt comfortable with, that's what I tried to do.

It was hard to make out the announcers' voices, for although the huge stadium from which the broadcast was originating was so close at hand, there was a good deal of static. Adding to the problem was the fact that the actual noise from the game, like the students singing their school songs, seemed to be overlapping with what we were hearing on the portable radio.

"Who's winning?" I asked the man in the suit.

"Waseda's ahead. At least for now, that is," he replied with a scowl.

All of a sudden it struck me! That umpire standing there just beyond the screen, mask removed as the teams changed sides, was none other than Umpire Kitami himself! Five years earlier he'd told me that, except for December, January and February, he came here every day it didn't rain—had he really kept that schedule up all this while! His blue windbreaker was faded, and his white canvas shoes soiled, but he was sporting a brand-new protector. Each time the team changed sides, he would walk back and write something on the blackboard affixed to the screen with a piece of chalk.

"Hey, Kitami!" I called to him. "It's been quite a while, hasn't it! Remember me? We met right here early one morning five years ago—it was still practically dark. You lit my cigarette. Before that, you were talking with a patrolman."

"Oh, now I remember you!" said Kitami with a look of surprise. "You're right, it has been a while. Today I'm copying Nidegawa of the Pacific League. Please stick around—it's quite a show!"

"What were you writing just now on the black-board?"

"That's the scoreboard."

"And how about that new protector—it looks pretty smart!"

"I borrowed it from one of the players. The mask, too. Each time they change sides, the catcher coming off the field lends me his mask."

Kitami went over to the bench to get his new mask, walked back to home plate, swept it off with his whisk broom, and shouted 'pura—!' in a loud voice. Another one of his countless innings had just begun. It was the cream-coloured team's turn at the plate, and their batting was marvellous. The first batter swung just as Kitami shot his right hand into the air and called 'tsuee!' The ball flew on a line into the gap in right-centre field, and the batter ended up with a triple. The next batter waited as Kitami called 'boru!' four times in succession and trotted down to first base. The next batter hit a deep fly to the outfield, scoring the runner from third. The following batter belted another long hit, scoring the runner from first and leaving himself standing on third base. Then there was a strikeout and another long fly. The teams changed, and Kitami came back to the screen to record the score.

"Hey, Kitami!" I called to him. "How do you spend your winters these days? Still taking other jobs during the off-season?"

"I spend my winters training—live off my savings," he answered when he'd finished writing down the score. "I've got to keep in shape—agility counts a lot in umpiring. Every day, I do radio calisthenics and go running. Some nights I run out here, and shout out my calls while I look at the stars. An umpire's eyes are important, and his voice is important, too!"

The white-clad team came to the plate, but as their batting was unremarkable, the spectators drifted away. The man carrying the portable radio disappeared, as did the swollen-faced fellow standing next to me—he had seemed quite down-and-out. There had been a middle-aged woman who looked cold and a man in his forties with a baseball cap and a puffy face, but now they were gone too. In their place, a lean dried-up looking old man presently came up to stand beside me. He was wearing a frock coat, and appeared to have just emerged from a wedding at the adjacent Meiji Memorial Hall, for a gaudy artificial flower was pinned to his lapel. It seemed likely that he had been a baseball player in his youth. He watched the game with great intensity, and at one point, apparently unable to control himself, made a brief trip around the backstop to check the scoreboard. Having done that, his expression became completely unperturbed.

There were six baseball diamonds on the grounds —from Field One to Field Six—and each was crammed with players. A single groundskeeper equipped with a bamboo rake and basket, made the rounds from field to field, collecting waste paper, cigarette butts and other trash and depositing them in a large gasoline drum. In the forest beyond the fields, a pale yellow banner was fluttering at the end of a tall pole.

I waited until someone hit a home run, then cut through the grove of trees across the spike-studded ground back to the paved road. The towering stand of horse chestnuts, having shed their leaves early, recalled a winter's scene, and the image of their imposing presence continued to swim in my head even after I had boarded the train. Seen at night, they must seem to pierce the sky itself. Were it winter, with the moon and stars all out, the sight would be uncanny indeed. And were Umpire Kitami there alone on the baseball field under the winter's sky, roaring out his calls of 'out' and 'safe,' and were I to see him standing there in the light of the moon and the stars, then, I thought, I would be able to bring his story to a conclusion.

I GUESS YOU FELLOWS JUST DON'T WANT ME
Nelson Algren

I once knew a here-and-there sort of fellow who was so here-then-there that the police would always pick him up before he could get somewhere.

The officers would never admit—no, not in a hundred years—that they kept picking this fellow up just for being *around.* "We're *forced* to pick him up," one told me, "because he's so *suspicious.*"

"It's not so simple a matter as mere suspicion," the desk sergeant tried to explain, "it's because he's suspicious of *himself.* If a man is suspicious of himself, why shouldn't we be?"

If the police had just said straight out that they picked him up because his neck was on crooked they would have been on solid ground. You could hardly fault the law for a man's neck being on one side. The law didn't put it on that way.

But, as though crookedneckedness wasn't enough to get him picked up, this fellow would stand around with his cap pulled down far enough over his eyes as to constitute intent to commit a misdemeanor if not a felony, on street corners where buses never stopped. If he'd just pulled that cap off his eyes and gone up to the bus-stop, crooked neck or no crooked neck, it wouldn't have made the least difference. He would have been picked up all the same. Because by that hour the buses are all back in the barns and *every* corner is a wrong corner. This fellow seemed bright enough in other ways. His trouble was he had an IQ beyond psychology.

Another affliction this fellow had was having a record over five inches long. The way he'd gotten it was by getting himself picked up only a block away from a bar where a pearl-handled .22-caliber pistol and ninety-eight dollars and sixty cents had just been stolen. Sure enough, this fellow was found to be carrying a pearl-handled .22-caliber pistol. The officers accused him of having *robbed* it.

"Why should I rob another man's weapon," he demanded to know, "when I've got ninety-eight dollars in my wallet?"

"How much you got in your pocket?" one of the shrewder officers asked immediately.

"Sixty cents," this fellow answered proudly. But when they took an account it was found he had a total of a hundred and four dollars in the wallet and twenty-six cents in his pockets. He was sentenced to six months for failing to account for the $5.66 discrepancy. He had to give the pistol back, too.

As soon as he got out he began doing everything he knew how to do to keep from getting a record a full half-foot long. And what he knew how to do better than anything was moving electric typewriters, computing machines, lamps, swivel chairs, and cherrywood desks out of the back doors of Milwaukee Avenue office-furniture stores while a couple of cops were guarding the front to see that no one walked down the alley. The fellow called this "helping out" because he did it unarmed.

When the cops handed him five or ten dollars he would accept it. But he would never take an adding machine, or a carton of fountain pens or a shipment of typewriter ribbons off the law. Which goes to show that even though his neck was on crooked his thinking was pretty straight.

Whether this fellow's affliction was hereditary or had been acquired by looking back over his shoulder I never did find out. And if I gave you another hundred years to guess what we nicknamed this fellow, you'd never hit it. Right off you'd say "Crooked-neck" or "Dizzy" or "Dodger" or "Rabbit" or something like that. But it wasn't *anything* like that. What we called this fellow was Ipso. Which was short for Ipso Facto.

Because you'd be talking to him here and, when you looked around, he was over there. So you'd ask him where he was going and he'd say, "I'm on my way—*ipso facto.*" Or, when the cops thought he was starting to look suspicious of himself again, they'd stop him and ask, "Who are you going to rob tonight, Ipso? Who are you waiting around here to kill? How much did you make picking pockets at Wrigley Field yesterday?"

"I wasn't at Cubs Park yesterday," Ipso would answer.

"*Where* were you?"

"Sox Park," Ipso would say; because he was ashamed to tell them he'd spent the whole day riding the roller-coaster at Riverview.

"The Sox are out of town," the cops would say, "get in, *Ipso Facto.*"

Now what Ipso Facto meant by *Ipso Facto* was "I'll see you around." But what the cops thought "Ipso Facto" meant was "Be damned quick about it." Ipso would accept the cops' interpretation.

Then, of course, in the query room it would come down to a matter of being booked on suspicion or of helping the boys out.

The first time Ipso was picked up he asked the officers, "What for?"

"You look suspicious," one explained; and held the car-mirror so Ipso would see himself in it.

"You're right," Ipso had to agree, "I really *do* look suspicious."

But when they wanted to take his prints that time, Ipso asked them, "What for? I haven't robbed nobody."

"But if you should change your mind we'd *need* them," the fingerprint man explained in a kindly manner.

"I see your point of view," Ipso had agreed; and put his hands on the pad.

He felt relieved after they'd gotten his prints.

"When they told me I could go home it was better than confession," Ipso admitted to me, "that was why I didn't go straight home."

"Where'd you go?"

"Nowheres. I just sat down in the cops' waiting room and read a copy of *St. Jude's Magazine*. When they asked me what I was hanging around for I told them I thought maybe they wanted me for a Lie Detector Test."

Ipso's draftboard was a bit startled when he materialized at the induction center. Being three inches over six feet, weighing only 129 pounds, and the manner in which his head was set on his shoulders wouldn't have attracted special attention had it not been for the tiny American flag waving from the left lens of Ipso's tortoise-shell specs. The pin holding the frame had been lost; so Ipso had inserted the stem of the tiny flag to keep the glasses from falling off. Removing the flag from its stem would not only have been unpatriotic, Ipso explained, but would also constitute a felony.

All the inducting officer could think to ask was, "Are you going to be on *our* side?"

"I'd like to die for my country," Ipso announced, "but I have bad teeth."

"That's all right," the officer decided, having recovered from his first surprise, "we don't want you to bite the enemy."

It was only his neck which deprived Ipso of becoming a force for law and order in Chicago. Had they ever let *him* ask the questions in the query room, he would have asked all the right questions:

"If you weren't planning to mug some drunk, when you were hanging around that bar, why don't you let us have your prints in event you should change your mind?"

"If you're not guilty of something, why are you trying to make fools of us by having us stand around asking you questions?"

"If you're so innocent what are you bleeding about?"

"If you're not *guilty* of something, you must be innocent of something—and that's even more serious."

Ipso hated work. He hated work so much that he not only hated people who went to work but he hated unemployed people who had friends who were working. All he did, himself, besides moving office furniture, was to drive a cab a couple nights a week.

He drove sitting in the middle of the seat. Had he sat under the wheel his flag, projecting out of the window, would have caused the driver behind to think he was about to make a U-turn.

When a passenger would ask why he drove in this position, Ipso would answer, "I was a pursuit pilot, sir." Why a stupid answer like that worked I never understood. Wouldn't you think *somebody* would have said, "Get the hell under that wheel where you belong?" Yet nobody ever did.

We were playing the Kosciusko Arrows, for five dollars a man, on a hot, dry, dusty Sunday morning, on the lot bounded by Ashland Avenue and Bosworth Street. We were two runs behind with one out in the ninth when Ipso came to bat with a man on second. The manager flashed the bunt sign to the third-base coach; who flashed it to Ipso.

Ipso stepped back out of the box, because he didn't get the signal. The coach flashed it again but it was no use. Ipso had forgotten it.

"Bunt you meathead!" the manager shouted at the top of his lungs from the bench. "B-U-N-T—BUNT!"

The pitcher gave Ipso a fast ball and he laid down a perfect sacrifice bunt—and *slid* into first base.

He waited there, while the right fielder and the first baseman hunted for the ball, long enough to adjust his flag. Then he took off and slid into second base. The pitcher went over to help the right fielder help the first baseman and right fielder find the ball. Ipso dusted himself off again. Then he adjusted his flag.

"I guess you fellows just don't want me," he finally told the second baseman; and took off for third. This time he used a hook slide.

The Kosciusko second baseman went over to help the pitcher help the right fielder help the first baseman to find the ball. Ipso dusted himself off again. His flag was still in place.

"I guess you don't want me neither," he told the third baseman. And took off home.

Ten feet from the plate he took the ball out of his pocket and tossed it to the catcher; who tagged him out so hard he knocked Ipso down.

Ipso didn't get up right away. He just lay there, turning his lopsided head one way and another and saying to himself, "I had it coming! I had it coming!" Miraculously, the flag was still waving.

All Ipso would answer for some days after that, when asked for an explanation, was "*ipso facto.*" But, about a month after, sitting in a bar, I asked him why he'd given up that ball.

"If I'd scored a tying run on a stolen ball I wouldn't be a *good* guy," he told me. "I *deserved* to be tagged out."

"That is highly honorable of you, Ipso," I had to admit, "but how come your conscience didn't bother you, the night before, when you were hauling two thousand dollars' worth of somebody else's furniture down the alley? How could you get conscience-stricken about a sixty-nine-cent baseball the next morning?"

"What does *costs* have to do with it," Ipso asked me. "Sports is one thing and robbin' is another. Everybody stands a pinch now and then—but *nobody* steals first base."

"Then it was stealing first base, and not stealing the ball, that made you get yourself tagged out?"

"Of *course*. Lots of good guys go robbin'. But *no* good guy slides into first."

"Frank Frisch did it at the Polo Grounds," I had to remind Ipso, "and started a riot."

"I wish you would've told me that before the game," Ipso reflected wistfully, "we'd all be five bucks richer today."

And adjusted his little flag.

RONNIE ON THE MOUND
Jack Kerouac

During infield practice the Chryslers are out on the field in their golden-yellow uniforms and the warm-up pitcher is little Theo K. Vance, bespectacled and scholarly, testing out his blazing fireball at catcher Babe Blagden, the veteran of more years in the league than he'd care to admit to any babe he tried to pick up last night in the Loop—it's a spring night in Chicago, the occasion a crucial game between the Chicago Chryslers (tied for the league lead with St. Louis at 21–11 all) and the Pittsburgh Plymouths, the usual door mats of the league now rejuvenated not only with a new manager, old Pie Tibbs, an all-time all-star great centerfielder and slugger, but with new additions like the kid outfielder Oboy Roy Turner, the steady rookie Leo Sawyer at short (son of veteran Vic Sawyer) and then new star pitcher Ronnie Melaney just up from the minors with a dazzling record and rumors of a blazing fast ball. It's May in the Loop town, the wind blows softly from the lake, with a shade of autumnal coolness in the air presaging the World Series excitement to come, even the lowly Plymouths at a 14-won and 18-lost record hoping to be up there by that time now that they have that new wild line-up—but it's just really another game, another night, the usual gathering, cigar smoke in the stands, hot dogs, the call of beer sellers, the latecoming fans, the kids yelling in the bleachers (Friday night) and the old umpire like W.C. Fields in black coat and bursting pants bending to brush the plate as on a thousand other occasions in his old spittoon life—but the thrill runs through the crowd to see the rookie making his debut on the big-league mound: Ronnie Melaney, nineteen, handsome, with dark eyes, pale skin, nervous hands, rubbing his hands down his green-striped trousers, kicking the mound, handling the resin bag and eyeing the bright lamps all around the stadium, newspapermen in the press box leaning forward to report his showing. Old Frank "Pie" Tibbs is out there on the mound giving Ronnie last-minute pats on the pants. "Take it easy kid, these Chryslers can be beat just like the bushwallopers back home." "Thanks, Mr. Tibbs," gulps Ronnie as he takes a step off the mound and pretends to fiddle with his shoes as the umpire calls "Batter up" and the stands vibrate with the excitement of the opening pitch of the game. The first batter will be Lefty Murphree the new sensation, called a "sophomore," in his second year of play with the Chryslers, whose speed (16 doubles) and general .300 hitting has sykrocketed the Chryslers up to top tie position, a murderous hitter, second in the league also in stolen bases with 9 (behind the incomparable Pancho Villa of Los Angeles), a left-handed beauty, stepping in now with a delicate pinch at his cap tip and a knock on his spikes and a spit to the side, as the old umpire handles his bellywhomper and straightens it out and prepares to half squat to squint at that pitch and call 'em straight. Now Murphree is in the box leveling his bat around in easy aiming strokes and is the first big-leaguer to be looking down the slot at Ronnie Melaney.

The sign is for a fast ball: *Let 'em see it, boy!* thinks the catcher (antique Jake Guewa of thirty years on the very same Pittsburgh team—a hard, browned, seamy little man with guts of iron, a weak hitter but a clutch hitter, who maybe after six games hitless and arid can suddenly win a game with an unobtrusive single in the bottom of the ninth). "Come on Daddy Kid!" Ronnie dangles the ball from his strong right hand, nods, steps on the rubber, winds back and forth a little rock, throws up the left leg, comes around like a whip and balls one straight at Murphree's strike zone and Murphree swings a mean white bat and the ball whistles past the umpire's crowned noggin for a hang-in foul strike into the screen and umpire J.C. Gwynn raises right hand and shouts "Streeike!" and the game is on and the crowd goes "Whooee!"

Old Jake Guewa takes a peak at the bench and Manager Pie Tibbs gives him the sign for a curve; Ronnie's curve is a good one with a hopper, many's the old seamed scout watched it from behind the screen in the Texas League. Ronnie nods and gulps, he likes to concentrate on his fast ball, but orders are orders. He winds back and forth as a gust of wind comes and ripples the flags around the stadium, someone whistles, someone hoots and the white pellet is seen flying home high in the night toward the tense Murphree—the umpire throws up his left arm, yells, "Ball one" and the crowd goes, "Oh, oh." Guewa has the ball where it exploded *plow* into his glove, holds it aloft as such, walks a few feet ahead of the plate, says something to Ronnie, who strains to listen and comes forward a few steps. Guewa fires it at him, hard, as if to wake him up, turns and goes back with the inestimable sorrow of the baseball catcher to squat and as if to sigh again behind that old plate and Murphree knocks the spikes with the bat (one and one is the count, the kid's first major-league count), grits his teeth, sets that foot back on the rubber and sees the sign for fast ball and says to himself, *I'll burn this guy right down!* and whams it around, wild and high again. "Ball Two!" "Hey!" yells the crowd. "He's wild!" "Throw the bum out!" "Where'd you get the bushman!" "Come on, kid, settle down!" "He's got fire in that ball but we better call the fire dee-part-ment"; laughter, discussion, conversation between women about how cute he is, kids yelling with glee about nothing they can understand, a bottle breaking somewhere far back in the johns. Melaney is behind in the count and now he begins to sweat and takes the sign for sinker and nods gravely—he's afraid to look toward the bench where maybe now Manager Tibbs is frowning. Murphree stands in there, leveling the bat around, careful as a hawk, eyes right on Ronnie, chewing with no feeling. Ronnie winds up and delivers with his heart as big as a toad: strike down the middle which Murphree only glances at, because he's had his own orders to let this one go—the ball has come in high, like a vision, but sunk in across the chest perfectly spotted, landing in old Guewa's glove like a shot of a gun, *plow!* "Yay!" yells a fan. "He'll make it! You'll be awright, baby!" And now the count is two and two and Jake gives the sign for a fast ball, Ronnie steels himself, remembers the calm with which he used to deliver pitches like this on drowsy afternoons in Dallas and Fort Worth and even before that in the Sunset League in Arizona, and in a dream he lets go his next pitch, high, too high, just off, ball three! And now it's a full count.

Manager Pie Tibbs is staring anxiously toward the mound, trying to think what to order; finally he sends the sign to the catcher, curve ball, who transmits it to Ronnie, who gulps because a curve ball is harder to control—*But I'll make it true!* There is a silence now in the stadium, you can hear little clicks of teletypes up in the press box, and small familiar sounds like a distant car horn in the street, and the usual whistles and catcalls: "He's a bum left, let 'im have it!" "Another two bagger, boy!" (These cries are from the Chrysler bench, from Hophead Deane the crazy first-baseman and from utility men like Ernie Shaw and veteran Johnny Keggs and kids like Phil Drayton the speed-boy pinch-runner.) Ronnie winds up now and lets her go at Lefty Murphree, who's ready and raps the bat around and connects with a dead knock that signifies he's topped the ball and it bounces down in front of him and goes skittering straight at first-baseman Wade Hazard who just stands as if knock-kneed to let it pop into his glove and nonchalantly (almost spitting) he straightens up and trots to the first base bag well ahead of the racing, smoky Murphree, out, and Murphree streaks across the bag a dead pigeon and Ronnie Melaney's first man up has grounded out to first.

But here comes mighty Herb Jangraw to the plate; a second ago he was kneeling and spitting with three bats between his big mitts, dreaming of something else, waiting for his turn, now here he comes for his licks and it's only the beginning of Ronnie Melaney's career in the world. The crowd lets out a yowl of joy to see the old time great slugger in a slump this year, but still as explosive as ever potentially, a man who has hit home runs out of sight in every ball park in the league, six-foot-four, 210 pounds, a rangy body, mighty arms, a great, ragged, ruinous face—drinks cases of beer by himself, a big jaw, a big cud, a big splurt of brown tobacco juice on the green fresh grass, he doesn't care, hitches his mighty pants and steps in, also left-handed, but with an immense long 45-inch bat that puts the fear of God into Ronnie to see it. "Phew," says the kid—only one out and two to go, and then only one inning and eight to go, and then only one game and thirty, forty for the year, and then only one year and twenty to go (if lucky) and then death O Lord. Jake Guewa steps out a ways, winks at Ronnie, gives him the sign for a sinker, goes back and squats; the old umpire leans in, Ronnie toes the rubber, rocks, rocks one time extry, throws up the left leg and burns one down, twisting his wrist as hard as he can to make that sinker *sink* dear God or Jangraw'll golf it out of sight and Pittsburgh. He does golf it, hits it with a woodsy whack, it goes arcing weakly to the left, the third-baseman Joe Martin makes a leap but it means nothing, he knows he can't get it, he even lets his good glove go as a sign of *O well*; the glove sails up and the ball sails out to left field, where Oboy Roy scutters up to recover it and fires it to second at little Homer Landry, as Jangraw gallumps down to first and makes a halfhearted turn and goes back to stand on the bag with a single to left, arms akimbo and spitting brown juice and nodding as Wade Hazard makes a smiling remark at him and the first-base umpire yells some joke and the fans are buzzing and sitting down again. But what now? What with the next batter, the mighty Babe Blagden, one of the greatest hitters of all time and currently batting .323—in only 29 games he's had 31 hits and already delivered 8 homers (3 behind Jangraw) and catching up to the league leaders after he'd originally decided (in the spring) to give up active playing and be a coach, then persuaded to pinch hit, which he did with three home runs in a row or so, and so now back in the regular lineup and booming as good as ever.

Now Manager Pie Tibbs is stalking up and down before the bench with that familiar walk of his, well-known to two generations of baseball fans, that cat stalk, only now there are lines in his face and he has to decide weighty issues. The fans are jeering Ronnie, "It's only the beginning kiddo!" "Let's see that famous fast ball, Babe loves that fast ball!" "Beer! Get me cold beer!" A cold sweat is on Ronnie's brow, he wipes it away like grease, he rubs his hands in the sand, on the resin bag, something's wrong with his body juices—*I've gotta get outa this inning!* he prays—he gets the sign and gets ready to deliver.

It's a fast ball, fast as he can make it, to catch Blagden off balance, Babe is a right-hand powerhouse and swings with his wrists alone. He likes it and steps in with a short dusty push of his cleated foot and toothpicks the bat around and clacks it a weak popup into the air off the mound which Ronnie himself takes with a reassuring hand wave to the others. "I got it," he calls.

So Jangraw is left standing on first base and now there's two outs and can Ronnie make it? Babyface Kolek, the recent hot hitter of the league rewarded with cleanup spot on the Chryslers, is stepping in and the stands are in an uproar. Kolek is such a clever clutch-hitter Manager Pie Tibbs is worried and comes out to the mound to talk to Ronnie; Pie is also worried about the kid's debut, his beginning inning will be so important in his development, besides who wants Jangraw sent around from first to score and put the Chryslers out ahead in the first inning.

"Boy, I want you to take it cagey with this Kiolex, he's a mean little bastat, let him have an assortment, start with a curve and keep it outside." "Yessir, Mr. Tibbs." "Lissen, kid, I don't have to come out here in the first inning, but I notice you're nervous…let old Jake tell you what to do now, aim straight." Ronnie, in a dream, toes the rubber, eyes Jangraw leading off first. Pie is back in the dugout, sitting, hunched, watching, Ronnie pumps fast and pours her in, at the left-handed, squatting, keen-eyed Kolek, who lets it by his letters for a perfect strike. "Two more boy!" yells Jake Guewa, whanging the ball back, smarting Ronnie's hand. He pours another one in high, the count is even and still in the balance—"Just a few more pitches!" He sweats…now he pauses, wipes his hands, wishes for a drink of water, or a Coke, swallows, takes the sign for change of pace fast ball and again checks on big Jangraw on first, with Wade Hazard hovering behind him, both doing a little, slow, big man hop. Ronnie turns his face from them and his arm responds, hard, whiplash, down-the-wrist twists, the ball sails home, sinks too far, low, for ball two—"What's the matter with me! Do I have to do everything in this world?" "Come on, kid!" yells the old third base coach Pep McDill who's been with the Plymouths since the beginning of time, now a bowlegged pot-bellied old-timer with no real cares but plenty of sympathy, whom Ronnie as a kid had seen skittering around shortstop in Pittsburgh like a little rabbit. Sighing, Ronnie does the fast rock and comes in with his sinker, Kolek's eyes light up and he lunges for it, his right foot shows the cleated sole, Ronnie sees the bat come around and blinks as it explodes hard and whistles over his head and into center field where Tommy Turner is running like a smooth hare to recover and whip it on down to third, after some difficulty, and even slow-footed Jangraw has made it there on the long single and there are men on first and third and two out and things are tight.

O Lord, thinks Ronnie, *I'll get the boot sure, starting off like this!* Manager Pie Tibbs looks for the first time toward the bull pen in left field, this he's never done before. *That's the sign*, thinks Ronnie, his heart sinking. *Another boner and I'm out in the showers.* It will be K.L. Jordan facing him, bespectacled, book-keeperish thin, but one of the most consistent hitters in baseball, currently whacking .307 in 32 games, with a slew of clutch hits to his credit, a dangerous man, the whole Chicago line-up packed with enthusiastic dynamite. Jake Guewa gives the sign for fast ball, Jordan's weakness; it will be a case of burn him down. Ronnie eyes the men on first and third one after the other, pauses, the whole game hinges on his action, and he blows her in and Jordan likes it and easily, with an expression of glint in his spectacles though there is unconcern on the face itself, and placks it down on the grass where again it rolls to Wade Hazard at first who leaps, startled to see it, and goes over a few feet and takes it in and trots a few feet to first and steps on the bag, sealing Ronnie's courage into the records—and Ronnie slowly walks off the mound, letting off a big sigh that can be seen deflating his chest from the farthest gloomiest seat in the upper deep center-field bleachers, and as he does he takes one side look of longing at his wife in the stands and she holds up her fingers in the sign of "All straight," and Ronnie is made.

A GAME OF CATCH
Richard Wilbur

Monk and Glennie were playing catch on the side lawn
of the firehouse when Scho caught sight of them. They
were good at it, for seventh-graders, as anyone could
see right away. Monk, wearing a catcher's mitt, would
lean easily sidewise and back, with one leg lifted and
his throwing hand almost down to the grass, and then
lob the white ball straight up into the sunlight. Glennie
would shield his eyes with his left hand and, just as the
ball fell past him, snag it with a little dart of his glove.
Then he would burn the ball straight toward Monk, and
it would spank into the round mitt and sit, like a still-
life apple on a plate, until Monk flipped it over into his
right hand and, with a negligent flick of his hanging
arm, gave Glennie a fast grounder.

They were going on and on like that, in a kind of
slow, mannered, luxurious dance in the sun, their faces
perfectly blank and entranced, when Glennie noticed
Scho dawdling along the other side of the street and
called hello to him. Scho crossed over and stood at the
front edge of the lawn, near an apple tree, watching.

"Got your glove?" asked Glennie after a time. Scho
obviously hadn't.

"You could give me some easy grounders," said Scho. "But don't burn 'em."

"All right," Glennie said. He moved off a little, so the three of them formed a triangle, and they passed the ball around for about five minutes, Monk tossing easy grounders to Scho, Scho throwing to Glennie, and Glennie burning them in to Monk. After a while, Monk began to throw them back to Glennie once or twice before he let Scho have his grounder, and finally Monk gave Scho a fast, bumpy grounder that hopped over his shoulder and went into the brake on the other side of the street.

"Not so hard," called Scho as he ran across to get it.

"You should've had it," Monk shouted.

It took Scho a little while to find the ball among the ferns and dead leaves, and when he saw it, he grabbed it up and threw it toward Glennie. It struck the trunk of the apple tree, bounced back at an angle, and rolled steadily and stupidly onto the cement apron in front of the firehouse, where one of the trucks was parked. Scho ran hard and stopped it just before it rolled under the truck, and this time he carried it back to his former position on the lawn and threw it carefully to Glennie.

"I got an idea," said Glennie. "Why don't Monk and I catch for five minutes more, and then you can borrow one of our gloves?"

"That's all right with me," said Monk. He socked his fist into his mitt, and Glennie burned one in.

"All right," Scho said, and went over and sat under the tree. There in the shade he watched them resume their skillful play. They threw lazily fast or lazily slow—high, low, or wide—and always handsomely, their expressions serene, changeless, and forgetful.

When Monk missed a low backhand catch, he walked indolently after the ball and, hardly even looking, flung it sidearm for an imaginary put-out. After a good while of this, Scho said, "Isn't it five minutes yet?"

"One minute to go," said Monk with a fraction of a grin.

Scho stood up and watched the ball slap back and forth for several minutes more, and then he turned and pulled himself up into the crotch of the tree.

"Where you going?" Monk asked.

"Just up the tree," Scho said.

"I guess he doesn't want to catch," said Monk.

Scho went up and up through the fat light-gray branches until they grew slender and bright and gave under him. He found a place where several supple branches were knit to make a dangerous chair, and sat there with his head coming out of the leaves into the sunlight. He could see the two other boys down below, the ball going back and forth between them as if they were bowling on the grass, and Glennie's crew-cut head looking like a sea urchin.

"I found a wonderful seat up here," Scho said loudly. "If I don't fall out." Monk and Glennie didn't look up or comment, and so he began jouncing gently in his chair of branches and singing "Yo-ho, heave ho" in an exaggerated way.

"Do you know what, Monk?" he announced in a few moments. "I can make you two guys do anything I want. Catch that ball, Monk! Now you catch it, Glennie!"

"I was going to catch it anyway," Monk suddenly said. "You're not making anybody do anything when they're already going to do it anyway."

"I made you say what you just said," Scho replied joyfully.

"No, you didn't," said Monk, still throwing and catching but now less serenely absorbed in the game.

"That's what I wanted you to say," Scho said.

The ball bounded off the rim of Monk's mitt and plowed into a gladiolus bed beside the firehouse, and Monk ran to get it while Scho jounced in his treetop and sang, "I wanted you to miss that. Anything you do is what I wanted you to do."

"Let's quit for a minute," Glennie suggested.

"We might as well, until the peanut gallery shuts up," Monk said.

They went over and sat cross-legged in the shade of the tree. Scho looked down between his legs and saw them on the dim, spotty ground, saying nothing to one another. Glennie soon began abstractedly spinning his glove between his palms; Monk pulled his nose and stared out across the lawn.

"I want you to mess around with your nose, Monk," said Scho, giggling. Monk withdrew his hand from his face.

"Do that with your glove, Glennie," Scho persisted. "Monk, I want you to pull up hunks of grass and chew on it."

Glennie looked up and saw a self-delighted, intense face staring down at him through the leaves. "Stop being a dope and come down and we'll catch for a few minutes," he said.

Scho hesitated, and then said, in a tentatively mocking voice, "That's what I wanted you to say."

"All right, then, nuts to you," said Glennie.

"Why don't you keep quiet and stop bothering people?" Monk asked.

"I made you say that," Scho replied, softly.

"Shut up," Monk said.

"I made you say that, and I want you to be standing there looking sore. And I want you to climb up the tree. I'm making you do it!"

Monk was scrambling up through the branches, awkward in his haste, and getting snagged on twigs. His face was furious and foolish, and he kept telling Scho to shut up, shut up, shut up, while the other's exuberant and panicky voice poured down upon his head.

"*Now* you shut up or you'll be sorry," Monk said, breathing hard as he reached up and threatened to shake the cradle of slight branches in which Scho was sitting.

"I *want*—" Scho screamed as he fell. Two lower branches broke his rustling, crackling fall, but he landed on his back with a deep thud and lay still, with a strangled look on his face and his eyes clenched. Glennie knelt down and asked breathlessly, "Are you O.K., Scho? Are you O.K.?" while Monk swung down through the leaves crying that honestly he hadn't even touched him, the crazy guy just let go. Scho doubled up and turned over on his right side, and now both the other boys knelt beside him, pawing at his shoulder and begging to know how he was.

Then Scho rolled away from them and sat partly up, still struggling to get his wind but forcing a species of smile onto his face.

"I'm sorry, Scho," Monk said. "I didn't mean to make you fall."

Scho's voice came out weak and gravelly, in gasps. "I meant— you to do it. You—had to. You can't do— anything—unless I want—you to."

Glennie and Monk looked helplessly at him as he sat there, breathing a bit more easily and smiling fixedly, with tears in his eyes. Then they picked up their gloves and the ball, walked over to the street, and went slowly away down the sidewalk, Monk punching his fist into the mitt, Glennie juggling the ball between glove and hand.

From under the apple tree, Scho still bent over a little for lack of breath, croaked after them in triumph and misery, "I want you to do whatever you're going to do for the whole rest of your life!"

THE CENTERFIELDER
Sergio Ramírez

The flashlight picked out one prisoner after another until it came to rest on a bed where a man was asleep, his back to the door. His bare torso glistened with sweat.

"That's him, open up," said the guard, peering through the bars.

The warder's key hung from a length of electric cable he used as a belt. It grated in the rusty lock. Inside, the guards beat their rifle butts on the bedframe until the man struggled to his feet, shielding his eyes from the glare.

"Get up, you're wanted."

He was shivering with cold as he groped for his shirt, even though the heat had been unbearable all night, and the prisoners were sleeping in their underpants or stark naked. The only slit in the wall was so high up that the air never circulated much below the ceiling. He found his shirt, and poked his feet into his laceless shoes.

"Get a move on!" the guard said.

"I'm coming, can't you see?"

"Don't get smart with me, or else…"

"Or else what?"

"You know what else!"

The guard stood to one side to let him out of the cell. "Walk, don't talk," he snapped, jabbing him in the ribs with the rifle. The man flinched at the cold metal.

They emerged into the yard. Down by the far wall, the leaves of almond trees glittered in the moonlight. It was midnight, and the slaughtering of animals had begun in the next-door abattoir. The breeze carried a smell of blood and dung.

What a perfect field for baseball! The prisoners must make up teams to play, or take on the off-duty guards. The backstop would be the wall, which left about three hundred and fifty feet from home plate to centerfield. You'd have to field a hit from there running backwards toward the almond trees. When you picked up the ball the diamond would seem far away; the shouts for you to throw would be muffled by the distance; the batter would be rounding second base—and then I'd reach up, catch a branch, and swing myself up. I'd stretch forward, put my hands carefully between the broken bottles on the top of the wall, then edge over with my feet. I'd jump down, ignoring the pain as I crashed into the heap of garbage, bones, bits of horn, broken chairs, tin cans, rags, newspapers, dead vermin. Then I'd run on, tearing myself on thistles, stumbling into a drain of filthy water, but running on and on, as the dry crack of rifles sounded far behind me.

"Halt! Where d'you think you're going?"

"To piss, that's all."

"Scared are you?"

It is almost identical to the square back home, with the rubber trees growing right by the church steps. I was the only one on our team who had a real leather glove: all the others had to catch barehanded. I'd be out there fielding at six in the evening when it was so dark I could hardly see the ball. I could catch them like doves in my hand, just by the sound.

"Here he is, Captain," the guard called, poking his head around a half-open door. From inside came the steady hum of air conditioning.

"Bring him in, then leave us."

He felt immediately trapped in this bare, whitewashed room. Apart from a chair in the center, and the captain's desk up against the far wall, the only adornments were a gilt-framed portrait and a calendar with red and blue numbers. To judge by the fresh plaster, the air conditioning had only recently been installed.

"What time were you picked up?" the captain asked, without looking up.

He stood there at a loss for a reply, wishing with all his heart that the question had been aimed at somebody else—perhaps at someone hiding under the table.

"Are you deaf—I'm talking to you. What time were you taken prisoner?"

"Sometime after six, I reckon," he mumbled, so softly he was convinced the captain hadn't heard him.

"Why do you think it was after six? Can't you tell me the exact time?"

"I don't have a watch, sir, but I'd already eaten, and I always eat at six."

Come and eat, Ma would shout from the sidewalk outside the house. Just one more inning, I'd say, then I'll be there. But son, it's dark already, how can you see to play? I'm coming, there's only one inning left. The violin and the harmonium would be tuning up for Mass in the church as the ball flew safely into my hands for the last out. We'd won yet again.

"What job do you do?"

"I'm a cobbler."

"Do you work in a shop?"

"No, I do repairs at home."

"You used to be a baseball player, didn't you?"

"Yes, once upon a time."

"And you were known as 'Whiplash' Parrales, weren't you?"

"Yes, they called me that because of the way I threw the ball in."

"And you were on the national team that went to Cuba?"

"That's right, twenty years ago. I went as center-fielder."

"But they kicked you out…"

"When we got back."

"You made quite a name for yourself with that arm of yours." The captain's angry stare soon dashed the smile from Parrales' lips.

The best piece of fielding I ever did was at home when I caught a fly ball on the steps of the church itself. I took it with my back to the bases, but fell sprawling on my face and split my tongue. Still, we won the game and the team carried me home in triumph. My mother left her tortilla dough and came to care for my wound. She was sorry and proud at the same time: "Do you have to knock your brains out to prove you're a real sport?"

"Why did they kick you off the team?"

"On account of my dropping a fly and us losing the game."

"In Cuba?"

"We were playing Aruba. I bungled it, they got two runs, and we'd lost."

"Several of you were booted out, weren't you?"

"The fact is, we all drank a lot, and you can't do that in baseball."

"Aha!"

He wanted to ask if he could sit down because his shins were aching so, but didn't dare move an inch. Instead he stood stock still, as though his shoes were glued to the floor.

The captain laboriously wrote out something. He finally lifted his head, and Parrales could see the red imprint of a cap across his forehead.

"Why did they bring you in?"

He shrugged and stared at him blankly.

"Well, why?"

"No," he answered.

"No, what?"

"No, I don't know."

"Aha, so you don't know."

"No."

"I've got your file here," the capital said, flourishing a folder. "Shall I read you a few bits so you can learn about yourself?" He stood up.

From centerfield you can barely hear the ball smack the catcher's mitt. But when the batter connects, the sound travels clearly and all your senses sharpen to follow the ball. As it flies through the distance to my loving hands, I wait patiently, dancing beneath it until finally I clasp it as though I'm making a nest for it.

"At five PM on July 28th a green canvas-topped jeep drew up outside your house. Two men got out: one was dark, wore khaki trousers, and sun glasses. The other was fair-skinned, wore blue jeans and a straw hat. The one with dark glasses was carrying a PanAm dufflebag; the other had an army backpack. They went into your house, and didn't come out again until ten o'clock. They didn't have their bags with them."

"The one with glasses...," nervous, he choked on endless saliva, "he was my son, the one in glasses."

"I know that."

Again there was silence. Parrales' feet were perspiring inside his shoes, making them as wet as if he had just crossed a stream.

"The bag contained ammunition for a fixed machine gun, and the rucksack was full of fuses. When had you last seen your son before that?"

"Not for months," he murmured.

"Speak up, I can't hear you."

"Months—I don't remember how many, but several months. He quit his job at the ropeworks one day, and we didn't see him again after that."

"Weren't you worried about him?"

"Of course—he's my son, after all. We asked, made official enquiries, but got nowhere." Parrales pushed his false teeth back into place, worried in case the plate worked loose.

"Did you know he was in the mountains with the rebels?"

"We did hear rumors."

"So when he turned up in the jeep, what did you think?"

"That he was coming home. But all he did was say hello, then leave again a few hours later."

"And ask you to look after his things?"

"Yes, he said he'd send for them."

"Oh, he did, did he?"

The captain pulled more purple-typed sheets out of the folder. He sifted through them, then laid one out on the desk.

"It says here that for three months you were handling ammunition, firearms, fuses and subversive literature, and that you let enemies of the government sleep in your house."

Parrales said nothing. He took out a handkerchief to blow his nose. He looked gaunt and shrunken in the lamplight, as though already reduced to a skeleton.

"And you weren't aware of a thing, were you?"

"You know what sons are."

"Sons of bitches, you mean."

Parrales stared down at the protruding tongues and the mud caking his tattered shoes.

"How long is it since you last saw you son?"

He looked the captain full in the face. "You know he's been killed, so why ask me that?"

The last inning of the game against Aruba, zero to zero, two outs, and the white ball was floating gently home to my hands as I waited, arms outstretched; we were about to meet for ever when the ball clipped the back of my hand, I tried to scoop it up, but it bounced to the ground—far off I could see the batter sliding home, and all was lost. Ma, I needed warm water on my wounds, like you always knew, I was always brave out on the field, even ready to die.

"Sometimes I'd like to be kind, but it's impossible," the captain said, advancing around the desk. He tossed the folder back into the drawer, and turned to switch off the air conditioning. Again the room was plunged into silence. He pulled a towel from a hook and draped it about his shoulders.

"Sergeant!" he shouted.

The sergeant stood to attention in the doorway. He led the prisoner out, then reappeared almost immediately.

"What am I to put in the report?"

"He was a baseball player, so make up anything you like. Say he was playing with the other prisoners, that he was centerfielder and chased a hit down to the wall, then climbed up an almond tree and jumped over the wall. Put down that we shot him as he was escaping across the slaughterhouse yard."

PLAYING BALL ON HAMPSTEAD HEATH
Mordecai Richler

Summer.

Drifting through Soho in the early evening, Jake stopped at the Nosh Bar for a sustaining salt-beef sandwich. He had only managed one squirting mouthful and a glance at the unit trust quotations in the *Standard* (S&P Capital was steady, but Pan Australian had dipped again) when he was distracted by a bulging-bellied American in a Dacron suit. The American's wife, unsuccessfully shoehorned into a mini-skirt, clutching a *London A to Z* to her bosom. The American opened a fat credit-card-filled wallet, briefly exposing an international medical passport which listed his blood type; he extracted a pound note and slapped it into the waiter's hand. "I suppose," he said, winking, "I get twenty-four shillings change for this?"

The waiter shot him a sour look.

"Tell your boss," the American continued, unperturbed, "that I'm a Galicianer, just like him."

"Oh, Morty," his wife said, bubbling.

And the juicy salt beef sandwich turned to leather in Jake's mouth. It's here again, he realized, heart sinking, the season.

Come summer, American and Canadian show business plenipotentiaries domiciled in London had more than the usual hardships to contend with. The usual hardships being the income tax tangle, scheming and incompetent natives, uppity *au pairs* or nannies, wives overspending at the bazaar (Harrod's, Fortnum's, Asprey's), choosing suitable prep schools for the kids, doing without real pastrami and pickled tomatoes, fighting decorators and smog, and of course keeping warm. But come summer, tourist liners and jets began to disgorge demanding hordes of relatives and friends of friends, long (and best) forgotten schoolmates and army buddies, on London, thereby transmogrifying the telephone, charmingly inefficient all winter, into an instrument of terror. For there was not a stranger who phoned and did not exude warmth and expect help in procuring theater tickets and a night on the town ("What we're really dying for is a pub crawl. The swinging pubs. Waddiya say, old chap?") or an invitation to dinner at home. ("Well, Yankel, did you tell the Queen your Uncle Labish was coming? Did she bake a cake?")

The tourist season's dialogue, the observations, the complaints, was a recurring hazard to be endured. You agreed, oh how many times you agreed, the taxis were cute, the bobbies polite, and the pace slower than New York or, in Jake's case, Montreal. "People still know how to enjoy life here. I can see that." Yes. On the other hand, you've got to admit...the bowler hats are a scream, hotel service is lousy, there's nowhere you can get a suit pressed in a hurry, the British have snobby British accents and hate all Americans. Jealousy. "Look at it this way, it isn't home." Yes, a thousand times yes. All the same, everybody was glad to have made the trip, it was expensive but broadening, the world was getting smaller all the time, a global village, only next time they wouldn't try to squeeze so many countries into twenty-one days. "Mind you, the American Express was very, very nice everywhere. No complaints in that department."

Summer was charged with menace, with schnorrers and greenhorns from the New Country. So how glorious, how utterly delightful, it was for the hard-core show biz expatriates (those who weren't in Juan-les-Pins or Dubrovnik) to come together on a Sunday morning for a sweet and soothing game of softball, just as the Raj of another dynasty had used to meet on the cricket pitch in Malabar.

Sunday morning softball on Hampstead Heath in summer was unquestionably the fun thing to do. It was a ritual.

Manny Gordon tooled in all the way from Richmond, stowing a fielder's mitt and a thermos of martinis in the boot, clapping a sporty tweed cap over his bald head and strapping himself and his starlet of the night before into his Aston-Martin at nine AM. C. Bernard Farber started out from Ham Common, picking up Al Levine, Bob Cohen, Jimmy Grief and Myer Gross outside Mary Quant's on the King's Road. Moey Hanover had once startled the staff at the Connaught by tripping down the stairs on a Sunday morning, wearing a peak cap and T-shirt and blue jeans, carrying his personal Babe Ruth bat in one hand

and a softball in the other. Another Sunday Ziggy Alter had flown in from Rome, just for the sake of a restorative nine innings.

Frankie Demaine drove in from Marlow-on-Thames in his Maserati. Lou Caplan, Morty Calman, and Cy Levi usually brought their wives and children. Monty Talman, ever mindful of his latest twenty-one-year-old girlfriend, always cycled to the Heath from St. John's Wood. Wearing a maroon track suit, he usually lapped the field eight or nines times before anyone else turned up.

Jake generally strolled to the Heath, his tattered fielder's mitt and three enervating bagels filled with smoked salmon concealed under the *Observer* in his shopping bag. Some Sundays, like this one, possibly his last for a while, Nancy brought the kids along to watch.

The starting line-up on Sunday, June 28, 1963 was:

AL LEVINE'S TEAM	LOU CAPLAN'S BUNCH
Manny Gordon, ss.	Bob Cohen, *3b.*
C. Bernard Farber, *2b.*	Myer Gross, ss.
Jimmy Grief, *3b.*	Frankie Demaine, *lf.*
Al Levine, *cf.*	Morty Calman, *rf.*
Monty Talman, *1b.*	Cy Levi, *2b.*
Ziggy Alter, *lf.*	Moey Hanover, *c.*
Jack Monroe, *rf.*	Johnny Roper, *cf.*
Sean Fielding, *c.*	Jason Storm, *1b.*
Alfie Roberts, *p.*	Lou Caplan, *p.*

Jake, like five or six others who had arrived late and hung over (or who were unusually inept players), was a sub. A utility fielder, Jake sat on the bench with Lou Caplan's Bunch. It was a fine, all but cloudless morning, but looking around Jake felt there were too many wives, children, and kibitzers about. Even more ominous, the Filmmakers' First Wives Club or, as Ziggy Alter put it, the Alimony Gallery, was forming, seemingly relaxed but actually fulminating, on the grass behind home plate.

First Al Levine's Team and then Lou Caplan's Bunch, both sides made up mostly of men in their forties, trotted out, sunken bellies quaking, discs suddenly tender, hemorrhoids smarting, to take a turn at fielding and batting practice.

Nate Sugarman, once a classy shortstop, but since his coronary the regular umpire, bit into a digitalis pill, strode onto the field, and called, "Play ball!"

"Let's go, boychick."

"We need a hit," Monty Talman, the producer, hollered.

"*You* certainly do," Bob Cohen, who only yesterday had winced through a rough cut of Talman's latest fiasco, shouted back snidely from the opposite bench.

Manny, hunched over the plate cat-like, trying to look menacing, was knotted with more than his usual fill of anxiety. If he struck out, his own team would not be too upset because it was early in the game, but Lou Caplan, pitching for the first time since his Mexican divorce, would be grateful, and flattering Lou was a good idea because he was rumored to be ready to go with a three-picture deal for Twentieth; and Manny had not been asked to direct a big-budget film since *Chase*. *Ball one, inside.* If, Manny thought, I hit a single I will be obliged to pass the time of day with that stomach-turning queen Jason Storm, 1b., who was in London to make a TV pilot film for Ziggy Alter. *Strike one, called.*

He had never hit a homer, so that was out, but if come a miracle he connected for a triple, what then? He would be stuck on third sack with Bob Cohen, strictly second featuresville, a born loser, and Manny didn't want to be seen with Bob, even for an inning, especially with so many producers and agents about. K-nack! *Goddammit, it's a hit! A double, for Chrissake!*

As the players on Al Levine's bench rose to a man, shouting encouragement—

"Go, man. Go."

"Shake the lead out, Manny. Run!"

—Manny, conscious only of Lou Caplan glaring at him ("It's not my fault, Lou."), scampered past first base and took myopic, round-shouldered aim on second, wondering should he say something shitty to Cy Levi, 2b., who he suspected was responsible for getting his name on the blacklist years ago.

Next man up to the plate, C. Bernie Farber, who had signed to write Lou Caplan's first picture for Twentieth, struck out gracefully, which brought up Jimmy Grief. Jimmy swung on the first pitch, lifting it high and foul, and Moey Hanover, c., called for it, feeling guilty because next Saturday Jimmy was flying to Rome and Moey had already arranged to have lunch with Jimmy's wife on Sunday. Moey made the catch, which brought up Al Levine, who homered, bringing in Manny Gordon ahead of him. Monty Talman grounded out to Gross, ss., retiring the side.

Al Levine's Team, first inning: two hits, no errors, two runs.

Leading off for Lou Caplan's Bunch, Bob Cohen smashed a burner to center for a single and Myer Gross fanned, bringing up Frankie Demaine and sending all the outfielders back, back, back. Frankie whacked the third pitch long and high, an easy fly had Al Levine been playing him deep left instead of inside right, where he was able to flirt hopefully with Manny Gordon's starlet, who was sprawled on the grass there in the shortest of possible Pucci prints. Al Levine was the only man on either team who always played wearing shorts—shorts revealing an elastic bandage which began at his left kneecap and ran almost as low as the ankle.

"Oh, you poor darling," the starlet said, making a face at Levine's knee.

Levine, sucking in his stomach, replied, "Spain," as if he were tossing the girl a rare coin.

"Don't tell me," she squealed. "The beach at Torremolinos. Ugh!"

"No, no," Levine protested. "The civil war, for Chrissake. Shrapnel. Defense of Madrid."

Demaine's fly fell for a homer, driving in a panting Bob Cohen.

Lou Caplan's Bunch, first inning: one hit, one error, two runs.

Neither side scored in the next two innings, which were noteworthy only because Moey Hanover's game began to slip badly. In the second Moey muffed an easy pop fly and actually let C. Bernie Farber, still weak on his legs after a cleansing, all but foodless, week at Forest Mere Hydro, steal a base on him. The problem was clearly Sean Fielding, the young RADA graduate whom Columbia had put under contract because, in profile, he looked like Peter O'Toole. The game had only just started when Moey Hanover's wife, Lilian, had ambled over to Al Levine's bench and stretched herself out on the grass, an offering, beside Fielding, and the two of them had been giggling together and nudging each other ever since, which was making Moey nervy. Moey, however, had not spent his young manhood at a yeshiva to no avail. Not only had he plundered the Old Testament for most of his winning *Rawhide* and *Bonanza* plots, but now that his Lilian was obviously in heat again, his hard-bought Jewish education, which his father had always assured him was priceless, served him splendidly once more. Moey remembered his *David ha'Melech: And it came to pass in the morning, that David wrote a letter to Joab, and sent it by the hand of Uriah. And he wrote in the letter, saying, Set Uriah in the forefront of the hottest battle, and retire ye from him, that he may be smitten, and die.*

Amen.

Lou Caplan yielded two successive hits in the third and Moey Hanover took off his catcher's mask, called for time, and strode to the mound, rubbing the ball in his hands.

"I'm all right," Lou said. "Don't worry. I'm going to settle down now."

"It's not that. Listen, when do you start shooting in Rome?"

"Three weeks tomorrow. You heard something bad?"

"No."

"You're a friend now, remember. No secrets."

"No. It's just that I've had second thoughts about Sean Fielding. I think he's very exciting. He's got lots of appeal. He'd be a natural to play Domingo."

As the two men began to whisper together, players on Al Levine's bench hollered, "Let's go, gang."

"Come on. Break it up, Moey."

Moey returned to the plate, satisfied that Fielding was as good as in Rome already. May he do his own stunts, he thought.

"Play ball," Nate Sugarman called.

Alfie Roberts, the director, ordinarily expected soft pitches from Lou, as he did the same for him, but today he wasn't so sure, because on Wednesday his agent had sent him one of Lou's properties to read and—Lou's first pitch made Alfie hit the dirt. That settles it, he thought, my agent already told him it doesn't grab me. Alfie struck out as quickly as he could. Better be put down for a rally-stopper than suffer a head fracture.

Which brought up Manny Gordon again, with one out and runners on first and third. Manny dribbled into a double play, retiring the side.

Multi-colored kites bounced in the skies over the Heath. Lovers strolled on the tow paths and locked together on the grass. Old people sat on benches, sucking in the sun. Nannies passed, wheeling toddlers with titles. The odd baffled Englishman stopped to watch the Americans at play.

"Are they air force chaps?"

"Filmmakers, actually. It's their version of rounders."

"Whatever is that enormous thing that woman is slicing?"

"Salami."

"*On the Heath?*"

"Afraid so. One Sunday they actually set up a bloody folding table, right over there, with cold cuts and herrings and mounds of black bread and a whole bloody side of smoked salmon. *Scotch. Ten and six a quarter, don't you know?*

"On the Heath?"

"Champagne *in paper cups.* Mumm's. One of them had won some sort of award."

Going into the bottom of the fifth, Al Levine's Team led 6–3, and Tom Hunt came in to play second base for Lou Caplan's Bunch. Hunt, a Negro actor, was in town shooting *Othello X* for Bob Cohen.

Moey Hanover lifted a lazy fly into left field, which Ziggy Alter trapped rolling over and over on the grass until—just before getting up—he was well placed to look up Natalie Calman's skirt. Something he saw there so unnerved him that he dropped the ball, turning pale and allowing Hanover to pull up safely at second.

Johnny Roper walked. Which brought up Jason Storm, to the delight of a pride of British fairies who stood with their dogs on the first base line, squealing and jumping. Jason poked a bouncer through the infield and floated to second, obliging the fairies and their dogs to move up a base.

With two out and the score tied 7–7 in the bottom half of the sixth, Alfie Roberts was unwillingly retired and a new pitcher came in for Al Levine's Team. It was Gordie Kaufman, a writer blacklisted for years, who now divided his time between Madrid and Rome, asking a hundred thousand dollars a spectacular. Gordie came in to pitch with the go-ahead run on third and Tom Hunt stepping up to the plate for the first time. Big black Tom Hunt, who had once played semi-pro ball in Florida, was a militant. If he homered, Hunt felt he would be put down for another buck nigger, good at games, but if he struck out, which would call for rather more acting skill than was required of him on the set of *Othello X*, what then? He would enable a bunch of fat, foxy, sexually worried Jews to feel big, goysy. Screw them, Hunt thought.

Gordie Kaufman had his problems too. His stunning villa on Mallorca was run by Spanish servants, his two boys were boarding at a reputable British public school, and Gordie himself was president, sole stockholder, and the only employee of a company that was a plaque in Liechtenstein. And yet—and yet—Gordie still subscribed to the *Nation;* he filled his Roman slaves with anti-apartheid dialogue and sagacious Talmudic sayings; and whenever the left-wing *pushke* was passed around he came through with a nice check. I must bear down on Hunt, Gordie thought, because if he touches me for even a scratch single I'll come off a patronizing ofay. If he homers, God forbid, I'm a shitty liberal. And so with the count 3 and 2, and a walk, the typical social-democrat's compromise, seemingly the easiest way out for both men, Gordie gritted his teeth, his proud Trotskyite past getting the best of him, and threw a fast ball right at Hunt, bouncing it off his head. Hunt threw away his bat and started for the mound, fist clenched, but not so fast that players from both sides couldn't rush in to separate the two men, both of whom felt vindicated, proud, because they had triumphed over impersonal racial prejudice to hit each other as individuals on a fun Sunday on Hampstead Heath.

Come the crucial seventh, the Filmmaker's First Wives Club grew restive, no longer content to belittle their former husbands from afar, and moved in on the baselines and benches, undermining confidence with their heckling. When Myer Gross, for instance, came to bat with two men on base and his teammates shouted, "Go, man. Go," one familiar grating voice floated out over the others. "Hit, Myer. Make your son proud of you, *just this once.*"

What a reproach the first wives were. How steadfast! How unchanging! Still Waiting For Lefty after all these years. Today maybe hair had grayed and chins doubled, necks had gone pruney, breasts drooped and stomachs dropped, but let no man say these crones had aged in spirit. Where once they had petitioned for the Scotsboro Boys, broken with their families over mixed marriages, sent their boy friends off to defend Madrid, split with old comrades over the Stalin-Hitler Pact, fought for Henry Wallace, demonstrated for the Rosenbergs, and never, never yielded to McCarthy…today they clapped hands at China Friendship Clubs, petitioned for others to keep hands off Cuba and Vietnam, and made their sons chopped liver sandwiches and sent them off to march to Aldermaston.

The wives, alimonied but abandoned, had known the early struggling years with their husbands, the self-doubts, the humiliations, the rejections, the cold-water flats, and the blacklist, but they had always remained loyal. They hadn't altered, their husbands had.

Each marriage had shattered in the eye of its own self-made hurricane, but essentially the men felt, as Ziggy Alter had once put it so succinctly at the poker table, "Right, wrong, don't be silly, it's really a question of who wants to grow old with Anna Pauker when there are so many juicy little things we can now afford."

So there they were, out on the grass chasing fly balls on a Sunday morning, short men, overpaid and unprincipled, all well within the coronary and lung cancer belt, allowing themselves to look ridiculous in the hope of pleasing their new young wives and girlfriends. There was Ziggy Alter, who had once written a play "with content" for the Group Theatre. Here was Al Levine, who used to throw marbles under horses' legs at demonstrations and now raced two horses of his own at Epsom. On the pitcher's mound stood Gordie Kaufman, who had once carried a banner that read *No Pasarán* through the streets of Manhattan and now employed a man especially to keep Spaniards off the beach at his villa on Mallorca. And sweating under a catcher's mask there was Moey Hanover, who had studied at a yeshiva, stood up to the committee, and was now on a sabbatical from Desilu.

Usually the husbands were able to avoid their used-up wives. They didn't see them in the gaming rooms at the White Elephant or in the Mirabelle or Les Ambassadeurs. But come Brecht to Shaftesbury Avenue and without looking up from the second row center they could feel them squatting in their cotton bloomers in the second balcony, burning holes in their necks.

And count on them to turn up on a Sunday morning in summer on Hampstead Heath just to ruin a game of fun baseball. Even homering, as Al Levine did, was no answer to the drones.

"It's nice for him, I suppose," a voice behind Levine on the bench observed, "that on the playing field, with an audience, if you know what I mean, he actually appears virile."

The game dragged on. In the eighth inning Jack Monroe had to retire to his Mercedes-Benz for his insulin injection and Jake Hersh, until now an embarrassed sub, finally trotted onto the field. Hersh, thirty-three, one-time relief pitcher for Room 41, Fletcher's Field High (2–7), moved into right field, mindful of his disc condition and hoping he would not be called on to make a tricksy catch. He assumed a loose-limbed stance on the grass, waving at his wife, grinning at his children, when without warning a sizzling line drive came right at him. Jake, startled, did the only sensible thing: he ducked. Outraged shouts and moans from the bench reminded Jake where he was, in a softball game, and he started after the ball.

"Fishfingers."

"*Putz!*"

Runners on first and third started for home as Jake, breathless, finally caught up with the ball. It had rolled to a stop under a bench where a nanny sat watching over an elegant perambulator.

"Excuse me," Jake said.

"Americans," the nurse said.

"I'm a Canadian," Jake protested automatically, fishing the ball out from under the bench.

Three runs scored. Jake caught a glimpse of Nancy, unable to contain her laughter. The children looked ashamed of him.

In the ninth inning with the score tied again, 11–11, Sol Peters, another sub, stepped cautiously to the plate for Lou Caplan's Bunch. The go-ahead run was on second and there was only one out. Gordie Kaufman, trying to prevent a bunt, threw right at him and Sol, forgetting he was wearing his contact lenses, held the bat in front of him to protect his glasses. The ball hit the bat and rebounded for a perfectly laid down bunt.

"Run, you shmock."

"Go, man."

Sol, terrified, ran, carrying the bat with him.

Monty Talman phoned home.

"Who won?" his wife asked.

"We did. 13–12. But that's not the point. We had lots of fun."

"How many you bringing back for lunch?"

"Eight."

"Eight?"

"I couldn't get out of inviting Johnny Roper. He knows Jack Monroe is coming."

"I see."

"A little warning. Don't, for Chrissake, ask Cy how Marsha is. They're separating. And I'm afraid Manny Gordon is coming with a girl. I want you to be nice to her."

"Anything else?"

"If Gershon phones from Rome while the guys are there please remember I'm taking the call upstairs. And please don't start collecting glasses and emptying ashtrays at four o'clock. It's embarrassing. Bloody Jake Hersh is coming and it's just the sort of incident he'd pick on and joke about for months."

"I never coll—"

"All right, all right. Oh, shit, something else. Tom Hunt is coming."

"The actor?"

"Yeah. Now listen, he's very touchy, so will you please put away Sheila's doll."

"Sheila's doll?"

"If she comes in carrying that bloody golliwog I'll die. Hide it. Burn it. Hunt gets script approval these days, you know."

"All right, dear."

"See you soon."

THE PITCHER
Andre Dubus

They cheered and clapped when he and Lucky Ferris came out of the dugout, and when the cheering and clapping settled to sporadic shouts he had already stopped hearing it, because he was feeling the pitches in his right arm and watching them the way he always did in the first few minutes of his warm-up. Some nights the fast ball was fat or the curve hung or the ball stayed up around Lucky's head where even the hitters in this Class C league would hit it hard. It was a mystery that frightened him. He threw the first hard one and watched it streak and rise into Lucky's mitt; and the next one; and the next one; then he wasn't watching the ball anymore, as though it had the power to betray him. He wasn't watching anything except Lucky's target, hardly conscious of that either, or of anything else but the rhythm of his high-kicking windup, and the ball not thrown but released out of all his motion; and now he felt himself approaching that moment which he could not achieve alone: a moment that each time was granted to him. Then it came: the ball was part of him, as if his arm stretched sixty feet six inches to Lucky's mitt and slammed the ball into leather and sponge and Lucky's hand. Or he was part of the ball.

Now all he had to do for the rest of the night was

concentrate on prolonging that moment. He had trained himself to do that, and while people talked about his speed and curve and change of pace and control, he knew that without his concentration they would be only separate and useless parts; and instead of nineteen and five on the year with an earned run average of two point one five and two hundred and six strikeouts, going for his twentieth win on the last day of the season, his first year in professional ball, three months short of his twentieth birthday, he'd be five and nineteen and on his way home to nothing. He was going for the pennant too, one half game behind the New Iberia Pelicans who had come to town four nights ago with a game and a half lead, and the Bulls beat them, Friday and Saturday, lost Sunday, so that now on Monday in this small Louisiana town, Billy's name was on the front page of the local paper alongside the news of the war that had started in Korea a little over a month ago. He was ready. He caught Lucky's throw, nodded to him, and walked with head down toward the dugout and the cheers growing louder behind it, looking down at the bright grass, holding the ball loosely in his hand.

He spoke to no one. He went to the far end of the dugout that they left empty for him when he was pitching. He was too young to ask for that, but he was good enough to get it without asking; they gave it to him early in the year, when they saw he needed it, this young pitcher Billy Wells who talked and joked and yelled at the field and the other dugout for nine innings of the three nights he didn't pitch, but on his pitching night sat quietly, looking neither relaxed nor tense, and only spoke when politeness required it. Always he was polite. Soon they made a space for him on the bench, where he sat now knowing he would be all right. He did not think about it, for he knew as the insomniac does that to give it words summons it up to dance; he knew that the pain he had brought with him to the park was still there; he even knew it would probably always be there; but for a good while now it was gone. It would lie in wait for him and strike him again when he was drained and had a heart full of room for it. But that was a long time from now, in the shower or back in the hotel, longer than the two and a half hours or whatever he would use pitching the game; longer than a clock could measure. Right now it seemed a great deal of his life would pass before the shower. When he trotted out to the mound they stood and cheered and, before he threw his first warm-up pitch, he tipped his cap.

He did not make love to Leslie the night before the game. All season, he had not made love to her on the night before he pitched. He did not believe, as some ballplayers did, that it hurt you the next day. *It's why they call it the box score anyway*, Hap Thomas said on the bus the night after going hitless; *I left me at least two basehits in that whorehouse last night*. Like most ballplayers in the Evangeline League, Thomas had been finished for a long time: a thirty-six year old outfielder who had played three seasons—not consecutively—in Triple A ball, when he was in his twenties. Billy didn't make love the night before a game because he still wasn't used to night baseball; he still had the same ritual he'd had in San Antonio, playing high school and American Legion ball: he drank a glass of buttermilk then went to bed, where for an hour or more he imagined tomorrow's game, although it seemed the game already existed somewhere in the night beyond his window and was imagining him. When finally he slept, the game was still there with him, and in the morning he woke to it, remembered pitching somewhere between daydream and nightdream: and until time for the game he felt like a shadow cast by the memory and the morning's light, a shadow that extended from his pillow to the locker room, when he took off the clothes which had not felt like his all day and put on the uniform which in his mind he had been wearing since he went to bed the night before. In high school, his classes interfered with those days of being a shadow. He felt that he was not so much going to classes as bumping into them on his way to the field. But in summer when he played American Legion ball, there was nothing to bump into, there was only the morning's wait which wasn't really waiting because waiting was watching time, watching it win usually, while on those mornings he joined time and flowed with it, so that sitting before the breakfast his mother cooked for him he felt he was in motion toward the mound.

And he had played a full season less one game of pro ball and still had not been able to convince his mind and body that the night before a game was far too early to enter the rhythm and concentration that would work for him when he actually had the ball in his hand. Perhaps his mind and body weren't the ones who needed convincing; perhaps he was right when he thought he was not imagining the games, but they were imagining him: benevolent and slow-witted angels who had followed him to take care of him, who couldn't understand they could rest now, lie quietly the night before, because they and Billy had all next day to spend with each other. If he had known Leslie was hurt he could have told her, as simply as a man saying he was beset by the swollen agony of mumps, that he could not make love on those nights, it wasn't because he preferred thinking about tomorrow's game, but because those angels had followed him all the way to Lafayette, Louisiana. Perhaps he and Leslie could even have laughed about it, for finally it was funny, as funny as the story about Billy's Uncle Johnny whose two hounds had jumped the fence and faithfully tracked or followed him to a bedroom a few blocks from his house, and bayed outside the window: a bedroom Uncle Johnny wasn't supposed to be in, and more trouble than that, because to get there he had left a bedroom he wasn't supposed to leave.

Lafayette was funny too: a lowland of bayous and swamps and Cajuns. The Cajuns were good fans. They were so good that in early season Billy felt like he was barnstorming in some strange country, where everybody loved the Americans and decided to love baseball too since the Americans were playing it for them. They knew the game, but often when they yelled about it they yelled in French, and when they yelled in English it sounded like a Frenchman's English. This came from the colored section too. The stands did not extend far beyond third and first base, and where the first base stands ended there was a space of about fifty feet and, after that, shoved against each other, were two sections of folding wooden bleachers. The Negroes filled them, hardly noticed beyond the fifty feet of air and trampled earth. They were not too far down the right field line: sometimes when Billy ran out a ground ball he ended his sprint close enough to the bleachers to hear the Negroes calling to him in French, or in the English that sounded like French.

Two Cajuns played for the Bulls. The full name was the Lafayette Brahma Bulls, and when the fans said all of it, they said Bremabulls. The owner was a rancher who raised these bulls, and one of his prizes was a huge and dangerous-looking hump-necked bull whose grey coat was nearly white; it was named Huey for their governor who was shot and killed in the state capitol building. Huey was led to home plate for opening day ceremonies, and after that he attended every game in a pen in foul territory against the right field fence. During batting practice the left handers tried to pull the ball into the pen. Nobody hit him, but when the owner heard about it he had the bull brought to the park when batting practice was over. By then the stands were filling. Huey was brought in a truck that entered through a gate behind the colored bleachers, and the Negroes would turn and look behind them at the bull going by. The two men in the truck wore straw cowboy hats. So did the owner, Charlie Breaux. When the Cajuns said his first and last names together they weren't his name anymore. And since it was the Cajun third baseman, E.J. Primeaux, a wiry thirty year old who owned a small grocery store which his wife ran during the season, who first introduced Billy to the owner, Billy had believed for the first few days after reporting to the club that he pitched for a man named Mr. Chollibro.

One night someone did hit Huey: during a game, with two outs, a high fly ball that Hap Thomas could have reached for and caught; he was there in plenty of time, glancing down at the pen's fence as he moved with the flight of the ball, was waiting safe from collision beside the pen, looking now from the ball to Huey who stood just on the other side of the fence, watching him; Hap stuck his arm out over the fence and Huey's head; then he looked at Huey again and withdrew his arm and stepped back to watch the ball strike Huey's head with a sound the fans heard behind third base. The ball bounced up and out and Hap barehanded it as Huey trotted once around the pen. Hap ran toward the dugout, holding the ball up, until he reached the first base umpire who was alternately signalling safe and pointing Hap back to right field. Then Hap flipped him the ball and, grinning, raised both arms to the fans behind the first base line, kept them raised to the Negroes as he ran past their bleachers and back to Huey's pen, taking off his cap as he approached the fence where Huey stood again watching, waved his cap once over the fence and horns, then trotted to his position, thumped his glove twice, then lowered it to his knee, and his bare hand to the other, and crouched. The fans were still laughing and cheering and calling to Hap and Huey and Chollibro when two pitches later the batter popped up to Caldwell at short.

In the dugout Primeaux said: "Hap, I seen many a outfielder miss a fly ball because he's wall-shy, but that's the first time I ever seen one miss because he's *bull*-horn shy." And Hap said: "In this league? That's nothing. No doubt about it, one of these nights I'll go out to right field and get bit by a cottonmouth so big he'll chop my leg in two." "Or get hit by lightning," Shep Caldwell said. In June lightning had struck a center-fielder for the Abbeville Athletics; struck the metal peak of his cap and exited into the earth through his spikes. When the Bulls heard the announcement over their public address system, their own sky was cloudy and there were distant flashes; perhaps they had even seen the flash that killed Tommy Lyons thirty miles away. The announcement came between innings when the Bulls were coming to bat; the players and fans stood for a minute of silent prayer. Billy was sitting beside Hap. Hap went to the cooler and came back with a paper cup and sat looking at it but not drinking, then said: "He broke a leg, Lyons did. I played in the Pacific Coast League with him one year. 'Forty-one. He was hitting three-thirty; thirty-something home runs; stole about forty bases. Late in the season he broke his leg sliding. He never got his hitting back. Nobody knew why. Tommy didn't know why. He went to spring training with the Yankees then back to the Pacific Coast League, and he kept going down. I was drafted by then, and next time I saw him was two years ago when he came to Abbeville. We had a beer one night and I told him he was headed for the major leagues when he broke his leg. No doubt about it. He said he knew that. And he still didn't understand it. Lost something: swing; timing. Jesus, he used to hit the ball. Now they fried him in front of a bunch of assholes in Abbeville. How's that for shit." For the rest of the game most of the players watched their sky; those who didn't were refusing to. They would not know until next day about the metal peak on Lyons' cap; but two innings after the announcement, Lucky went into the locker room and cut his off. When he came back to the dugout holding the blue cap and looking at the hole where the peak had been, Shep said: "Hell, Lucky, it never strikes twice." Lucky said: "That's because it don't have to," and sat down, stroking the hole.

Lafayette was only a town on the way to Detroit, to the Tigers; unless he got drafted, which he refused to think about, and thought about daily when he read of the war. Already the Tiger scout had watched Billy pitch three games and talked to him after each one, told him all he needed was time, seasoning; told him to stay in shape in the off-season; told him next year he would go to Flint, Michigan, to Class A ball. He was the only one on the club who had a chance for the major leagues, though Billy Joe Baron would probably go up, but not very far; he was a good first baseman and very fast, led the league in stolen bases, but he had to struggle and beat out drag bunts and ground balls to keep his average in the two-nineties and low three hundreds, and he would not go higher than Class A unless they outlawed the curve ball. The others would stay with the Bulls, or a team like the Bulls. And now Leslie was staying in this little town that she wasn't supposed to see as a town to live in longer than a season, and staying too in the little furnished house they were renting, with its rusted screen doors and its yard that ended in the back at a woods which farther on became a swamp, so that Billy never went off the back porch at night and if he peered through the dark at the grass long enough he was sure he saw cottonmouths.

She came into the kitchen that morning of the final game, late morning after a late breakfast so he would eat only twice before pitching, when he was already—or still, from the night before—concentrating on his twentieth win; and the pennant too. He wanted that: wanted to be the pitcher who had come to a third place club and after one season had ridden away a pennant winner. She came into the kitchen and looked at him more seriously than he'd ever seen her, and said: "Billy, it's a terrible day to tell you this but you said today was the day I should pack."

He looked at her from his long distance then focused in closer, forced himself to hear what she was saying, felt like he was even forcing himself to see her in three dimensions instead of two, and said: "What's the matter, baby?"

"I'm not going."

"Not going where?"

"San Antonio. Flint. I'm staying here."

Her perspiring face looked so afraid and sorry for him and determined all at once, that he knew he was finished, that he didn't even know what was happening but there would never be enough words he could say. Her eyes were brimming with tears, and he knew they were for herself, for having come to this moment in the kitchen, so far from everything she could have known and predicted; deep in her eyes, as visible as stars, was the hard light of something else, and he knew that she had hated him too, and he imagined her hating him for days while he was on the road: saw her standing in this kitchen and staring out the screen door at the lawn and woods, hating him. Then the picture completed itself: a man, his back to Billy, stood beside her and put his arm around her waist.

"Leslie?" and he had to clear his throat, clear his voice of the fear in it: "Baby, have you been playing around?"

She looked at him for such a long time that he was both afraid of what she would say, and afraid she wouldn't speak at all.

"I'm in love, Billy."

Then she turned and went to the back door, hugging her breasts and staring through the screen. He gripped the corners of the table, pushed his chair back, started to rise, but did not; there was nothing to stand for. He rubbed his eyes, then briskly shook his head.

"It wasn't just that you were on the road so much. I was ready for that. I used to tell myself it'd be exciting a lot of the time, especially in the big leagues. And I'd tell myself in ten years it'd be over anyway, some women have to—"

"*Ten?*" Thinking of the running he did, in the outfield on the days he wasn't pitching, and every day at home between seasons, having known long ago that his arm was a gift and it would last until one spring when it couldn't do the work anymore, would become for the first time since it started throwing a baseball just an ordinary arm; and what he could and must do was keep his lungs and legs strong so they wouldn't give out before it did. He surprised himself: he had not known that, while his wife was leaving him, he could proudly and defensively think of pitching in his early thirties. He had a glimpse of the way she saw him, and he was frightened and ashamed.

"All right: fifteen," she said. "Some women are married to sailors and soldiers and it's longer. It wasn't the road trips. It was when you were home: you weren't here. You weren't here, with me."

"I was here all day. Six, seven hours at the park at night. I don't know what that means."

"It means I'm not what you want."

"How can you tell me what I want?"

"You want to be better than Walter Johnson."

From his angle he saw very little of her face. He waited. But this time she didn't speak.

"Leslie, can't a man try to be the best at what he's got to do and still love his wife?" Then he stood: "Goddamnit, who *is* he?"

"George Lemoine," she said through the screen.

"George Le*moine*. Who's George Le*moine*?"

"The dentist I went to."

"What dentist you went to?"

She turned and looked at his face and down the length of his arms to his fists, then sat at the opposite end of the table.

"When I lost the filling. In June."

"*June*?"

"We didn't start then." Her face was slightly lowered, but her eyes were raised to his, and there was another light in them: she was ashamed but not remorseful, and her voice had the unmistakable tone of a woman in love; they were never so serious as this, never so threatening, and he was assaulted by images of Leslie making love with another man. "He went to the games alone. Sometimes we talked down at the concession stand. We—" Now she looked down, hid her eyes from him, and he felt shut out forever from the mysteries of her heart.

All his life he had been confident. In his teens his confidence and hope were concrete: the baseball season at hand, the season ahead, professional ball, the major leagues. But even as a child he had been confident and hopeful, in an abstract way. He had barely suffered at all, and he had survived that without becoming either callous or naive. He was not without compassion when his life involved him with the homely, the clumsy, the losers. He simply considered himself lucky. Now his body felt like someone else's, weak and trembling. His urge was to lie down.

"And all those times on the road I never went near a whorehouse."

"It's not the same."

He was looking at the beige wall over the sink, but he felt that her eyes were lowered still. He was about to ask what she meant, but then he knew.

"So I guess when I go out to the mound tonight he'll be moving in, is that right?"

Now he looked at her, and when she lifted her face, it had changed; she was only vulnerable.

"He has to get a divorce first. He has a wife and two kids."

"Wait a minute. *Wait* a minute. He's got a wife and two *kids*? How *old* is this son of a bitch?"

"Thirty-four."

"God*damnit*, Leslie! How dumb can you be? He's getting what he wants from you, what makes you think he won't be smart enough to leave it at that? God*damn*."

"I believe him."

"You believe him. A dentist anyhow. How can you be married to a ballplayer and fall for a dentist anyhow? And what'll you do for money? You got that one figured out?"

"I don't need much. I'll get a job."

"Well you won't have much either, because I'm going over there and kill him."

"Billy." She stood, her face as admonitory as his mother's. "He's got enough troubles. All summer I've been in trouble too. I've been sad and lonesome. That's the only way this could ever happen. You know that. All summer I've been feeling like I was running alongside the players' bus waving at you. Then he came along."

"And picked you up."

He glared at her until she blushed and lowered her eyes. Then he went to the bedroom to pack. But she had already done it: the suitcase and overnight bag stood at the foot of the bed. He picked them up and walked fast to the front door. Before he reached it she came out of the kitchen, and he stopped.

"Billy. I don't want you to be hurt; and I know you won't be for long. I hope someday you can forgive me. Maybe write and tell me how you're doing."

His urge to drop the suitcase and overnight bag and hold her and ask her to change her mind was so great that he could only fight it with anger; and with the clarity of anger he saw a truth which got him out the door.

"You want it all, don't you? Well, forget it. You just settle for what you chose."

Scornfully he scanned the walls of the living room, then Leslie from feet to head; then he left, out into the sun and the hot still air, and drove into town and registered at a hotel. The old desk clerk recognized him and looked puzzled but quickly hid it and said: "Y'all going to beat them New Iberia boys tonight?"

"Damn right."

The natural thing to do now was go to Lemoine's office, walk in while he was looking in somebody's mouth: *It's me you son of a bitch* and work him over with the left hand, cancel his afternoon for him, send him off to another dentist. What he had to do was unnatural. And as he climbed the stairs to his room he thought there was much about his profession that was unnatural. In the room he turned off the air conditioning and opened the windows, because he didn't want his arm to be in the cool air, then lay on the bed and closed his eyes and began pitching to the batting order. He knew them all perfectly; but he did not trust that sort of perfection, for it was too much like confidence, which was too much like complacency. So he started with Vidrine, the lead-off man. Left-handed. Went with the pitch, hit to all fields; good drag-bunter but only fair speed and Primeaux would be crowding him at third; choke-hitter, usually got a piece of the ball, but not that quick with the bat either; couldn't hit good speed. Fastballs low and tight. Change on him. Good base runner but he had to get a jump. Just hold him close to the bag. Then Billy stopped thinking about Vidrine on base. Thing was to concentrate now on seeing his stance and the high-cocked bat and the inside of the plate and Lucky's glove. He pushed aside the image of Vidrine crouching in a lead off first, and at the same time he pushed from his mind Leslie in the kitchen telling him; he saw Vidrine at the plate and, beyond him, he saw Leslie going away. She had been sitting in the box seat but now she walked alone down the ramp. Poor little Texas girl. She even sounded like a small town in Texas: Leslie Wells. Then she was gone.

The home run came with one out and nobody on in the top of the third inning after he had retired the first seven batters. Rick Stanley hit it, the eighth man in the order, a good field no hit third baseman in his mid-twenties. He had been in the minors for seven years and looked like it: though trimly built, and the best third baseman Billy had ever seen, he had a look about

him of age, of resignation, of having been forced—
when he was too young to bear it well—to compromise
what he wanted with what he could do. At the plate he
looked afraid, and early in the season Billy thought
Stanley had been beaned and wasn't able to forget it.
Later he realized it wasn't fear of beaning, not fear at
all, but the strain of living so long with what he knew. It
showed in the field too. Not during a play, but when it
was over and Stanley threw the ball to the pitcher and
returned to his position, his face looking as though it
were adjusting itself to the truth he had forgotten when
he backhanded the ball over the bag and turned and
set and threw his mitt-popping peg to first; his face
then was intense, reflexive as his legs and hands and
arm; then the play was over and his face settled again
into the resignation that was still new enough to be
terrible. It spread downward to his shoulders and then
to the rest of him and he looked old again. Billy wished
he had seen Stanley play third when he was younger
and still believed there was a patch of dirt and a bag
and a foul line waiting for him in the major leagues.

One of Billy's rules was never to let up on the bottom
of the batting order, because when one of them got a
hit it hurt more. The pitch to Stanley was a good one.
Like many players, Stanley was a poor hitter because he
could not consistently be a good hitter; he was only a
good hitter for one swing out of every twelve or so; the
other swings had changed his life for him. The
occasional good one gave the fans, and Stanley too by
now, a surprise that always remained a surprise and so
never engendered hope. His home run was a matter of
numbers and time, for on this one pitch his concentration and timing and swing all flowed together,

making him for that instant the hitter of his destroyed dream. It would happen again, in other ball parks, in other seasons; and if Stanley had been able to cause it instead of having it happen to him, he would be in the major leagues.

Billy's first pitch to him was a fast ball, waist high, inside corner. Stanley took it for a strike, with that look on his face. Lucky called for the same pitch. Billy nodded and played with the rosin bag to keep Stanley waiting longer; then Stanley stepped out of the box and scooped up dust and rubbed it on his hands and the bat handle; when he moved to the plate again he looked just as tense and Billy threw the fast ball; Stanley swung late and under it. Lucky called for the curve, the pitch that was sweet tonight, and Billy went right into the windup, figuring Stanley was tied up tightly now, best time to throw a pitch into all that: he watched the ball go in fast and groin-high, then fall to the left and it would have cut the outside corner of the plate just above Stanley's knees; but it was gone. Stanley not only hit it so solidly that Billy knew it was gone before looking, but he got around on it, pulled it, and when Billy found it in the left-centerfield sky it was still climbing above James running from left and LeBlanc from center. At the top of its arc, there was something final about its floodlit surface against the real sky, dark up there above the lighted one they played under.

He turned his back to the plate. He never watched a home run hitter cross it. He looked out at LeBlanc in center; then he looked at Harry Burke at second, old Harry, the manager, forty-one years old and he could still cover the ground, mostly through cunning; make the pivot—how many double plays had he turned in his life?—and when somebody took him out with a slide Billy waited for the cracking sound, not just of bone but the whole body, like a dried tree limb. Hap told him not to worry, old Harry was made of oiled leather. His face looked as if it had already outlived two bodies like the one it commanded now. Never higher than Triple A, and that was long ago; when the Bulls hired him and then the fans loved him he moved his family to Lafayette and made it his home, and between seasons worked for an insurance company, easy money for him, because he went to see men and they drank coffee and talked baseball. He had the gentlest eyes Billy had ever seen on a man. Now Harry trotted over to him.

"We got twenty-one outs to get that back for you."

"The little bastard hit that pitch."

"Somebody did. Did you get a close look at him?"

Billy shook his head and went to the rubber. He walked the fat pitcher Talieferro on four pitches and Vidrine on six, and Lucky came to the mound. They called him Lucky because he wasn't.

"One run's one thing," Lucky said. "Let's don't make it three."

"The way y'all are swinging tonight, one's as good as nine." For the first time since he stepped onto the field, Leslie that morning rose up from wherever he had locked her, and struck him.

"Hey," Lucky said. "Hey, it's early."

"Can't y'all hit that fat son of a bitch?"

"We'll hit him. Now you going to pitch or cry?"

He threw Jackson a curve ball and got a double play around the horn, Primeaux to Harry to Baron, who did a split stretching and got Jackson by a half stride.

He went to his end of the bench and watched Talieferro, who for some reason pronounced his name Tolliver: a young big left-handed pitcher with the kind of belly that belonged to a much older man, in bars on week-end afternoons; he had pitched four years at the local college, this was his first season of pro ball, he was sixteen and nine and usually lost only when his control was off. He did not want to be a professional ballplayer. He had a job with an oil company at the end of the season, and was only pitching and eating his way through a Louisiana summer. Billy watched Lucky adjust his peakless cap and dust his hands and step to the plate, and he pushed Leslie back down, for she was about to burst out of him and explode in his face. He looked down at the toe plate on his right shoe, and began working the next inning, the middle of the order, starting with their big hitter, the centerfielder Remy Gauthreaux, who was finished too, thirty years old, but smart and dangerous and he'd knock a mistake out of the park. Low and away to Gauthreaux. Lucky popped out to Stanley in foul territory and came back to the dugout shaking his head.

Billy could sense it in all the hitters in the dugout, and see it when they went to the plate: Talieferro was on, and they were off. It could be anything: the pennant game, when every move counted; the last game of the season, so the will to be a ballplayer was losing to that other part of them which insisted that when they woke tomorrow nothing they felt tonight would be true; they would drive home to the jobs and other lives that waited for them; most would go to places where people had not even heard of the team, the league. All of that would apply to the Pelicans too; it could be that none of it applied to Talieferro: that rarely feeling much of anything except digestion, hunger, and gorging, he had no conflict between what he felt now and would start feeling tomorrow. And it could be that he simply had his best stuff tonight, that he was throwing nearly every pitch the way Stanley had swung that one time.

Billy went to the on-deck circle and kneeled and watched Harry at the plate, then looked out at Simmons, their big first baseman: followed Gauthreaux in the order, a power hitter but struck out about a hundred times a year: keep him off balance, in and out, and throw the fast one right into his power, and right past him too. Harry, choking high on the bat, fouled off everything close to the plate then grounded out to short, and Billy handed his jacket to the batboy and went through cheers to the plate. When he stepped in Talieferro didn't look at him, so Billy stepped out and stared until he did, then dug in and cocked the bat, a good hitter so he had played right field in high school and American Legion when he wasn't pitching. He watched the slow easy fat man's wind-up and the fast ball coming out of it: swung for the fence and popped it to second, sprinting down the line and crossing the bag before the ball came down. When he turned he saw Talieferro already walking in, almost at the third base line. Harry brought Billy's glove out to the mound and patted his rump.

"I thought you were running all the way to Flint."

In the next three innings he pitched to nine men. He ended the fifth by striking out Stanley on curve balls; and when Talieferro led off the sixth Billy threw a fast ball at his belly that made him spin away and fall into the dust. Between innings he forced himself to believe in the hope of numbers: the zeroes and the one on the scoreboard in right-center, the inning number, the outs remaining for the Bulls; watched them starting to hit, but only one an inning, and nobody as far as second base. He sat sweating under his jacket and in his mind pitched to the next three Pelicans, then the next three just to be sure, although he didn't believe he would face six of them next inning, or any inning, and he thought of eighteen then fifteen then twelve outs to get the one run, the only one he needed, because if it came to that, Talieferro would tire first. When Primeaux struck out leading off the sixth, Billy looked at Hap at the other end of the bench, and he wanted to be down there with him. He leaned forward and stared at his shoes. Then the inning was over and he gave in to the truth he had known anyway since that white vision of loss just before the ball fell.

Gauthreaux started the seventh with a single to right, doing what he almost never did: laid off pulling and went with the outside pitch. Billy worked Simmons low and got the double play he needed, then he struck out the catcher Lantrip, and trotted off the field with his string still going, thirteen batters since the one-out walk to Vidrine in the third. He got the next six. Three of them grounded out, and the other three struck out on the curve, Billy watching it break under the shiny blur of the bat as it would in Flint and wherever after that and Detroit too: his leg kicking and body wheeling and arm whipping around in rhythm again with his history which had begun with a baseball and a friend to throw it to, and had excluded all else, or nearly all else, and had included the rest somewhere alongside him, almost out of his vision (once between innings he allowed himself to think about Leslie, just long enough to forgive her); his history was his future too and the two of them together were twenty-five years at most until the time when the pitches that created him would lose their speed, hang at the plate, become hits in other men's lives instead of the heart of his; they would discard him then, the pitches would. But he loved them for that too, and right now they made his breath singular out of the entire world, so singular that there was no other world: the war would not call him because it couldn't know his name; and he would refuse the grief that lurked behind him. He watched the final curve going inside then breaking down and over and Lucky's mitt popped and the umpire twisted and roared and pointed his right fist to the sky.

He ran to the dugout, tipping his cap to the yelling Cajuns, and sat between Hap and Lucky until Baron flied out to end the game. After the showers and good-byes he drove to the hotel and got his still-packed bags and paid the night clerk and started home, out of the lush flatland of marsh and trees, toward Texas. Her space on the front seat was filled as with voice and touch. He turned on the radio. He was not sleepy, and he was driving straight through to San Antonio.

THE GREATEST SLUMP OF ALL TIME
David Carkeet

"Apples" Bagwell loses it in the late innings. His shoulders slump, his curve hangs, and his fastball yawns. Into the seventh or eighth he is great, almost perfect. But then he loses it, and it always takes Grammock a few more baserunners than it should to come out from the dugout and mumble around the mound and finally signal to the bullpen. Apples comes off the field looking like a puppy about to be whipped and sighs into the dugout. He just fills that dugout with his sigh.

People talk about it. He gets tired, some say. He has a fear of losing, say others, remembering his early years in the bigs. Some believe he becomes overconfident and lets up. The profile is baffling. Late innings. A lead. A stunning performance through six or seven frames.

E.T.A. Whitaker, a bespectacled first baseman with a good mind and a social worker for a wife, finally figures it out. He takes Apples to breakfast, choosing a secluded booth at the rear of the hotel coffee shop.

"Tough game last night," E.T.A. says to Apples as he gives his menu to the waitress. "For you, I mean." Apples lost his stuff in the seventh, but Butch came in and saved the game. The team is only three games out now, with a month of the regular season left.

"Yeah," says Apples.

"Grammock shoulda left you in, Apples," says the waitress, who is buxom and toothy. "He shoulda let you work it out. You're the best."

Apples shrugs and a pitiful look, one familiar to E.T.A. of late, crosses his face.

"She likes you, you know," says E.T.A., testing his theory after the waitress has gone.

Apples looks down at the table. His lids are heavy, his cheeks pale and lifeless. "Let Jaime have her," he says without feeling. Jaime is their right fielder. He has an unquenchable lust for women and an active English vocabulary of sixty-five words.

"He has," says E.T.A. "She told him she wants you."

Apples sighs and sinks deeper into gloom.

E.T.A. knows that the way out and the way in are one and the same. "The writers are talking about you for the Cy Young Award this year, Apples."

"Great," says Apples. His face doesn't say "great." Someone watching from across the room would think he was recalling famous airline disasters.

"We're all really happy for you," says E.T.A. "The whole team." Then, twisting the knife, "We all love you, Apples. Deeply. We really do."

It works. Apples begins to sob. His face turns into a contorted mass of red flesh under his hands. The waitress, who has brought his pineapple pancakes, sees what is happening and thinks he is upset about last night's game. She crawls into the next booth and leans over him from behind and begins to knead his shoulders like a trainer, whispering comforting words into his ear.

E.T.A. watches with pity which, he begins to notice with concern, is mixed with self-pity.

"Success depresses him," E.T.A. says to shortstop Scrappy Hawthorn as they walk back to the third-base line after a warm-up run. "Give him praise and he crumbles. On the mound he sees a victory coming and he folds. He's afraid of winning."

"That don't make no sense," says Scrappy. Unlike E.T.A., who is a modern athlete in every sense and an interviewer's delight, Scrappy talks like a Coolidge-era ballplayer.

"I didn't think so at first either," says E.T.A. "But then I saw that if you think you're inferior, being good at things will only make you feel like more of a bum."

Scrappy frowns and turns to him. "Apples feels like a bum?"

E.T.A. nods. They have reached the baseline and turn to run the twelve paces again, gliding easily with synchronized strides. As they slow and turn to walk back, E.T.A. says, "Maybe deep down we all think we're bums. After all, you know yourself better than anyone else does. You know how stupid and cruel you can be. Heap success on top of that and you've got a real formula for the blues." He pats Scrappy on the fanny and they turn and run once more. E.T.A. slows to a stop and turns, but Scrappy continues running in a wide arc and jogs back to the dugout alone.

E.T.A., temporarily relieved by their talk, plays well that day. Scrappy goes oh-for-five. In the field *twice* he trips over second base as he tries to make unassisted double plays, and *twice* his throw sails wide of E.T.A.'s desperate reach. The second throw is much more cautious, and much worse, than the first. Then, in the ninth, he instinctively dives to his right to make an impossible game-ending catch of a line drive, his body stretched out straight as a javelin. The cheers rains down on him in the clubhouse. That night he has trouble falling asleep. He wakes before dawn and stares at the ceiling until it is time for breakfast, when he must go into society and be congratulated again.

The next day Scrappy shares his inarticulate thoughts with Bubba Phelps, the second baseman. Bubba laughs without sympathy and apparently without understanding, and then commits a judgment error in the field and later is picked off first base—a base given to him not on the merits of a hit, but because he was too slow, too torpid, too sodden with thought, to move out of the way of a high, inside pitch that grazed him on the arm. All day, and then at night, he sees that pitch again and again, only it is higher, heading for his face, and he is even slower to get out of its way.

To ease his mind, Bubba raps with Eddie Johnson, the swift center fielder. Eddie gives him wisdom and comfort. Later, when the team's flight is delayed by a mechanical problem, Eddie smashes two metal chairs in the airport lounge in a fit of impatience. He unburdens himself to his teammates in the outfield, Buford Ellenbogen and Jaime, and from Buford the word travels back into the infield to the fast-talking third baseman, Frank Joiner; Frank gives it to Narvel Adams, the catcher, and in no time at all Narvel is matching batterymate Apples sigh for sigh.

As the days wear on and the players collectively bring the team into first place, their symptoms diversify and specialize. Apples, of course, is the chief mumbler and moper. He has polished his flatness of affect beyond improvement. Between innings of work Grammock, a former pitching coach, criticizes and corrects him, telling him to bear down, goddammit, and push off the be-Jesus mound. He listens and feels each word adding measurable weight to his body. When he returns to the mound his motion is even more ponderous than before.

Frank is different. He plays well and looks normal, but his mind is full of spiders. He thinks people are talking about him. On the road he lurks just inside the door of his hotel room, listening to his teammates going down to breakfast, wondering why they haven't asked him to join them. He hears words that could be about him—words like "am" and "my"—and he aches for acceptance.

Narvel sighs a lot. This makes him light-headed and dizzy. Though only twenty-four, he concludes that his body is deteriorating. Two years, maybe three, and he will announce his retirement.

Bubba fears someone is going to break into his apartment on a dark night while he is in bed. The intruder will of course steal from him, but he will also abuse him with words. Bubba feels that the man will have every right to do this.

Eddie compares himself with others and comes out sub-human. The way Scrappy runs the bases, the way Jaime goes back on the long ball—he can't match them. He doesn't belong in the majors. Every day he is ashamed to see his name still on his locker.

Scrappy can't sleep. He awakens at 4:00 every morning as if called by God. He lies awake and stares, then lurches in bed as if having sex with the air. Then he stares some more. His afternoon naps debilitate him further. The sleep he loses at night is unrecoverable.

Buford, once featured in the hometown newspaper for the way he ate four entrees in succession at a Denny's, has lost his appetite.

E.T.A. maintains that the world has gone to hell in a cardboard suitcase. His favorite word is "point," especially when it occurs with "no," or "what's the."

Jaime, newly impotent, is exploring suicide.

Narvel calls home. His mother answers and calls with elderly enthusiasm to his father, who picks up the phone in the Rathskeller.

"Narvel! How are you, boy?"

"Fine, Dad."

"Say, you guys are lookin' good. I mean good. A steady climb into first, tough resolve in the face of challenge, a widening lead in the division…I like the looks of it. I like it a lot. I like the whole pattern of the season. Another week of the same and I'd say you're uncatchable. I'd definitely say you're uncatchable. Of course I'm assuming lively run production from Eddie and a little more pizzazz in your starters, especially Apples. Nice play last night on that bad throw, by the way. You saved a run and kept the D.P. in order."

Narvel blinks heavily. His father is retired and lives for the game. This once gave Narvel pleasure.

"How are you?" asks Narvel. He knows his conversation is lifeless. He could never talk—not well, anyway.

"Us?" his father says loudly. "Fine, fine. Not bad for old folks. Your mom's back is giving her some trouble."

"I'm sorry—"

"It's nothing," says his mother. "Narvel, do you remember Mrs. Webster?"

"No."

"The Sunday School teacher?"

"No, I don't."

"He was too young, Ruth," says his father.

"She passed away," says his mother, ending the tale.

"Hunh," says Narvel. There is a long silence after this. Then he says, "Mom, Dad, do you remember an old diary I kept when I was little?"

"No," says his father.

"Of course," says his mother. "It's in the trunk in the attic." Her voice is chipper and sing-songy.

"Can you send it to me?"

"Of course."

"Gettin' sentimental, boy?" says his father suspiciously. "Seems to me you ought to be thinkin' of the future, not the past. Like tomorrow's doubleheader. Those guys will eat you for lunch if you let 'em."

"Yes, sir," he says, feeling reprimanded. His throat tightens and his voice thins out. "It's just that a bunch of us were talking about our childhoods and all, and I got wondering about mine and if it was, well, you know, what it was like and all, and I thought maybe the diary would help, because lately—"

"Of course, dear. I'll put it in the mail right away."

Narvel sighs in misery. His mother, as always, co-operates without understanding.

"The future is for the living, Narvel," his father says. "You guys have been lookin' pretty drab for a front-runner."

"Maybe it's our TV, Ralph. Ever since they built that high-rise—"

"I know a drab team when I see one," his father insists. "Do you hear me, Narvel? Talk to me."

"Yes, sir," he says, sighing again. His father understands but gives no support. Narvel suddenly sees himself as a soldier wounded in battle; his parents try to help him back to safety, but they arrive with a corpse mangled from mishandling.

Eddie plays with his daughter, Tina, and listens to his wife on the telephone. She is talking to Bubba's wife, making plans for the World Series. The playoffs start tomorrow and already she is planning for the Series. His resentment is like a cloak that warms him and darkens his life. He pulls it around himself tighter and tighter. She has come to expect satisfaction. She is never surprised when they win. She will never see his achievement for what it is—not just a well-paying job, but a glorious, precarious moment of trembling balance. An injury or a brief slump turning into a long one because he gives it too much thought—either of these could close it out and turn him into a regular guy with nothing more than a year or two of interesting history becoming less interesting as the years go by. And a bitch for a wife, because all baseball is to her is lots of money and a chance to shop in New York during the

Series. She who has never touched a baseball in her life, who sits with the other wives and cheers in ignorance. She still doesn't know what a hit is. If he flies out four times in a game she will say he got four hits. She cannot know how good he is. Neither can Tina, because she is so young. And when she is older? He imagines her future, a product of his wife's unassisted bungling because he is on the road so much: knocked up with nine kids and no man; or maybe a good Christian who prays her bruises away while her man drinks and beats up on her; or maybe a radical feminist who uses her dead father in her speeches as an example of persistent racism in the U.S. because in spite of his brains there was no room for him in baseball management after it came to an end for him in his third year because of an injury or a slump that he gave too much thought to.

A conference on the mound. It is a key game—the fourth game of the playoffs. After taking the first two from Chicago they have dropped one and fear dropping this one. Chicago would have the momentum then and would be strong for the fifth game. They are at home, up by one, in the top of the ninth. After a disputed call on a dive by Eddie for a ball hit behind second (ruled an out), Apples has hit a batsman (who stole second on the next pitch), intentionally walked a batter, and given up an infield single—a ludicrously topped ball that dribbled nowhere in particular and advanced everybody. The bases are loaded. Apples is down, but no more than usual.

Narvel shuffles out to him. Apples welcomes the rebuke implied by his approach. The infield moves to the mound. Narvel looks at their faces and sees ghosts.

"What are we gonna do?" asks Apples.

They all look down at their feet and kick at the dirt on the mound.

"I dunno, man," says Bubba. "Don't let him hit to me. I'm blue."

"And I'm tired," says sleepless Scrappy. "Make him pull it."

They all look up at the batter to see if he is right- or left-handed. They should know this already without having to look, but they don't concentrate. He is a switch hitter, and he will bat left-handed against Apples. If he pulls the ball sharply it will go to E.T.A. at first. They turn to him and he shrugs.

"Sure," he says indifferently. "I can handle it. And if I don't?" He flashes a macabre grin and his eyeglasses twinkle in the sunlight. "What does it matter? Everyone here'll be dead someday." He sweeps his eyes over the field and then up to the stands filled with hopeful supporters. His teammates follow his eyes and suddenly find themselves surrounded by sixty thousand skeletons.

"There are people dyin' every day," Narvel says thoughtfully. "People you don't even know."

"Whatever happens," says Apples—and a quiet urgency in his voice draws their close attention—"I want you guys to know I've really appreciated your support this year."

This is received glumly by all but E.T.A. He laughs loudly. "Jesus, Apples, what do you do when you're thirsty—drink ashes?" The infield begins to chuckle grimly and a dark figure approaches. Narvel sees him out of the corner of his eye and fancies it is the Grim Reaper, but it is only the home-plate ump. He tells them to stop clowning around and play ball. Meekly, guiltily, they obey.

Two things happen that decide it. First, Apples forgets there is already one out—the disputed call and subsequent hit batsman have blurred in his mind into just one hitter—so he pitches with no expectation of victory. With the bases loaded and nobody out he thinks, Chicago is bound to take it away from them. Then after the loss tomorrow he can stay home in bed for five months.

He puts the ball right where he should.

Second, E.T.A. gets mad. As he crouches with Apples' pitch and watches the switch hitter he is reminded of a minor league coach who tried to make *him* into a switch hitter, ruining his average for a full year and slowing his rise to the major leagues. He complained about it frequently and got a bad rap as a troublemaker. When the coach got reassigned somewhere E.T.A. resumed his left-handed hitting and left the farm the next season. For the misery he caused him with his ignorance, that coach nearly destroyed his career.

In rage E.T.A. whirls and guns the ball to second even before he knows he has fielded it cleanly, and in the same motion he is on his way back to first to cover, because he knows Apples won't make it, and he takes Scrappy's low return throw out of the dirt to his right, stretching his leg as if convinced that to tear something in it is to tear that coach's heart out, and the ump's call and the cheers from the stands send him and his team to the Series.

It has been asked if it is possible for a team to win the big one without a big stick, or with a bullpen that is weak, or with rookies at the corners. A related question that has not been asked is if it is possible for a team to win the big one with an outfield on Elavil.

"Poppin' pills again?" asks Grammock as he walks through the clubhouse and sees Buford and Eddie comparing prescriptions. Eddie protests that it is legal —they're not uppers, he says, they're anti-downers. Grammock shakes his head in silence and stalks off to his office, feeling that he just doesn't understand his boys anymore. He has tried his bench, hoping that platooning his regulars would get them out of the doldrums, but as soon as his bench performs well they go logy on him too. So he sticks with his starters. If he's going to put nine zombies on the field he wants it to be his best nine.

Scrappy, who is in sit-down psychotherapy, chal- lenges Eddie's treatment. He says that the outfielders will never truly know themselves if they rely solely on drugs.

"'Know thyself,' said Abe Lincoln," Scrappy informs him. "He knew hisself, you can bet."

"Like you?" Eddie asks mockingly.

"I'm workin' on it," Scrappy says with a tentativeness bordering on total capitulation. "It takes time."

"Yeah? How much time?"

Scrappy's eyes shift nervously. "A year, maybe Maybe longer."

Eddie laughs loudly.

"I...I got a lotta issues to work through," says Scrappy.

"Issues?" says Eddie. "Issues of what—the *Sporting News?* What kind of word is that, you dirtbrain?" His words surprise everyone. Though big, black, and witty,

Eddie has never been the club razzer. That was always Narvel's role, at least before he forgot how to talk.

Scrappy's face collapses and he begins to whine his arguments out. He says that drugs just cover up the sickness. Eddie says that if the sickness is bad only because of the symptoms, and if drugs take away the symptoms, then it's a harmless disease. It's as harmless, he says, as being allergic to moon dust: it makes no difference if you never go there.

Frank has been oiling his glove nervously and listening. He speaks up in a speedy, jerky way that is like his lateral movement at third base. "Scrappy's right. He's just got the wrong kind of therapy. What is your guy—an analyst?"

"I dunno," says Scrappy.

"How often do you go?"

"Once a week."

Frank purses his lips. "Maybe not, then."

"But he wants me to come three or four times a week."

"Ah. Does he ever talk about the here-and-now?"

Scrappy looks deeply uncertain.

"You know—what's going on in your life today," Frank explains.

"Nah. He's more, I dunno, innerested in pre-school I guess."

"Yeah," Frank says knowingly. "You got the wrong persuasion, Scrappy. You should get into cognitive therapy."

"What's that?" asks E.T.A., who has joined the group.

"It's clean and simple," says Frank. "People get depressed because they have bad thoughts about themselves. Cognitive therapy helps the patient see that these thoughts are distortions of reality. Like if Jaime here thought he was a for-shit ballplayer, if I was his therapist I'd remind him of his record for doubles last year and the catch he made on Frawley's ball last week. Stuff like that." Jaime smiles, happy to be discussed this way.

"And it works?" asks Eddie, his eyebrows dancing. He looks right at Frank, into the soul of his depression.

"Well, it's *working*" says Frank.

Eddie snorts. "And what if the bad thoughts are true? Like Jaime's batting average is way down this year, and he lost us the third game of the playoffs on that pansy throw. What does a therapist do when there's evidence that the patient is a washout?" Jaime has stopped smiling.

Frank is not prepared for this argument. "Maybe he kind of puts things in perspective," he says tentatively, gesturing broadly with his hands—hands that have been called "soft" for the way they absorb ground balls.

Eddie snorts again. "If you're throwing away money on a shrink like that you better hope we win the Series. And you better help us, like by improving your bunting, for God's sake. It stinks. Did your guy tell you that?"

"I'm just trying to get better," Frank says weakly. He is not talking about his bunting.

E.T.A. has observed this dialogue closely. Eddie's anger surprises him. He remembers his own flash of hatred for his old coach in the last game of the playoffs. He looks at Apples, Narvel, and the others. Their self-hatred is suddenly as obvious to him as it would be if they were systematically mutilating their bodies with their cleats.

"Listen up, guys," he calls out with a hint of his old

hopefulness. Heads turn. The faces are pale and listless, but they are interested. He speaks. His theory is simple: depression, he says, is hatred of others turned inward. It is anger unreasonable only in its direction. "We're like a little boy whose parents have yelled at him so he kicks his dog," he says, his hand darting nervously up to adjust his glasses. "Only we're the dog. We're kicking ourselves."

Buford asks him how he gets from anger to depression. They seem to him to be different emotions.

E.T.A., suddenly losing all faith in his position, says he doesn't know. Maybe it makes no sense, he admits, and maybe no one is mad at anybody he can think of, at least not right now, but all he is asking is that they give it some thought, not necessarily right now, but—

"I hate my wife," Eddie announces matter-of-factly. He looks at Scrappy, Jaime, and Frank. He has hurt them too, he sees, along with himself. His eyes moist, he says to each of them, "Hey, man…hey, man…"

"It's okay," Scrappy says softly.

"I hate *someone*," says Narvel, banging his fist into his palm. "I know I do. I can feel it." His words are followed by a long silence. It is the first time he has spoken in two days.

"When I was a kid," Bubba says suddenly, "this other kid who was older and a lot bigger than me used to wait for me and beat me up on my way to school. He had a whip, too, and sometimes he used that. He waited for me every day."

"I was an Army kid," says Frank, "and we moved around a lot, so I was switching schools all the time. It seemed like I'd never studied what the other kids had, so I was always behind. Couldn't draw or sing, either.

The teachers always found me handy as a negative example, and they would talk about me all the time in front of the other kids." He pauses, then says with a dreamy smile, "I hate a whole shitload of people."

The players form a tighter circle and continue to talk. Grammock steps out of his office and opens his mouth to ask Narvel something about the New York line-up. The words don't come out. He squints at his team—all hunched up together and muttering, as isolated and freaky as those goddamned Christian athletes in Bible study.

They win the first, third, and fifth games of the Series on skill, instinct, and constructive anger. They lose the second, fourth, and sixth games in the fog of depressive relapses. The pattern has not gone unnoticed, and the sportswriters, ignorant of the pathology, pursue a mathematical whimsy and predict victory for them in game seven. The players themselves do not know what to expect, or what to hope for. For a baseball team sickened by success, winning the World Series is definitely contraindicated. They wonder if, during the game, they will sabotage victory if they see it coming. But then perhaps a win is just the thing they need. How nice, how *insuring*, to have reached the absolute top. Good material for a cognitive therapist, that. And they are getting madder every day. Old angers grow stronger—Eddie, for example, is divorcing his wife and seeking custody of Tina—and new angers erupt: Jaime has decided that he hates women, and the nervousness his discovery arouses in the clubhouse is offset by the team thrill in the knowledge that the entire outfield, in spite of their medication, is now mad as hell.

Apples and Narvel are the only ones left to make progress. They have been slow, as E.T.A. puts it, "to get in touch with their anger." But even this changes for the good in the eleventh hour, at least for Apples. During a live radio interview in the dugout just before the seventh game, the normally placid pitcher flushes with sudden annoyance at a prying question, and as the looks back at the badly dressed broadcaster who has been tailing them all season, he recalls that it was this same man who once described him as "a tall, skinny, loosey-goosey kind of pitcher," and while Apples knows that this describes his motion perfectly, he resents the implication of awkwardness and ugliness. After all, that waitress back at the hotel wanted him, didn't she? He suddenly feels that the press has never dealt with him fairly, always suggesting that because he doesn't look like a pitcher he probably isn't. He responds to the question, not even remembering what it is, with a flurry of obscenity that leaves the broadcaster speechless. The interview is carried over the radio speakers in the clubhouse, and those players still there tying their shoelaces or looking at themselves with ambivalence in the mirror hear the words in astonishment and send out a cheer for their hurler.

As for Narvel, it is obvious from the way he returns Apples' fiery warm-up throws that he's still being blue. The team sees it. E.T.A., chewing on the bitterness of his minor league experience, knows the joy of rage, and he wants Narvel to know it too, so when the game starts he directs his encouraging chatter away from Apples to the catcher, saying, "C'mon babe, c'mon Narvel babe, get mad, babe, c'mon," and Scrappy, who has been watering with tears an ancient anger toward the incompetent and belittling grandmother who reared him, yells, "Work on it, Narvel, work on it," and Frank at third interrupts a steady stream of soft curses at a grade school teacher who said his painted trees in art class looked like apple cores to shout, "Who do ya hate, Narv, who do ya hate?"

Narvel accepts the encouragement gratefully. The game seems to proceed almost without him. He drops a few balls (but nobody's hurt), he gives some bad signs (but Apples just shakes them off), and he makes a bad throw on an attempted steal (but it's backed up by swift, dry-mouthed Eddie, who charges in from center and throws the runner out as he tries to advance to third). The game remains scoreless, the only threat coming from long balls hit to the wall in fury by Eddie, Frank, and E.T.A. New York has barely touched the ball because Apples is hot, giving up just two hits, bloop singles, into the bottom of the seventh. His cheeks are flaming red, and he gets hotter as he moves through his fateful innings. He imagines he is pitching over and over to the radio broadcaster, and he rejoices in his enemy's repeated failures at bat.

In the top of the ninth, back-to-back doubles by Bubba and Jaime give them a one-run lead. Both hits are line drives to the wall on the fly—clotheslines, ropes. It happens so quickly that they are ahead before they have time to think about it. A relief pitcher enters the game for New York, and while he takes his warm-up throws each of the next three batters waits and watches, alone with his thoughts. It is the top of the ninth, after all, and the more runs they score the more likely they are to win. When play resumes, Eddie and Scrappy promptly strike out. E.T.A. fares even more poorly. Remembering his minor league coach and wishing to prove himself once and for all, he bats right-handed for the first time in eight years. He ignores Grammock's baffled shouts from the dugout, and after two swinging strikes he makes contact but is called out for several of the most ignominious reasons in the rule book. His weak undercut sends the ball straight up, spinning madly but rising no more than five feet. As it drops back down it strikes his bat as it swings around in an awkward follow-through. The ball squirts down the first-base line, where it is struck again by his bat—which has slipped out of his unaccustomed right-handed grip—and then kicked by his foot as he stumbles out of the batter's box. The ump says he is out; the opposing catcher adds, "And then some." E.T.A takes his position in the field, gloating with a strange sense of revenge.

In the bottom of the ninth Apples retires the first batter on a pop-up to Frank that Narvel should have taken, but Frank and E.T.A. have agreed to cover for Narvel because of his deep funk. The second batter hits a ball sharply down the line at third that rolls around in the left-field corner. Buford, hungry and constipated, seems to take a day or two to come up with it, and he just barely holds him to a triple. The hometown crowd goes wild: the tying run is at third. Apples, expecting to lose now, whiffs the next batter on three pitches, and the visiting fans thunder with anticipation of the final, Series-winning out. Apples, expecting to win, walks the next batter on four pitches. He studies the runner's lead at first and remembers how the press has always criticized his pick-off move. He fires the ball to E.T.A. and the runner is safe by a wide margin. He goes into his stretch and fires again, making it a little closer. He hears Grammock yell something from the dugout but ignores it. His third throw to E.T.A. is wide and E.T.A must come off the bag to take it. The tying run at third dances down the line, itching to get home. Grammock is joined in his yelling by some fans behind the dugout. They shout "Get the batter, Apples! Get the last out!" Unhappy with his last throw, Apples tries again and is pleased with the improvement. Yes, this is definitely a part of the game he needs to work on. No time like the present. He tries a slightly different motion and E.T.A. blocks the ball with his chest as it bounces up out of the dirt.

Grammock jumps from the dugout and a voice from the stands yells, "Tell the moron to forget about the runner and work on the batter, Grammock." The voice is familiar to Apples—it is a friend or relative of one of the players—and he smiles toward it and toward the approaching Grammock with blank indifference. Grammock chastises him further, waving violently to the rest of the infield to stay back from the mound.

Apples sighs despondently and agrees to abandon his cause. After getting the sign from Narvel, he delivers a lackluster pitch that is outside by a foot, and Narvel surprises everyone by coming up quickly from behind the plate to try to pick the runner off at first. He too, it seems, has become caught up in Apples' obsession. But the ball doesn't go to E.T.A. at all. Instead it screams over the dugout toward the fans in the stands, and there is a shout and a *pwang!* as it flies into the tin crate of a beer vendor, knocking him backwards into a row of spectators. One voice rises above the others. It is Narvel's father, yelling, "What the hell are you doin' boy?" Beside him, Narvel's mother wipes spilled beer from her lap and softly weeps.

The runner at first advances to second on the throw. The runner at third comes home, tying the score, and he says something unkind and jeering to Narvel. Narvel does not hear him. His mind is numb. His body tingles with satisfaction.

The winning run at second is represented by a rookie—a pinch runner who nervously stands on one leg and grabs the ankle of the other, stretching his quadriceps. He chatters excitedly, and he reminds Bubba of the taunting teenage boy who always beat him up on his way to school. When Apples, inspired by the team's declining fortune, gets the next batter to hit a ground ball to Bubba for an easy play at first which will send the game into extra innings, Bubba guns the ball across the diamond to Frank at third in hopes of erasing the skinny bully once and for all. Though surprised, Frank takes the throw well—for he is good, his hands are soft, his cognitive therapist says so—and comes within inches of tagging the sliding runner. In the cloud of dust the call can go either way. Because Bubba's play was so stupid in the first place, the ump spreads his hands out wide and sticks his fanny up and yells, "He's there!"

The infield, agitated and without direction, draws together on the mound. E.T.A. says, "Well, the run that will beat us is at third."

"Yeah," says Frank. "We put him there too."

"You're a sport for sayin' 'we,' Frank," says Bubba. "It was my fault all the way."

"I put him on base to begin with," says Apples.

"And I got him to second," says Narvel.

E.T.A. grins. "A team effort. That's what we'll say to the press afterward. Better yet, we'll let Apples tell them." They all chortle, producing a cacophonous death rattle that reaches the fans in the first few rows and chills their hearts. "It's funny," continues E.T.A., "you'd think depressed people wouldn't want to be around other depressed people, but we seem to get along all right. I think it's even been good for team spirit."

"You didn't start this on purpose, did you, E.T.A.?" asks Bubba. "Jis' to bring us together? You wouldn't do that, would you, man?"

"He couldn't have," says Apples. "He didn't start it. I did."

"But he put it into words," says Bubba. "He made it contagious."

"Nobody started it," Frank says firmly. "It just happened. We were all ripe. Maybe everybody's ripe."

Scrappy nods slowly. "Ain't it a bitch the way it takes hold of you? And it's never over, is it? Even when you think you're gettin' better."

"It's never over until it's over," says Narvel.

As the infield pauses to ponder this, the ump steps out and rudely orders them to break it up. As he turns his back he received a blistering chorus of illegal epithets. Their anger is like a pitching machine gone wild, spraying the ball park with vengeful sallies. The ump flinches but keeps walking to the plate. He should eject them all, but he lets it pass. His judgment has been dulled by nine innings of Narvel's sighing listlessness at his feet.

In mutual consolation for their season in hell together, and to warm one another for the long, cold off-season ahead of them, the infield forms a hugging circle and squeezes hard. With a moaning cheer they break the circle and return to their positions. Apples bends down and picks up the rosin bag. He wants to give this one some thought, and the rule book says that with a man on base a pitcher may take as long as he likes.

Meanwhile, at third, Frank and the rookie pinch runner chat, as opposing players will do, even under the most tense of circumstances. The rookie, grown cocky with his progress to third base and his instant national importance, asks Frank why his club is so weird. Apple's delay behind the mound gives Frank ample opportunity to speak about the suffering of his team. He describes the symptoms and possible origins of clinical depression, stressing his team's particular nemesis: the psychic perils of success. Frank understands the problem well and speaks about it intelligently. The upshot of their discussion is that when Apple finally goes into his stretch and looks at the rookie at third and sighs so heavily that he balks, thus automatically scoring the runner (who must trot home and touch the plate to end the game—a formality, but a necessary formality), the rookie freezes in uncertainty at third base.

LOSERS
Brian Fawcett

I might have been a Little League all-star if I hadn't broken a finger in the last game of the season when I was twelve. I was a shortstop, with a slick glove that almost made up for my terrible hitting. I might have been a good hitter if an opposing pitcher hadn't lost control of a fast ball and hit me on the side of the head with it. After that happened I was more interested in keeping the ball from hitting me than in hitting it with my bat.

Two years later, in Pony League, I was again headed for an all-star berth at shortstop, still all field and no hit, when fate intervened again. My coach saw me fooling around with a roundhouse curve ball I could throw because of my double-jointed shoulders. The curve ball had a kind of lazy elegance that came from the way my shoulder came out of the socket when I threw. This made the ball curve across and down about eighteen inches.

The coach began to treat me as if I were a very short and pale Don Newcombe with glasses, and I, quite naturally, fell for it. I was a hero for the first two games I pitched, striking out nearly every batter I didn't walk or hit with the curve ball. I filled the league with batters just like me. No one knew where the ball would go when I threw it. I had the slight advantage of knowing it would end up roughly a foot and a half to the left and down from where it was supposed to go, even if I couldn't control where I sent it in the first place. But by the third or fourth game I pitched, a few of the more cunning kids in the league had figured it out, and I was in trouble.

Elegance has its own weaknesses, the greatest of which has to do with the fact that if a barbarian refuses to be dazzled, and watches it carefully, it eventually appears simple and obvious. By my fifth game, the barbarians were streaming over every hill, and because it never occurred to me to throw anything but my best pitch, I got shellacked.

I pulled myself in the second inning of the sixth game. I had a sore arm, the team had another shortstop, and I'd decided I was really more interested in my stamp collection. I quit cold and didn't go back.

I loved baseball. It was the only sport I really cared about, then or ever. But I'd quit, and I wouldn't go back, even though it meant that my major league career was gone, and therefore I would have to grow up. I couldn't get what I wanted from it. I couldn't win, so I let it all go, and began, very slowly, and in terror, to grow older.

Deep inside me a struggle was going on. It was between the part of me that wanted to be a hero, and which loved all the nonsense life in a small town offered, and the part of me that was a quitter, and didn't want anything to do with the barbarians and their nonsense. The struggle went on for a long time, until I discovered the one occupation that could resolve the contending parts: I became a writer.

One of the first things I did was leave town. If I was going to be a writer, I reasoned, I would have to figure out what writers really did, and what they thought about, and what they wrote. I needed equipment.

I decided I needed to know *everything,* so I went to university. At university everything that turned out to be important was the reverse of what I once thought was important. Life turned out to be a serious business, and business turned out to be the opposite of what my father had tried to convince me it was. Fine, I thought. Just fine.

I met new people, and they introduced me to even more serious ideas, and to other people who told me that the world was a singular and malevolent machine that was in the process of devouring everyone. I was a long way from home, and I loved it.

I gave up sports altogether because I thought, as many people did in those days, that sports were frivolous. I didn't want to be just any old kind of writer; I wanted to be a Great Writer, and things like running around on a playground chasing a ball covered with leather and stitches wasn't going to help me. If I was going to chase anything, it was going to be women. My hormones were telling me that wasn't at all frivolous, and I got the idea from somewhere that it was an important part of my training as a writer.

Like most young men, I had a fair amount of energy and very little to write about, so I chased women. I've heard that referred to as a sport, but for me it was much more serious—my earnestness was matched only by my incompetence, and my confusion whenever I succeeded.

Then, what people who grew up in the 1960s called "The Revolution" came. "Peace and Love," it said, and "No More Competition," and it expounded some confused ideas to the effect that there were more important things to do than chase women, and that anyway, women were not sports equipment, and they certainly were not funny. Right in the middle of all this, somebody asked me if I wanted to play some baseball.

I thought about it seriously for a while, and decided that it would be a good way of taking my mind off women, and an even better way of working out some new attitudes toward competition. Or so I said. The truth was that I was going crazy trying to figure out how to deal with everything that was coming at me. Being serious about everything wasn't turning out to be much fun.

Some of my new friends and I started a baseball team, and we joined an informal league of teams that each had some particular, and usually peculiar, hold on "The Revolution." There was a team of rock'n'roll musicians, a team of political radicals, a team of motorcycle hoodlums, two teams made up of writers, painters and serious musicians, a team of women, a gay team, a team of dope fiends (and a team of undercover cops to shadow them) and so on.

I wasn't the same kind of ball player any more, either. I'd been sitting around thinking for long enough that the rubber in my body had largely turned to jello, and my fielding was anything but slick.

On the other hand, the spectre of the ball aimed at my head had vanished, and I could hit. I hit consistently, and sometimes with power. What had once seemed mysterious and terrifying was reversed like everything else. Hitting was easy. I just hit the ball with the bat.

The position I liked least now was shortstop. When I was a kid, the sense of space and freedom in the middle of a baseball infield appealed to me. I seemed to have no direct responsibilities, except when I had to cover second base, and there were other players on each side of me. I was at the centre of things, and I could help anyone, do anything, or ignore whatever didn't come directly at me.

I'd been almost completely wrong about being a shortstop, of course; a shortstop is the one player on a ball field who is responsible to, and for, everyone and everything. My first few games as an adult shortstop, consequently, were filled with a series of tactical and physical errors. If I actually managed to field a ground ball, I was as likely to throw it to the pitcher or to the centre fielder as to the correct baseman. I was even more hopeless at pop flies, which I played as if I had a combination of vertigo and St. Vitus' Dance—I grew dizzy, fell into nonexistent potholes, or lost the ball in the sun even if it was a cloudy day.

Our second baseman, as myopic as I was, had similar problems but a different technique. Where I would dither in circles at some distance from the place where the fly was to land, he had a knack for being in the right spot without knowing it. He would stand perfectly still as if nothing at all were happening, at the last second make a wild dash for the ball and then, without looking up, attempt to catch it with his head.

We played the game in our own strange way, adjusting the rules to fit the "Spirit of Revolution." No one was allowed to wear spikes, and at first, uniforms were sneered at. Teams were supposed to be integrated, meaning that every team was supposed to have some women on it, including the women's teams, which had one or two males just to turn things properly around. We called it the "Cosmic League."

Our team soon became one of the better teams in the League, mostly because I gave up trying to play shortstop and went to first base where all I had to do was catch the infielder's throws, and my companion at second base went to right field, where he didn't have to catch much of anything. We were also the most argumentative team in the league, and were widely acclaimed as a bunch of jerks.

To my surprise, I was the biggest jerk on the team. I was prepared to do anything short of killing in order to win, and I was unsympathetic when team members made errors—excluding, naturally, my own. Worse, I didn't really like having women play on the team, particularly if they weren't as skillful as the rest of us.

I accounted for my un-cosmic behavior with the explanation that, well, I didn't use hallucinogenic drugs. My friends explained it by deciding that I was a jerk.

It was the sixth inning of a game that was important solely because it was Tuesday night, and tomorrow it was going to be Wednesday. Somebody decided his girlfriend had to play a few innings.

I asked why.

"Because it's Tuesday," he said.

"What's so special about Tuesday?" I asked, sensing that I was headed for a trap.

"It's the day before Wednesday," he replied, and sprang the trap. "What's so important about this game that she can't play a few innings?"

"Nothing," I said morosely. "She's just a lousy player, that's all."

"What's that got to do with it?" he said. "It's just a game."

"Tomorrow is Wednesday," I told him. "Let her play then."

"There's no game tomorrow."

"I don't care. I just hate losing on Tuesdays."

The truth was that I hated to lose on any day, more than I ever had as a kid. I lost that argument, probably, and a lot of other ones like it, and we probably lost a few games because I'd lost the arguments. I knew it didn't really matter, but there was something in me that I was vaguely ashamed of that told me it damned well did matter. It mattered so much to me that I made enemies of some friends over it, and finally, I quit the team, feeling as helpless as a brontosaurus blundering into a bog.

But The Revolution was in trouble too, and it was in trouble with baseball for the same reasons it was in trouble with a lot of fairly basic laws of behavioural physics. For one thing, if people practice anything, they'll get better at it—unless, of course, they get bored with it, or become afraid of it, and quit. Skill has its own unique set of demands, one of which is that it breeds ambition.

When our team became, with my departure, more studiously revolutionary, it began to lose all the time. The other teams were improving, and so were the people on our team who were ball players—which is to say, they were there not just because of the social and political merits of the League, but because they liked playing ball.

I joined another team, one made up mostly of people on the periphery of the drug world—I could never quite tell whether they were on the rehabilitative or merchandising side—but they played fairly good ball, even though most of them played in various conditions of altered consciousness. None of them wanted to become Great Writers, which most of my old team aspired to as I did, but they were clearly part of The Revolution, and some of their confusions about where The Revolution was, and what it was, were educative.

They kept individual batting statistics, which I liked a lot, and the team scorekeeper was generous about what could be classified as a hit and what couldn't. He might, for instance, award a hit even if the batter went out, provided that the ball took an interesting bounce along the way, or curved into the sun in a way that caught his fancy. Most of us, consequently, batted over .400.

They made me their catcher. I enjoyed catching, because it required a certain quickness, a good arm, not too much speed afoot, and a high pain threshold. My attention for the game was beginning to wane, and I found that catching enabled me to concentrate—if I didn't I would quickly get hurt. Along with the batter, I was the only player on the field who could see the pattern of the game, and I studied it, and the different hitters who came up, with renewed interest.

That summer both industry and government moved in on The Revolution—the one to make money out of it, and the other, or so it said, in search of innovative projects and new ways to understand the changes its bewildered civil servants thought were occurring. As part of one of the government's innumerable attempts to understand, and then to co-opt what the citizens were up to, someone gave the Cosmic League a grant.

We woke up the next morning and we were back in Pony League. There were formal schedules, league statistics, a rule book, and a championship trophy. Photographers came to the games, and the local underground newspaper began carrying wildly inaccurate accounts of league play. Crews of TV cameramen showed up to film The Revolution in action. The T-shirt manufacturers were making a killing, and drug dealers were doing even better.

The Revolution always seemed to get the giggles whenever it was taken seriously by the things it wanted to change, and this was no different. What began as an enjoyable re-evaluation of competition became bad theatre, and my adopted team turned into the leading theatre company in the league. I quit again.

Baseball had lost me before, but it seemed unwilling to let me go this time. I joined a team of disgruntled veterans who, like me, wanted to play serious ball, without the obligatory democracy or theatre. We had one heroic season. We lost every single game we played, and I rediscovered my curve ball.

We lost because we were good, not because there was something wrong with the way we played. And the more we lost, the better we all got at it, and the more we enjoyed ourselves. We found ways to lose to teams we couldn't possibly lose to, and ways to *almost* defeat teams we couldn't possibly win against. By the time our losing streak reached fifty games, we had teams lined up to play against us. They knew that we would play them on their terms, and that we would lose to them in precisely the right way. We made going into the ninth inning with a four run lead and then getting blown away for ten runs almost an art form.

A catcher with a mammoth curve ball isn't the same thing to a sandlot softball team as a skinny fourteen-year-old with a mammoth curve ball is to an ambitious Pony League baseball coach. The curve ball now was my own entertainment, and because it wasn't supposed to be there, I used it freely and without conscience. I threw it back to my pitcher, to second base whenever someone tried to steal it, and I could whip it around the head of a runner heading to first base on a bunt without the slightest danger of it hitting him.

Everyone else on the team was entertaining himself in his own way. Some of the entertainments weren't as spectacular as the curve ball, and others were more cerebral, but we had a sense of perspective that told us that it was for these kinds of entertainments that we were playing. We were losing, but we were losing The Revolution too, and maybe this was what it was all for: to teach us to lose.

It made me realize that I was never going to grow up properly, and it made me love baseball more than ever. I wasn't a Superstar, although I was just good enough to be able to convince myself that I was every once in while. A long ball would sail over the centre field fence, a throw to second would beat a base runner by ten feet, and *Presto!*

The next season, unfortunately, the team began to win. For me and a few others, it signalled that The Revolution was over, and that our side had lost. Our baseball skills had grown, which meant that we were all now *good* sandlot ball players, and that if we were willing to go to work for the telephone company or something like that, we could be playing Senior B softball. It got to some of us.

I wasn't among the ones it got to. I was beginning to find things to be a serious writer about, and sports certainly wasn't ever going to be one of them. The serious players started packing the team with hot dogs and ringers, younger kids who could play better ball than some of us, but couldn't play music, or write, or paint, or entertain themselves with the sheer delight of playing baseball for the fun of it.

The new players began to object to my curve ball, so I called a team meeting one night.

"Why are you being so heavy about all this?" I asked the ringleader.

He shrugged. There was a gleam in his eyes I remembered from somewhere.

"I dunno. Some of us just want to play good ball, that's all."

"Aw, come on," I said. "All we are is a bunch of pretty good fifth-rate ball players. That's all we'll ever be."

I saw the gleam disappear for a moment, and then brighten again. But when it came back, something else had flickered out.

"Well, so what," he replied. "It's better than just horsing around. There's too many guys on this team that don't want to play. All they do is horse around. It's gotta change."

My head was ringing. It was the message I'd heard all my life, and it still didn't make sense. Things didn't have to change at all, but if they did, I wasn't going to hang around to watch. Maybe it was time I moved on, and did what I was supposed to do.

"It's just a game," I said.

"We've got a serious game tomorrow," someone said. "If you don't like it, why don't you quit?"

It was Tuesday night, and my arm was sore—it had been sore, I realized, for years. I should never have thrown that curve ball in the first place—not, at least, if I wanted to play forever.

But forever belonged to them, and I didn't believe in it any more now than I ever had, and now I didn't even *want* to believe in it. I sat around for a while longer, talking about baseball, and when I got bored, I picked up my glove and walked outside into the night.

It wasn't very dark out there. I found my car easily and drove home.

THE THRILL OF THE GRASS
W.P. Kinsella

1981: the summer the baseball players went on strike.
The dull weeks drag by, the summer deepens, the strike
is nearly a month old. Outside the city the corn rustles
and ripens in the sun. Summer without baseball: a
disruption to the psyche. An unexplainable aimless-
ness engulfs me. I stay later and later each evening in
the small office at the rear of my shop. Now, driving
home after work, the worst of the rush hour traffic over,
it is the time of evening I would normally be heading
for the stadium.

I enjoy arriving an hour early, parking in a far corner
of the lot, walking slowly toward the stadium, rays of
sun dropping softly over my shoulders like tangerine
ropes, my shadow gliding with me, black as an
umbrella. I like to watch young families beside their
campers, the mothers in shorts, grilling hamburgers,
their men drinking beer. I enjoy seeing little boys
dressed in the home team uniform, barely toddling,
clutching hotdogs in upraised hands.

I am a failed shortstop. As a young man, I saw myself
diving to my left, graceful as a toppling tree, fielding
high grounders like a cat leaping for butterflies, bracing

my right foot and tossing to first, the throw true as if a steel ribbon connected my hand and the first base- man's glove. I dreamed of leading the American League in hitting—being inducted into the Hall of Fame. I batted .217 in my senior year of high school and aver- aged 1.3 errors per nine innings.

I know the stadium will be deserted; nevertheless I wheel my car down off the freeway, park, and walk across the silent lot, my footsteps rasping and mourn- ful. Strangle-grass and creeping charlie are already inching up through the gravel, surreptitious, surprised at their own ease. Faded bottle caps, rusted bits of chrome, an occasional paper clip, recede into the earth. I circle a ticket booth, sun-faded, empty, the door closed by an oversized padlock. I walk beside the tall, machinery-green, board fence. A half mile away a few cars hiss along the freeway; overhead a single-engine plane fizzes lazily. The whole place is silent as an empty classroom, like a house suddenly without children.

It is then that I spot the door-shape. I have to check twice to be sure it is there: a door cut in the deep green boards of the fence, more the promise of a door than the real thing, the kind of door, as children, we cut in the sides of cardboard boxes with our mother's paring knives. As I move closer, a golden circle of lock, like an acrimonious eye, establishes its certainty.

I stand, my nose so close to the door I can smell the faint odour of paint, the golden eye of a lock inches from my own eyes. My desire to be inside the ballpark is so great that for the first time in my life I commit a criminal act. I have been a locksmith for over forty years. I take the small tools from the pocket of my jacket, and in less time than it would take a speedy runner to circle the bases I am inside the stadium. Though the ballpark is open-air, it smells of abandonment; the walkways and seating areas are cold as basements. I breathe the odours of rancid popcorn and wilted cardboard.

The maintenance staff were laid off when the strike began. Synthetic grass does not need to be cut or watered. I stare down at the ball diamond, where just to the right of the pitcher's mound, a single weed, perhaps two inches high, stands defiant in the rain-pocked dirt.

The field sits breathless in the orangy glow of the evening sun. I stare at the potato-coloured earth of the infield, that wide, dun arc, surrounded by plastic grass. As I contemplate the prickly turf, which scorches the thighs and buttocks of a sliding player as if he were being seared by hot steel, it stares back in its uniform ugliness. The seams that send routinely hit ground balls veering at tortuous angles, are vivid, grey as scars.

I remember the ballfields of my childhood, the outfields full of soft hummocks and brown-eyed gopher holes.

I stride down from the stands and walk out to the middle of the field. I touch the stubble that is called grass, take off my shoes, but find it is like walking on a row of toothbrushes. It was an evil day when they stripped the sod from this ballpark, cut it into yard-wide swathes, rolled it, memories and all, into great green-and-black cinnamonroll shapes, trucked it away. Nature temporarily defeated. But Nature is patient.

Over the next few days an idea forms within me, ripening, swelling, pushing everything else into a corner. It is like knowing a new, wonderful joke and not being able to share. I need an accomplice.

I go to see a man I don't know personally, though I have seen his face peering at me from the financial pages of the local newspaper, and the *Wall Street Journal*, and I have been watching his profile at the baseball stadium, two boxes to the right of me, for several years. He is a fan. Really a fan. When the weather is intemperate, or the game not close, the people around us disappear like flowers closing at sunset, but we are always there until the last pitch. I know he is a man who attends because of the beauty and mystery of the game, a man who can sit during the last of the ninth with the game decided innings ago, and draw joy from watching the first baseman adjust the angle of his glove as the pitcher goes into his windup.

He, like me, is a first-base-side fan. I've always watched baseball from behind first base. The positions fans choose at sporting events are like politics, religion, or philosophy: a view of the world, a way of seeing the universe. They make no sense to anyone, have no basis in anything but stubbornness.

I brought up my daughters to watch baseball from the first-base side. One lives in Japan and sends me box scores from Japanese newspapers, and Japanese baseball magazines with pictures of superstars politely bowing to one another. She has a season ticket in Yokohama; on the first-base side.

"Tell him a baseball fan is here to see him," is all I will say to his secretary. His office is in a skyscraper, from which he can look out over the city to where the prairie rolls green as mountain water to the limits of the eye. I wait all afternoon in the artificially cool, glassy reception area with its yellow and mauve chairs, chrome and glass coffee tables. Finally, in the late afternoon, my message is passed along.

"I've seen you at the baseball stadium," I say, not introducing myself.

"Yes," he says. "I recognize you. Three rows back, about eight seats to my left. You have a red scorebook and you often bring your daughter…"

"Granddaughter. Yes, she goes to sleep in my lap in the late innings, but she knows how to calculate an ERA and she's only in Grade 2."

"One of my greatest regrets," says this tall man, whose moustache and carefully styled hair are polar-bear white, "is that my grandchildren all live over a thousand miles away. You're very lucky. Now, what can I do for you?"

"I have an idea," I say. "One that's been creeping towards me like a first baseman when the bunt sign is on. What do you think about artificial turf?"

"Hmmmf," he snorts, "that's what the strike should be about. Baseball is meant to be played on summer evenings and Sunday afternoons, on grass just cut by a horse-drawn mower," and we smile as our eyes meet.

"I've discovered the ballpark is open, to me anyway," I go on. "There's no one there while the strike is on. The wind blows through the high top of the grandstand, whining until the pigeons in the rafters flutter. It's lonely as a ghost town."

"And what is it you do there, alone with the pigeons?"

"I dream."

"And where do I come in?"

"You've always struck me as a man who dreams. I think we have things in common. I think you might like to come with me. I could show you what I dream, paint you pictures, suggest what might happen…"

He studies me carefully for a moment, like a pitcher trying to decide if he can trust the sign his catcher has just given him.

"Tonight?" he says. "Would tonight be too soon?"

"Park in the northwest corner of the lot about 1:00 AM. There is a door about fifty yards to the right of the main gate. I'll open it when I hear you."

He nods.

I turn and leave.

The night is clear and cotton warm when he arrives. "Oh, my," he says, staring at the stadium turned chrome-blue by a full moon. "Oh, my," he says again, breathing in the faint odours of baseball, the reminder of fans and players not long gone.

"Let's go down to the field," I say. I am carrying a cardboard pizza box, holding it on the upturned palms of my hands, like an offering.

When we reach the field, he first stands on the mound, makes an awkward attempt at a windup, then does a little sprint from first to about half-way to second. "I think I know what you've brought," he says, gesturing toward the box, "but let me see anyway."

I open the box in which rests a square foot of sod, the grass smooth and pure, cool as a swatch of satin, fragile as baby's hair.

"Ohhh," the man says, reaching out a finger to test the moistness of it. "Oh, I see."

We walk across the field, the harsh, prickly turf making the bottoms of my feet tingle, to the left-field corner where, in the angle formed by the foul line and the warning track, I lay down the square foot of sod. "That's beautiful," my friend says, kneeling beside me, placing his hand, fingers spread wide, on the verdant square, leaving a print faint as a veronica.

I take from my belt a sickle-shaped blade, the kind used for cutting carpet. I measure along the edge of the sod, dig the point in and pull carefully toward me. There is a ripping sound, like tearing an old bed sheet. I hold up the square of artificial turf like something freshly killed, while all the time digging the sharp point into the packed earth I have exposed. I replace the sod lovingly, covering the newly bared surface.

"A protest," I say.

"But it could be more," the man replies.

"I hoped you'd say that. It could be. If you'd like to come back…"

"Tomorrow night?"

"Tomorrow night would be fine. But there will be an admission charge…"

"A square of sod?"

"A square of sod two inches thick…"

"Of the same grass?"

"Of the same grass. But there's more."

"I suspected as much."

"You must have a friend…"

"Who would join us?"

"Yes."

"I have two. Would that be all right?"

"I trust your judgement."

"My father. He's over eighty," my friend says. "You might have seen him with me once or twice. He lives over fifty miles from here, but if I call him he'll come. And my friend…"

"If they pay their admission they'll be welcome…"

"And *they* may have friends…"

"Indeed they may. But what will we do with this?" I say, holding up the sticky-backed square of turf, which smells of glue and fabric.

"We could mail them anonymously to baseball executives, politicians, clergymen."

"Gentle reminders not to tamper with Nature."

We dance toward the exit, rampant with excitement.

"You will come back? You'll bring the others?"

"Count on it," says my friend.

They do come, those trusted friends, and friends of friends, each making a live, green deposit. At first, a tiny row of sod squares begins to inch along toward left-centre field. The next night even more people arrive, the following night more again, and the night after that there is positively a crowd. Those who come once seem always to return accompanied by friends, occasionally a son or younger brother, but mostly men my age or older, for we are the ones who remember the grass.

Night after night the pilgrimage continues. The first night I stand inside the deep green door, listening. I hear a vehicle stop; hear a car door close with a snug thud. I open the door when the sound of soft soled shoes on gravel tells me it is time. The door swings silent as a snake. We nod curt greetings to each other. Two men pass me, each carrying a grasshopper-legged sprinkler. Later, each sprinkler will sizzle like frying onions as it wheels, a silver sparkler in the moonlight.

During the nights that follow, I stand sentinel-like at the top of the grandstand, watching as my cohorts arrive. Old men walking across a parking lot in a row, in the dark, carrying coiled hoses, looking like the many wheels of a locomotive, old men who have slipped away from their homes, skulked down their sturdy sidewalks, breathing the cool, grassy, after-midnight air. They have left behind their sleeping, grey-haired women, their immaculate bungalows, their manicured lawns. They continue to walk across the parking lot, while occasionally a soft wheeze, a nibbling, breathy sound like an old horse might make, divulges their humanity. They move methodically toward the baseball stadium which hulks against the moon-blue sky like a small mountain. Beneath the tint of starlight, the tall light standards which rise above the fences and grandstand glow purple, necks bent forward, like sunflowers heavy with seed.

My other daughter lives in this city, is married to a fan, but one who watches baseball from behind third base. And like marrying outside the faith, she has been converted to the third-base side. They have their own season tickets, twelve rows up just to the outfield side of third base. I love her, but I don't trust her enough to let her in on my secret.

I could trust my granddaughter, but she is too young. At her age she shouldn't have to face such responsibility. I remember my own daughter, the one who lives in Japan, remember her at nine, all knees, elbows and missing teeth—remember peering in her room, seeing her asleep, a shower of well-thumbed baseball cards scattered over her chest and pillow.

I haven't been able to tell my wife—it is like my compatriots and I are involved in a ritual for true believers only. Maggie, who knew me when I still dreamed of playing professionally myself—Maggie, after over half a lifetime together, comes and sits in my lap in the comfortable easy chair which has adjusted through the years to my thickening shape, just as she has. I love to hold the lightness of her, her tongue exploring my mouth, gently as a baby's finger.

"Where do you go?" she asks sleepily when I crawl into bed at dawn.

I mumble a reply. I know she doesn't sleep well when I'm gone. I can feel her body rhythms change as I slip out of bed after midnight.

"Aren't you too old to be having a change of life," she says, placing her toast-warm hand on my cold thigh.

I am not the only one with this problem.

"I'm developing a reputation," whispers an affable man at the ballpark. "I imagine any number of private investigators following any number of cars across the city. I imagine them creeping about the parking lot, shining pen-lights on licence plates, trying to guess what we're up to. Think of the reports they must prepare. I wonder if our wives are disappointed that we're not out discoing with frizzy-haired teenagers?"

Night after night, virtually no words are spoken. Each man seems to know his assignment. Not all bring sod. Some carry rakes, some hoes, some hoses, which, when joined together, snake across the infield and outfield, dispensing the blessing of water. Others cradle in their arms bags of earth for building up the infield to meet the thick, living sod.

I often remain high in the stadium, looking down on the men moving over the earth, dark as ants, each sodding, cutting, watering, shaping. Occasionally the moon finds a knife blade as it trims the sod or slices away a chunk of artificial turf, and tosses the reflection skyward like a bright ball. My body tingles. There should be symphony music playing. Everyone should be humming 'America The Beautiful.'

Towards dawn, I watch the men walking away in groups, like small patrols of soldiers, carrying instead of arms, the tools and utensils which breathe life back into the arid ballfield.

Row by row, night by night, we lay the little squares of sod, moist as chocolate cake with green icing. Where did all the sod come from? I picture many men, in many parts of the city, surreptitiously cutting chunks out of their own lawns in the leafy midnight darkness, listening to the uncomprehending protests of their wives the next day—pretending to know nothing of it—pretending to have called the police to investigate.

When the strike is over I know we will all be here to watch the workouts, to hear the recalcitrant joints crackling like twigs after the forced inactivity. We will sit in our regular seats, scattered like popcorn throughout the stadium, and we'll nod as we pass on the way to the exits, exchange secret smiles, proud as new fathers.

For me, the best part of all will be the surprise. I feel like a magician who has gestured hypnotically and produced an elephant from thin air. I know I am not alone in my wonder. I know that rockets shoot off in half-a-hundred chests, the excitement of birthday mornings, Christmas eves, and home-town double-headers, boils within each of my conspirators. Our secret rites have been performed with love, like delivering a valentine to a sweetheart's door in that blue-steel span of morning just before dawn.

Players and management are meeting round the clock. A settlement is imminent. I have watched the stadium covered square foot by square foot until it looks like green graph paper. I have stood and felt the cool odours of the grass rise up and touch my face. I have studied the lines between each small square, watched those lines fade until they were visible to my eyes alone, then not even to them.

What will the players think, as they straggle into the stadium and find the miracle we have created? The old-timers will raise their heads like ponies, as far away as the parking lot, when the thrill of the grass reaches their nostrils. And, as they dress, they'll recall sprawling in the lush outfields of childhood, the grass as cool as a mother's hand on a forehead.

"Goodbye, goodbye," we say at the gate, the smell of water, of sod, of sweat, small perfumes in the air. Our secrets are safe with each other. We go our separate ways.

Alone in the stadium in the last chill darkness before dawn, I drop to my hands and knees in the centre of the outfield. My palms are sodden. Water touches the skin between my spread fingers. I lower my face to the silvered grass, which, wonder of wonders, already has the ephemeral odours of baseball about it.

THE HECTOR QUESADILLA STORY
T.C. Boyle

He was no Joltin' Joe, no Sultan of Swat, no Iron Man.
For one thing, his feet hurt. And God knows no
legendary immortal ever suffered so prosaic a com-
plaint. He had shin splints too, and corns and ingrown
toenails and hemorrhoids. Demons drove burning
spikes into his tailbone each time he bent to loosen his
shoelaces, his limbs were skewed so awkwardly that his
elbows and knees might have been transposed and the
once-proud knot of his *frijole*-fed belly had fallen like
an avalanche. Worse: he was old. Old, old, old, the
graybeard hobbling down the rough-hewn steps of the
senate building, the ancient mariner chewing on his
whiskers and stumbling in his socks. Though they
listed his birthdate as 1942 in the program, there were
those who knew better: it was way back in '54, during
his rookie year for San Buitre, that he had taken
Asunción to the altar, and even in those distant days,
even in Mexico, twelve-year-olds didn't marry.

When he was younger—really young, nineteen, twenty, tearing up the Mexican League like a saint of the stick—his ears were so sensitive he could hear the soft rasping friction of the pitcher's fingers as he massaged the ball and dug in for a slider, fastball, or change-up. Now he could barely hear the umpire bawling the count in his ear. And his legs. How they ached, how they groaned and creaked and chattered, how they'd gone to fat! He ate too much, that was the problem. Ate prodigiously, ate mightily, ate as if there were a hidden thing inside him, a creature all of jaws with an infinite trailing ribbon of gut. *Huevos con chorizo* with beans, *tortillas, camarones* in red sauce, and a twelve-ounce steak for breakfast, the chicken in *mole* to steady him before afternoon games, a sea of beer to wash away the tension of the game and prepare his digestive machinery for the flaming *machaca*-and-pepper salad Asunción prepared for him in the blessed evenings of the home stand.

Five foot seven, one hundred eighty-nine and three-quarters pounds. Hector Hernán Jesús y María Quesa-dilla. Little Cheese, they called him. Cheese, Cheese, Cheesus, went up the cry as he stepped in to pinch-hit in some late-inning crisis, Cheese, Cheese, Cheesus, building to a roar until Chavez Ravine resounded as if with the holy name of the Saviour Himself when he stroked one of the clean line-drive singles that were his signature or laid down a bunt that stuck like a finger in jelly. When he fanned, when the bat went loose in the fat brown hands and he went down on one knee for support, they hissed and called him *Viejo*.

One more season, he tells himself, though he hasn't played regularly for nearly ten years and can barely trot to first after drawing a walk. One more. He tells Asunción too—One more, one more—as they sit in the gleaming kitchen of their house in Boyle Heights, he with his Carta Blanca, she with her mortar and pestle for grinding the golden, petrified kernels of maize into flour for the *tortillas* he eats like peanuts. *Una más,* she mocks. What do you want, the Hall of Fame? Hang up your spikes, Hector.

He stars off into space, his mother's Indian features flattening his own as if the legend were true, as if she really had taken a spatula to him in the cradle, and then, dropping his thick lids as he takes a long slow swallow from the neck of the bottle, he says: Just the other day, driving home from the park, I saw a car on the freeway, a Mercedes with only two seats, a girl in it, her hair out back like a cloud, and you know what the license plate said? His eyes are open now, black as pitted olives. Do you? She doesn't. Cheese, he says. It said Cheese.

Then she reminds him that Hector Jr. will be twenty-nine next month and that Reina has four children of her own and another on the way. You're a grandfather, Hector—almost a great-grandfather, if your son ever settled down. A moment slides by, filled with the light of the sad, waning sun and the harsh Yucatano dialect of the radio announcer. *Hombres* on first and third, one down. *Abuelo,* she hisses, grinding stone against stone until it makes his teeth ache. Hang up your spikes, *abuelo.*

But he doesn't. He can't. He won't. He's no grandpa with hair the color of cigarette stains and a blanket over his knees, he's no toothless old gasser sunning himself in the park—he's a big-leaguer, proud wearer of the Dodger blue, wielder of stick and glove. How can he get old? The grass is always green, the lights always shining, no clocks or periods or halves or quarters, no punch-in and punch-out: this is the game that never ends. When the heavy hitters have fanned and the pitchers' arms gone sore, when there's no joy in Mudville, taxes are killing everybody, and the Russians are raising hell in Guatemala, when the manager paces the dugout like an attack dog, mind racing, searching high and low for the canny veteran to go in and do single combat, there he'll be—always, always, eternal as a monument—Hector Quesadilla, utility infielder, with the .296 lifetime batting average and service with the Reds, Phils, Cubs, Royals, and L.A. Dodgers.

So he waits. Hangs on. Trots his aching legs round the outfield grass before the game, touches his toes ten agonizing times each morning, takes extra batting practice with the rookies and slumping millionaires. Sits. Watches. Massages his feet. Waits through the scourging road trips in the Midwest and along the East Coast, down to muggy Atlanta, across to stormy Wrigley, and up to frigid Candlestick, his gut clenched round an indigestible cud of meatloaf and instant potatoes and wax beans, through the terrible night games with the alien lights in his eyes, waits at the end of the bench for a word from the manager, for a pat on the ass, a roar, a hiss, a chorus of cheers and catcalls, the marimba pulse of bat striking ball, and the sweet looping arc of the clean base hit.

And then comes a day, late in the season, the home-boys battling for the pennant with the big-stick Braves and the sneaking Jints, when he wakes from honeyed dreams in his own bed that's like an old friend with the sheets that smell of starch and soap and flowers, and feels the pain stripped from his body as if at the touch of a healer's fingertips. Usually he dreams nothing, the night a blank, an erasure, and opens his eyes on the agonies of the martyr strapped to a bed of nails. Then he limps to the toilet, makes a poor discolored water, rinses the dead taste from his mouth, and staggers to the kitchen table, where food, only food, can revive in him the interest in drawing another breath. He butters tortillas and folds them into his mouth, spoons up egg and melted jack cheese and *frijoles refritos* with the green *salsa*, lashes into his steak as if it were cut from the thigh of Kerensky, the Atlanta relief ace who'd twice that season caught him looking at a full-count fastball with men in scoring position. But not today. Today is different, a sainted day, a day on which sunshine sits in the windows like a gift of the Magi and the chatter of the starlings in the crapped-over palms across the street is a thing that approaches the divine music of the spheres. What can it be?

In the kitchen it hits him: *pozole* in a pot on the stove, *carnitas* in the saucepan, the table spread with sweetcakes, *buñuelos*, and the little marzipan *dulces* he could kill for. *Feliz cumpleaños*, Asunción pipes as he steps through the doorway. Her face is lit with the smile of her mother, her mother's mother, the line of gift givers descendant to the happy conquistadors and joyous Aztecs. A kiss, a *dulce*, and then a knock at the door and Reina, fat with life, throwing her arms around him while her children gobble up the table, the room, their grandfather, with eyes that swallow their faces. Happy birthday, Daddy, Reina says, and Franklin, her youngest, is handing him the gift.

And Hector Jr.?

But he doesn't have to fret about Hector Jr., his firstborn, the boy with these same great sad eyes who'd sat in the dugout in his Reds uniform when they lived in Cincy and worshipped the pudgy icon of his father until the parish priest had to straighten him out on his hagiography; Hector Jr., who studies English at USC and day and night writes his thesis on a poet his father has never heard of, because here he is, walking in the front door with his mother's smile and a store-wrapped gift—a book, of course. Then Reina's children line up to kiss the *abuelo*—they'll be sitting in the box seats this afternoon—and suddenly he knows so much: he will play today, he will hit, oh yes, can there be a doubt? He sees it already. Kerensky, the son of a whore. Extra innings. Koerner or Manfredonia or Brooksie on third. The ball like an orange, a mango, a muskmelon, the clean swipe of the bat, the delirium of the crowd, and the gimpy *abuelo*, a big-leaguer still, doffing his cap and taking a tour of the bases in a stately trot, Sultan for a day.

Could things ever be so simple?

In the bottom of the ninth, with the score tied at 5 and Reina's kids full of Coke, hotdogs, peanuts, and ice cream and getting restless, with Asunción clutching her rosary as if she were drowning and Hector Jr.'s nose stuck in some book, Dupuy taps him to hit for the pitcher with two down and Fast Freddie Phelan on second. The eighth man in the lineup, Spider Martinez from Muchas Vacas, D.R., has just whiffed on three straight pitches, and Corcoran, the Braves' left-handed relief man, is all of a sudden pouring it on. Throughout the stadium a hush has fallen over the crowd, the torpor of suppertime, the game poised at apogee. Shadows are lengthening in the outfield, swallows flitting across the face of the scoreboard, here a fan drops into his beer, there a big mama gathers up her purse, her knitting, her shopping bags and parasol, and thinks of dinner. Hector sees it all. This is the moment of catharsis, the moment to take it out.

As Martinez slumps toward the dugout, Dupuy, a laconic, embittered man who keeps his suffering inside and drinks Gelusil like water, takes hold of Hector's arm. His eyes are red-rimmed and paunchy, doleful as a basset hound's. Bring the runner in, champ, he rasps. First pitch fake a bunt, then hit away. Watch Booger at third. Uh-huh, Hector mumbles, snapping his gum. Then he slides his bat from the rack—white ash, tape-wrapped grip, personally blessed by the archbishop of Guadalajara and his twenty-seven acolytes—and starts for the dugout steps, knowing the course of the next three minutes as surely as his blood knows the course of his veins. The familiar cry will go up—Cheese, Cheese, Cheesus—and he'll amble up to the batter's box, knocking imaginary dirt from his spikes, adjusting the straps of his golf gloves, tugging at his underwear, and fiddling with his batting helmet. His face will be impenetrable. Corcoran will work the ball in his glove, maybe tip back his cap for a little hair grease, and then give him a look of psychopathic hatred. Hector has seen it before. Me against you. My record, my career, my house, my family, my life, my mutual funds and beer distributorship against yours. He's been hit in the elbow, the knee, the groin, the head. Nothing fazes him. Nothing. Murmuring a prayer to Santa Griselda, patroness of the sun-blasted Sonoran village where he was born like a heat blister on his mother's womb, Hector Hernán Jesús y María Quesadilla will step into the batter's box, ready for anything.

But it's a game of infinite surprises.

Before Hector can set foot on the playing field, Corcoran suddenly doubles up in pain, Phelan goes slack at second, and the catcher and shortstop are hustling out to the mound, tailed an instant later by trainer and pitching coach. First thing Hector thinks is groin pull, then appendicitis, and finally, as Corcoran goes down on one knee, poison. He'd once seen a man shot in the gut at Obregón City, but the report had been loud as a thunderclap, and he hears nothing now but the enveloping hum of the crowd. Corcoran is rising shakily, the trainer and pitching coach supporting him while the catcher kicks meditatively in the dirt, and now Mueller, the Atlanta *cabeza*, is striding big-bellied out of the dugout, head down as if to be sure his feet are following orders. Halfway to the mound, Mueller flicks his right hand across his ear quick as a horse flicking its tail, and it's all she wrote for Corcoran.

Poised on the dugout steps like a bird dog, Hector waits, his eyes riveted on the bullpen. Please, he whispers, praying for the intercession of the Niño and pledging a hundred votary candles—at least, at least. Can it be?—yes, milk of my mother, yes—Kerensky himself strutting out onto the field like a fighting cock. Kerensky!

Come to the birthday boy, Kerensky, he murmurs, so certain he's going to put it in the stands he could point like the immeasurable Bambino. His tired old legs shuffle with impatience as Kerensky stalks across the field, and then he's turning to pick Asunción out of the crowd. She's on her feet now, Reina too, the kids come alive beside her. And Hector Jr., the book forgotten, his face transfigured with the look of rapture he used to get when he was a boy sitting on the steps of the dugout. Hector can't help himself: he grins and gives them the thumbs-up sign.

Then, as Kerensky fires his warm-up smoke, the loudspeaker crackles and Hector emerges from the shadow of the dugout into the tapering golden shafts of the late-afternoon sun. That pitch, I want that one, he mutters, carrying his bat like a javelin and shooting a glare at Kerensky, but something's wrong here, the announcer's got it screwed up: BATTING FOR RARITAN, NUMBER 39, DAVE TOOL. What the—? And now somebody's tugging at his sleeve and he's turning to gape with incomprehension at the freckle-faced batboy, Dave Tool striding out of the dugout with his big forty-two-ounce stick, Dupuy's face locked up like a vault, and the crowd, on its feet, chanting Tool, Tool, Tool! For a moment he just stands there, frozen with disbelief. Then Tool is brushing by him and the idiot of a batboy is leading him toward the dugout as if he were an old blind fisherman poised on the edge of the dock.

He feels as if his legs have been cut out from under him. Tool! Dupuy is yanking him for Tool? For what? So he can play the lefty-righty percentages like some chess head or something? Tool, of all people. Tool, with his thirty-five home runs a season and lifetime BA of .234; Tool, who's worn so many uniforms they had to expand the league to make room for him—what's he going to do? Raging, Hector flings down his bat and comes at Dupuy like a cat tossed in a bag. You crazy, you jerk, he sputters. I woulda hit him, I woulda won the game. I dreamed it. And then, his voice breaking: It's my birthday, for Christ's sake!

But Dupuy can't answer him, because on the first pitch Tool slams a real worm burner to short and the game is going into extra innings.

By seven o'clock, half the fans have given up and gone home. In the top of the fourteenth, when the visitors came up with a pair of runs on a two-out pinch-hit home run, there was a real exodus, but then the Dodgers struck back for two to knot it up again. Then it was three up and three down, regular as clockwork. Now, at the end of the nineteenth, with the score deadlocked at 7 all and the players dragging themselves around the field like gut-shot horses, Hector is beginning to think he may get a second chance after all. Especially the way Dupuy's been using up players like some crazy general on the Western Front, yanking pitchers, juggling his defense, throwing in pinch runners and pinch hitters until he's just about gone through the entire roster. Asunción is still there among the faithful, the foolish, and the self-deluded, fumbling with her rosary and mouthing prayers for Jesus Christ Our Lord, the Madonna, Hector, the home team, and her departed mother, in that order. Reina too, looking like the survivor of some disaster, Franklin and Alfredo asleep in their seats, the *niñitas* gone off somewhere—for Coke and dogs, maybe. And Hector Jr. looks like he's going to stick it out too, though he should be back in his closet writing about the mystical so-and-so and the way he illustrates his poems with gods and men and serpents. Watching him, Hector can feel his heart turn over.

In the bottom of the twentieth, with one down and Gilley on first—he's a starting pitcher but Dupuy sent him in to run for Manfredonia after Manfredonia jammed his ankle like a turkey and had to be helped off the field—Hector pushes himself up from the bench and ambles down to where Dupuy sits in the corner, contemplatively spitting a gout of tobacco juice and saliva into the drain at his feet. Let me hit, Bernard, come on, Hector says, easing down beside him.

Can't, comes the reply, and Dupuy never even raises his head. Can't risk it, champ. Look around you—and here the manager's voice quavers with uncertainty, with fear and despair and the dull edge of hopelessness—I got nobody left. I hit you, I got to play you.

No, no, you don't understand—I'm going to win it, I swear.

And then the two of them, like old bankrupts on a bench in Miami Beach, look up to watch Phelan hit into a double play.

A buzz runs through the crowd when the Dodgers take the field for the top of the twenty-second. Though Phelan is limping, Thorkelsson's asleep on his feet, and Dorfman, fresh on the mound, is the only pitcher left on the roster, the moment is electric. One more inning and they tie the record set by the Mets and Giants back in '64, and then they're making history. Drunk, sober, and then drunk again, saturated with fats and nitrates and sugar, the crowd begins to come to life. Go, Dodgers! Eat shit! Yo Mama! Phelan's a bum!

Hector can feel it too. The rage and frustration that had consumed him back in the ninth are gone, replaced by a dawning sense of wonder—he could have won it then, yes, and against his nemesis Kerensky too—but the Niño and Santa Griselda have been saving him for something greater. He sees it now, knows it in his bones: he's going to be the hero of the longest game in history.

As if to bear him out, Dorfman, the kid from Albuquerque, puts in a good inning, cutting the bushed Braves down in order. In the dugout, Doc Pusser, the team physician, is handing out the little green pills that keep your eyes open and Dupuy is blowing into a cup of coffee and staring morosely out at the playing field. Hector watches as Tool, who'd stayed in the game at first base, fans on three straight pitches, then he shoves in beside Dorfman and tells the kid he's looking good out there. With his big cornhusker's ears and nose like a tweezer, Dorfman could be a caricature of the green rookie. He says nothing. Hey, don't let it get to you, kid—I'm going to win this one for you. Next inning or maybe the inning after. Then he tells him how he saw it in a vision and how it's his birthday and the kid's going to get the victory, one of the biggest of all time. Twenty-four, twenty-five innings maybe.

Hector had heard of a game once in the Mexican League that took three days to play and went seventy-three innings, did Dorfman know that? It was down in Culiacán. Chito Marití, the converted bullfighter, had finally ended it by dropping down dead of exhaustion in center field, allowing Sexto Silvestro, who'd broken his leg rounding third, to crawl home with the winning run. But Hector doesn't think this game will go that long. Dorfman sighs and extracts a bit of wax from his ear as Pantaleo, the third-string catcher, hits back to the pitcher to end the inning. I hope not, he says, uncoiling himself from the bench; my arm'd fall off.

Ten o'clock comes and goes. Dorfman's still in there, throwing breaking stuff and a little smoke at the Braves, who look as if they just stepped out of *The Night of the Living Dead*. The home team isn't doing much better. Dupuy's run through the whole team but for Hector, and three or four of the guys have been in there since two in the afternoon; the rest are a bunch of ginks and gimps who can barely stand up. Out in the stands, the fans look grim. The vendors ran out of beer an hour back, and they haven't had dogs or kraut or Coke or anything since eight-thirty.

In the bottom of the twenty-seventh Phelan goes berserk in the dugout and Dupuy has to pin him to the floor while Doc Pusser shoves something up his nose to calm him. Next inning the balls-and-strikes ump passes out cold, and Dorfman, who's beginning to look a little fagged, walks the first two batters but manages to weasel his way out of the inning without giving up the go-ahead run. Meanwhile, Thorkelsson has been dropping ice cubes down his trousers to keep awake, Martinez is smoking something suspicious in the can, and Ferenc Fortnoi, the third baseman, has begun talking to himself in a tortured Slovene dialect. For his part, Hector feels stronger and more alert as the game goes on. Though he hasn't had a bite since breakfast he feels impervious to the pangs of hunger, as if he were preparing himself, mortifying his flesh like a saint in the desert.

And then, in the top of the thirty-first, with half the fans asleep and the other half staring into nothingness like the inmates of the asylum of Our Lady of Guadalupe, where Hector had once visited his halfwit uncle when he was a boy, Pluto Morales cracks one down the first-base line and Tool flubs it. Right away it looks like trouble, because Chester Bubo is running around right field looking up at the sky like a birdwatcher while the ball snakes through the grass, caroms off his left foot, and coasts like silk to the edge of the warning track. Morales meanwhile is rounding second and coming on for third, running in slow motion, flat-footed and hump-backed, his face drained of color, arms flapping like the undersized wings of some big flightless bird. It's not even close. By the time Bubo can locate the ball, Morales is ten feet from the plate, pitching into a face-first slide that's at least three parts collapse, and that's it, the Braves are up by one. It looks black for the hometeam. But Dorfman, though his arm has begun to swell like a sausage, shows some grit, bears down, and retires the side to end the historic top of the unprecedented thirty-first inning.

Now, at long last, the hour has come. It'll be Bubo, Dorfman, and Tool for the Dodgers in their half of the inning, which means that Hector will hit for Dorfman. I been saving you, champ, Dupuy rasps, the empty Gelusil bottle clenched in his fist like a hand grenade. Go on in there, he murmurs, and his voice fades away to nothing as Bubo pops the first pitch up in back of the plate. Go on in there and do your stuff.

Sucking in his gut, Hector strides out onto the brightly lit field like a nineteen-year-old, the familiar cry in his ears, the haggard fans on their feet, a sickle moon sketched in overhead as if in some cartoon strip featuring drunken husbands and the milkman. Asunción looks as if she's been nailed to the cross, Reina wakes with a start and shakes the little ones into consciousness, and Hector Jr. staggers to his feet like a battered middleweight coming out for the fifteenth round. They're all watching him. The fans whose lives are like empty sacks, the wife who wants him home in front of the TV, his divorced daughter with the four kids and another on the way, his son, pride of his life, who reads for the doctor of philosophy while his crazy *padrecito* puts on a pair of long stockings and chases around after a little white ball like a case of arrested development. He'll show them. He'll show them some *cojones*, some true grit and desire: the game's not over yet.

On the mound for the Braves is Bo Brannerman, a big mustachioed machine of a man, normally a starter but pressed into desperate relief service tonight. A fine pitcher—Hector would be the first to admit it—but he just pitched two nights ago and he's worn thin as wire. Hector steps up to the plate, feeling legendary. He glances over at Tool in the on-deck circle, and then down at Booger, the third-base coach. All systems go. He cuts at the air twice and then watches Brannerman rear back and release the ball: strike one. Hector smiles. Why rush things? Give them a thrill. He watches a low outside slider that just about bounces to even the count, and then stands like a statue as Brannerman slices the corner of the plate for strike two. From the stands, a chant of *Viejo, Viejo,* and Asunción's piercing soprano, Hit him, Hector!

Hector has no worries, the moment eternal, replayed through games uncountable, with pitchers who were over the hill when he was a rookie with San Buitre, with pups like Brannerman, with big-leaguers and Hall of Famers. Here it comes, Hector, 92 MPH, the big *gringo* trying to throw it by you, the matchless wrists, the flawless swing, one terrific moment of suspended animation—and all of a sudden you're starring in your own movie.

How does it go? The ball cutting through the night sky like a comet, arching high over the center fielder's hapless scrambling form to slam off the wall while your legs churn up the base paths, you round first in a gallop, taking second, and heading for third...but wait, you spill hot coffee on your hand and you can't feel it, the demons apply the live wire to your tailbone, the legs give out and they cut you down at third while the stadium erupts in howls of execration and abuse and the *niñitos* break down, faces flooded with tears of humiliation, Hector Jr. turning his back in disgust and Asunción raging like a harpy, *Abuelo! Abuelo! Abuelo!*

Stunned, shrunken, humiliated, you stagger back to the dugout in a maelstrom of abuse, paper cups, flying spittle, your life a waste, the game a cheat, and then, crowning irony, that bum Tool, worthless all the way back to his washerwoman grandmother and the drunken muttering whey-faced tribe that gave him suck, stands tall like a giant and sends the first pitch out of the park to tie it. Oh, the pain. Flat feet, fire in your legs, your poor tired old heart skipping a beat in mortification. And now Dupuy, red in the face, shouting: The game could be over but for you, you crazy gimpy old beaner washout! You want to hide in your locker, bury yourself under the shower-room floor, but you have to watch as the next two men reach base and you pray with fervor that they'll score and put an end to your debasement. But no, Thorkelsson whiffs and the new inning dawns as inevitably as the new minute, the new hour, the new day, endless, implacable, world without end.

But wait, wait: who's going to pitch? Dorfman's out, there's nobody left, the astonishing thirty-second inning is marching across the scoreboard like an invading army, and suddenly Dupuy is standing over you—no, no, he's down on one knee, begging. Hector, he's saying, didn't you use to pitch down in Mexico when you were a kid, didn't I hear that someplace? Yes, you're saying, yes, but that was—

And then you're out on the mound, in command once again, elevated like some half-mad old king in a play, and throwing smoke. The first two batters go down on strikes and the fans are rabid with excitement, Asunción will raise a shrine, Hector Jr. worships you more than all the poets that ever lived, but can it be? You walk the next three and then give up the grand slam to little Tommy Oshimisi! Mother of God, will it never cease? But wait, wait, wait: here comes the bottom of the thirty-second and Brannerman's wild. He walks a couple, gets a couple out, somebody reaches on an infield single and the bases are loaded for you, Hector Quesadilla, stepping up to the plate now like the Iron Man himself. The wind-up, the delivery, the ball hanging there like a *piñata*, like a birthday gift, and then the stick flashes in your hands like an archangel's sword, and the game goes on forever.

AUGUST NIGHTS
Hugh Hood

◆ The Banner ◆

"What'll we paint on it; what can you do with a name like Orlando Saint-James?"

"Could we put, 'Don't make Orlando Furioso?'"

"I don't understand you, Treesha. What does that mean?"

I said, "It's the name of some poem. And don't call me 'Treesha.' You know perfectly well what my name is."

"Patsy," said Sally. She spilled a little tin of silver paint.

"Not Patsy."

"Patty? Little Peppermint Patty?"

"You know my name."

She wiped silver paint on her T-shirt which made the cotton stiff. It stood out over her nipples. "You're such a straight arrow," she said, "you must have a sour pickle up your asshole."

"Maybe I do and maybe I don't."

"'Patricia,' for God's sakes!"

"At least I don't rub my thighs with Coppertone. At least I don't wear shorts that look like they're painted on my butt. I don't wear a skirt on the Métro and change in the toilet during BP."

Sally can't keep her mind on anything. "What about 'Ollie's Dollies'?" she said, surprising me. I thought it was cute.

"Let me think about it. What kind of cartoon would go with it?"

"You could draw us like a team of ball-girls."

"Listen Sally," I said, "we don't want to make ourselves into a pair of Baseball Annies. I bet you they're already talking about you in the bullpen."

She said, "That's why I wear shorts. I don't want them looking up my skirt any more than you do, Treesha. Why can't I call you that anyway? When Cookie Money asked about you, I told him you were called Treesha and he thought that was wonderful."

"When was that?"

"After the first game of the Pirates' doubleheader when he came out to loosen up before starting in the nightcap. I told him you said he should be starting every day."

"What did he say?"

"He said, 'I don't tell Hammacher how to manage the club and he don't tell me now to play second base.'"

"No, I mean what did he say about me?"

"He said, 'Treesha, Treesha, Treemonisha, she must be one foxy sister.'"

"Well I be dog!" I said. I felt pleased. "Cookie Money can call me anything he likes. He gets the job done in the field and at the plate."

"Orlando says Cookie sometimes doesn't execute."

"Ballplayers shouldn't knock each other," I said.

"They're just young guys away from home, Treesha, with the same desires as the guys in the office."

"One foxy sister?"

"That's what he say, girl."

"When we finish this, let's make one for Cookie," I said.

"Hokey-cokey."

"He'd be easy to come up with: 'Money talks.' 'We're in the Money.'"

"Money is the root of boll weevils."

"Take your Money out in Cookies."

"Keep it clean, soul sister," said Sally, "let's finish this banner. Who'll carry the banner? Sister Sarah will carry the banner."

"Hard-hearted Hannah, the vamp of Savannah, can carry the banner," I said, pulling the sheet straight out on the floor of my bedroom. There was just enough space for it between the bed and vanity. It was an old sheet, pale pink, queen size, without any holes. I took a narrow brush and began to draw in two chicks in ball-girl costumes like the ones those girls in Philly wear, Mary-Sue and that other one. Mary-Sue got married early this season but then she was back on the third-base foul line right after. I wonder what her husband thinks about it. She gets on TV all the time and I have to admit she has great legs. Better than mine but not as great as Sally's. Sally Slither! That's what the guys on the team call her. You can see them looking up from the track or the bullpen or the players' field entrance whenever we're up beside the foul pole in right.

"Hey Slither, Sally Slither, hey look this way."

She pretends not to notice. Gene Frumkin, the long man in the bullpen, keeps passing up notes on the end of a stick. She throws them away every time, just crumples them up and flips them back onto the warning track. She showed me one. All it said was, "Phone number???"

"Who does he think he is?"

"He has a three-year contract," I said.

"He can be gone, just like that, if he doesn't produce," Sally said. "He's only the tenth man on the staff."

"It could be worse," I said. "He could be the tenth man on the Jays' staff."

"That's a bad ball club," we said simultaneously.

"Imagine DH-ing with the Jays," Sally said.

"Would you go out with the DH on the Jays?"

She had to think it over. "He'd be old and slow but able to hit with power. No, I don't think I could bring myself to do that. Who is it this year? It used to be Solaita."

"Solaita only hit against righthanders and, anyway, he's now in Samoa or Japan or somewhere."

I waited and Sally started to giggle and we said together, 'Well, that's what happens when you can't hit the curve ball."

"That applies to everything in life," I said.

I brushed in the drawings of us as ball-girls, trying to make the likenesses as close as possible. I gave us very short shorts and I made the figure of Sally longer and taller than mine. I'm not obese or anything, I'm just not as tall as she is. I drew us in team jackets with the logo very carefully lined-in, and I gave Sally the number 100% on the sleeves of her jacket; you could read it easily. I put Cookie Money's number on my jacket just for fun, a big number 44. I made our faces really recognisable. I'm a taffy-blond and Sally has long shiny bronze-coloured hair down to her hips almost. Of course, she doesn't wear it out loose in the bleachers or even in the 300-level seats over the bullpen where we usually sit. It would blow all around if she didn't loop it up under her baseball cap.

"They look just like us," she said, looking at what I'd done. "Now paint in Ollie's head and shoulders just above us and in between. Make it good."

That's not as easy as it sounds. Ollie keeps growing a little bit of fuzz low down on his cheeks and under his chin. When it gets hairy and gross, he shaves it off; then he'll go with a moustache for a few weeks. He's very unpredictable. I gave him a clean shave in the picture and when it was finished anybody would have identified it as *"Orlando Saint-James, National League All-Star Right Fielder, 1977, 1978, 1980, GO OLLIE GO"* (which was how I lettered it). Above that, in huge blue letters I put *"OLLIE'S DOLLIES"* with wiggly speed-lines leading down to the cartoons of Sally and me. Stretched out on the floor, it looked cool.

When we got it to the stadium we took it out to Section 345 where we usually sit. The ushers know us and they mostly let us do things that ordinary fans couldn't get away with. We got to our seats around six-fifteen in time to watch the Cubbies' infield practice. They had another fifteen minutes to go which gave us plenty of time. Sally had a big staple gun, one of those industrial appliances which can fasten anything to anything. I think she borrowed it from her father's workbench. It's a tool you have to be careful with. If you drove a staple into yourself, would it ever hurt! We draped the banner over the railing just above the bullpen and the player's field entrance. I held the edge of the material rolled over the bar and Sally stapled it into place, tacking it in lightly at first until we had it attached along the whole width of the sheet. We let it flop down so that it was hanging below us against the base of the stands. It began to curl lazily and blow around in the breeze; we could see that it needed to be stapled along the bottom edge. Some of the Cubbie outfielders started looking over at us and laughing. The old punk of an usher wouldn't let us climb down onto the field even though Sally could have done it easily.

The Cubs went on hollering at us, "Slither, Slither, hey Slither, hey Sally, come on down and pin it up."

I think we're pretty well-known around the league. I noticed the camera crew looking over our way so I started jumping up and down and waving my arms. It was the middle of August and very warm. I started to sweat. The TV guys focussed on us and I could see our image on the monitor. I knew they'd try to get a shot of us during the telecast. It's something you get used to, especially when you're with Sally. By now the out-fielders were standing right below us at the edge of the track. Some of the things they said were pretty crude but most of them were nice.

"Who's the little blonde?"

"Hey hey hey Sally Slither, how's your big buddy Ollie?"

"Who's the greatest right-fielder since Ruth?"

"Winfield?"

Sally gave the finger to the guy who said that.

"Parker?"

"Clemente?"

"Clemente's dead," I yelled at them just as Cookie Money came onto the field; he was carrying three gloves—Cookie's the best utility man in OB—which meant he might be figuring on playing tonight. He looked up at us and smiled. Cookie's never going to get

500 at-bats in a season but he's been around long enough to get in his four years for the pension and he can play almost anywhere, outfield, infield, even catch a little. He had the outsized catcher's mitt with him—he'd be catching Angel-spit Busby's knuckleball during the warmup. He put his three gloves carefully on the bench in the bullpen enclosure beside the telephone and came over and looked right up into Section 345.

"Hello, Treesha," he said.

"Hello."

"You girls need a little help? Here, let me tack that thing down for you before it blow away in the cool breeze."

"It isn't that cool," I said. I was wet under my arms and my hair would be going stringy.

"Throw me down your stapler," he said.

Sally looked down at him and leaned over as far as she could. An usher came down the steps and held her around the waist. Two of the TV crew aimed hand-held cameras at us. One of them said, "Let them check this out in the booth."

"Catch," said Sally.

She dropped the gun. Cookie made a funny little basket-catch letting the gun drop almost to the track and scooping it out of the dirt at the last minute.

"The great hands," he said to himself. He stretched the sheet taut over a kind of plywood frame around the dugout roof where he could easily staple it to the wood.

"Don't let it get out of line," said Sally loudly.

The Cubs were strolling away towards their dugout. One of them turned around and said, "Hey Money, you setting things up for the big man?"

We could see the banner spread out straight and tight on the TV monitor. It looked sensational. *OLLIE'S DOLLIES*. We were sure they'd shoot it during the telecast.

At 7:12 PM Ollie came on the field down by the umpire's entrance behind home plate. He must have been doing some interviews in the press room because he usually comes out from the dugout just before game time. He's had this thing with the nerve in the back of his leg and a wrist problem so he can't work out as hard as he'd like. He tells Sally a lot of things about his physical condition, ever since she visited him in the hospital when he had the fracture. I guess he was in the hospital for six weeks and all his folks live in L.A. Ollie isn't married. He's really just a big kid. He can't be more than a year or two older than Sally and I.

He sauntered out behind the first base and did some leg-stretching exercises, bending one knee and then the other, stretching the hamstring away out on one leg and bending the other knee deep. He did three wind sprints and then went into the dugout. He didn't seem to notice the sign but Cookie, who was chasing wandering knuckleballs, looked up at us and winked.

"He saw it all right, ladies. Don't worry your heads none about that."

Once the game got started Ollie kept looking over at the banner and grinning. In the fifth inning he made a spectacular catch against the fence to end a Cubbies' rally. We were going crazy in the stands and he looked up at us and tipped his cap. I'm sure they saw it on the network. Late in the game he went after a long foul ball, out in the corner past the bullpen; he must have spotted us running over to watch the catch. The ball landed in some unoccupied bleachers' seats out-of-play and rebounded onto the field, but you couldn't see that from home plate. He flipped the ball back into the stands right in front of us, real sneaky, at the same time signalling it was out of reach. I got to the ball first. I've still got it. I copied his signature onto it from the official team guide in blue ballpoint.

It was obvious that he'd be player-of-the-game which meant that we wouldn't get to see him later because he'd be on the post-game show and wouldn't get his shower till too late. We kept shouting at him through the late innings.

"Ollie, we've got a CAKE, A CAKE FOR FRIDAY," I yelled, right off the end of my tongue or the top of my head or somewhere. He started laughing and then the game was over.

◆ The Cake ◆

We knew it was his birthday but we didn't know for sure how old he was until I checked him in the *Baseball Encyclopaedia* and it turned out he was only a year older than us, turning twenty-four. He'd been with the club since he was barely twenty when they brought him up for a look in September, and all through the next four seasons. He was selected as an All-Star in his first full season when he was twenty-one and again the next year. Then he missed a year when he had injuries and trouble with Hammacher; the club claimed he was a disciplinary problem. That was all just contract-jockeying; they were trying to intimidate his agent. Last winter he signed his new contract, another three-year deal, but this time worth three million dollars. Right away he got selected for the All-Star game again. Ollie can't handle anger, his own or the club's, and he hates to fight. I know what his problem is, and I feel I understand what he's going through better than anybody. He's really only a boy. He's practically world-famous. He's making all this money. He has groupies and Base-ball Annies hanging onto him whenever he goes on the road. He misses his Mom and family. Just because he can run, throw, hit, hit with power and judge the right-field wall in the stadium perfectly, everybody wants him to behave like a third-base coach or somebody like that, a manager's best buddy. Everybody knows they gave him Cookie Money for a roommate to quiet him down because Cookie is the sweetest, quietest guy on the club, not old, not a veteran, but not a threat either.

I mixed up this really disgusting icing for Ollie's cake, a blend of vegetable colouring, gelatine for stiffener and whipped cream chilled together for twenty-four hours before we iced the cake. I mixed it in the team colours in three bowls and whipped plenty of icing sugar and vanilla into it. When I say it was disgusting I mean you could hardly keep yourself from pigging out on it. It was stiff and sweet and creamy, sexy as anything. The cake was easy. We just baked three big white layers in different-sized tins. On Friday afternoon I took off from work sick and went home and plastered the icing between the three layers. I used mostly white icing to go between but I swirled in some of the red and the blue to give a marble effect. I pressed the three layers down, one on top of the other. The icing bulged out around the sides. I swirled some around my ring finger and licked it off and it was really weird gunk. You could eat it with a knife and fork.

I had to wait till Sally came over before I iced the top and sides because I'd promised her she could do some. She got to my place around four-thirty, dressed to kill. I could see she had big plans for the evening, a single game with the Cardinals beginning at 7:35 PM. Plenty of time to do the cake and the candles and the writing on top. Of course, Sally had to get undressed before she went near the bowls of icing. She was wearing bikini-briefs and no bra. I'll bet it's the first time anybody ever iced a birthday cake for an outfielder while topless.

"If I get this stuff on my shorts I'll never get it off."

"You're not wearing your shorts, Sally."

"That's why I took them off, dingaling," she said, licking her fingers. She kept smearing the sides of the cake with the tips of her fingers like a first-grader in finger-painting class.

"Don't mess up the cake," I said. She had topping on her legs and her panties.

"I know what I'm doing," she said. She kept building up layers of different-coloured icing until the top of the cake looked like a pennant or a swatch of bunting, all striped. We had some big fat candles and there was room on the cake for two dozen of them, which gives you an idea of the size. When she'd done what she thought was enough, she went into the bathroom and cleaned herself off. I think she took a shower but I'm not sure. I was too busy putting on the writing with a bag of blue icing and a decorating nozzle:

HAPPY TWENTY-FOURTH BIRTHDAY OLLIE
FROM SLITHER AND TREESHA

I put Sally's name first because she knows Ollie a bit better than I do even though I was the first one to actually get to talk to him one night in the roller rink near the players' parking area. We call it the roller rink because it's a big smooth space built up between several connecting ramps which go up to the 700 level and down past the 200 level to the indoor parking spaces for VIPs where some of the players disappear after the games if they're not going home on the Métro. That's where Sally and I met Ollie one night in 1979 just before he had his injury problem. Afterwards she started slithering into the hospital to talk to him while the rest of the team was on the road. During the off-season he used to call her up about once a month from L.A., just to talk.

"I can *talk* to you," he'd say, according to Sally. I never heard him say anything like that. He mostly says things a few words at a time like, "Do you dig?" or "Whoo-eee."

We stuck the cake in the refrigerator while we finished getting dressed to give it a chance to chill and to keep it out of the way; it was over two feet tall. I had to slide a couple of racks out of the bottom compartment to make room for it. It was in the fridge for over an hour and when we took it out the icing was set solid. We got it into a big cardboard carton and down the elevator and onto the Métro. It was heavy so we took turns carrying it while the other one went in front of keep the passengers from bumping into it.

Crossing town, we began to experience technical difficulties. We couldn't find a place to sit down until we passed the Berri-de Montigny station. It was terribly smelly and hot in the car because of the crowd. By the time we reached the stadium, the icing was starting to run. I took the box from Sally and made her walk along in front of me. Boy, that thing was heavy. I could smell the sugar in the heat. It wasn't cooler when we got up into the stadium and went out to our seats; it looked like we might be getting into one of those late-August heat waves.

The lights were already turned on when we got to Section 345 and there was a heavy haze hanging over the building, a smog-effect. We ripped the top off the carton as soon as we reached our seats; sure enough the icing was beginning to drip and sag. I was afraid that it might go liquid on us and drip down all over the seats, which would have made a terrible mess, but it just clung to the edges and sides of the top layer like rubber festoons.

It was crowded in the stadium; there were no empty seats near us. We sat the cake down on one of the pair that belonged to us and inserted the ticket stub in the icing where the usher could check the seat number. We took turns sitting in the other seat; when one of us had to stand she could lean over the railing to talk to the guys in the bullpen. Cookie was down there and Gene Frumkin and some others we knew. We told them to tell Orlando about the cake so that he could look up and see it. By the top of the third inning he'd spotted it and he waved to us. I was sitting beside it just then and I got my arms under it and held it up high where he could see it. When I lifted it up in front of my face, my arms pulled my T-shirt up out of my jeans, leaving my stomach bare. Some real cretin stuck his finger in my belly-button and wiggled it around. I nearly dropped the cake on the man in front of me, a sour old Pepsi who was complaining about icing on his collar.

He certainly wasn't the one who'd tickled my stomach; there wasn't any way I could identify the person who'd done it. This made me feel frightened but there was nobody I could tell about it. I tried to say something to Sally when we went to the ladies' room but she was on such a high I couldn't get anything across to her.

"Honestly Sally, he stuck his finger right in here. I could feel the fingernail and he scratched me."

"They're just a bunch of old farts from the east end. Forget about it. Nobody will dare lay a finger on you."

"But that's exactly what he did and I didn't like it. It scared me."

"Baby, that's one of the risks you have to take. Come on, let's go back and shake our cake."

A crowd of men had formed around the cake when we got back to our seats, looking like they wouldn't mind a slice of it, but we just pushed our way through them and grabbed it. It was the fifth-inning break and the grounds' crew was out raking the basepaths during the stop in the action. Orlando saw us come down to the railing with the cake; he gave a big smile and trotted over from right field to call up to us from the warning track.

"Lower it down," he said. I had to hold on to Sally's bum while she leaned way over, balancing the cake between her arms.

The announcer said, *"C'est aujourd'hui le vingt-quatrième anniversaire du voltigeur de droit Orlando 'Ollie' Saint-James."*

The crowd gave us a standing ovation; dozens of them took pictures. Ollie stuck his finger in the icing, then in his mouth. He smiled up at us.

"It's cool," he said. "I like that. Be around the parking lot after the game, the 'B' lot. We'll take the cake home and have a ball."

There was a big laugh and a cheer when I hauled Sally up in my arms. She nearly over-balanced once but we managed to get back to our places to watch the rest of the game. We won without coming to bat in the bottom of the ninth.

The crowd took its time getting out of the park; it was more than twenty minutes before we could get down to the players' parking lot. Most of the fans who hung around after the game seemed to be over by the front of the building between the beer gardens and the Métro entrance. Hardly any of them came back where the cars were. It's surprising how many of the players take the Métro home. It's easy and convenient and quick and most of them look pretty ordinary away from the field. Frumkin looks like a used-car salesman. He's got a wife somewhere but you'd never know it to see him in action. A real punker.

Angel-spit Busby looks impossible. If you don't know him for sure, you wouldn't believe he existed.

We waited in a shadowy corner where the ramps come down at two different angles to a flat space broken up by a row of cast concrete pillars which support the upper levels. This would have been waste space only somebody thought to use it for a small parking lot where about fifty cars fit between pillars. I don't much like to hang around here because there are plenty of dark spaces behind the uprights where somebody could come out and make a grab at you. I think we may be the only girls who know about the place or maybe the only ones smart enough to figure on running into one of the stars in the dark.

Ollie brings his car to the stadium once or twice during a home stand when he plans to go out somewhere after a game. Tonight he took a fairly long time to get dressed. It got very quiet in the shadows under the ramps. There's a door in the cement wall that only seems to open from inside. I've tried the handle often. It leads to a corridor directly to the home team's clubhouse. You can't open it from outside unless you know how. A couple of players came out and drove away in their cars and then Hammacher, the manager. He looked over and spotted us lurking there and he scowled. All of a sudden he said, "Don't fill Ollie up with that shit, Slither." We didn't know he knew anything about either of us. We stood there with our mouths open while he drove off. He honked softly twice and winked at us as he drove past us and down the ramp.

A few minutes after that, Ollie came out and picked us up. It was like a dream. He kept staring at the cake and licking his lips. "A cake for me. Man, you so *nice!* We gonna eat the whole thing."

We got in his car and balanced the cake on the back seat. He drove us down the ramp and out under the huge fluorescent-light standards by the entrance. His car was an enormous purple boat, I swear to God, purple or mauve or fuchsia. It glittered and sparkled under the orange lights.

Ollie and Cookie share an apartment together just below Sherbrooke in a highrise on Guy. You drive into the building up a lane running in from Saint-Mathieu. When we came to the end of the lane, while the garage doors were opening automatically with a rumbling whir, Ollie put the car in park and Sally slithered over right beside him. She was just about sitting on his lap.

They looked at me without saying a word. I opened the door on the right side and got out. Then the big fuchsia barge rolled in through the door. That was the last I saw of the cake.

I wandered through to Guy along the walkway beside the building. It was past midnight. I don't like walking alone at that time of night but the lights are so bright there and the Friday-night crowds so thick that I didn't feel too frightened. I crossed Guy and went and sat on a bench in the parkette at the corner of de Maisonneuve. I might have been sitting there for an hour when I suddenly realised that a man was standing beside the bench looking down at me.

"Don't you have a home to go to, Treesha?" he said. It was Cookie Money. I think he'd just come out of the Métro station across the street. A utility infielder-outfielder, wouldn't you know?

I said, "Certainly I have a home and anyway why aren't you in bed? You've got a day game tomorrow."

"Uh-uh, re-scheduled twi-night doubleheader. I don't think I can go upstairs yet anyhow."

"Oh Cookie, I'll make a banner and a cake for you."

He said, "I don't need no banner."

◆ The Roller Rink ◆

In September they were only in town at Labour Day and the week after. Then they had to travel all around the N.L. East to play the other contenders and work off seven doubleheaders from postponements that had piled up over the summer. We hardly got to see them the first week of the month. Two short series with the

Mets and the Buccos and the weather turned cold. Sally wouldn't talk about anything but her night with Orlando Saint-James. Nothing happened. Amazing! That's all. Nothing happened.

"He ate it all?"

"He was going to eat the candles but I hid them."

"You're kidding!"

"He loved his cake, Treesha, every tiny crumb."

"And nothing…?"

"Not a thing," she said smugly, "he thinks I'm still in my teens." She put her arm up beside her cheek and squinted along it, admiring the peach fuzz on her skin. I could have slapped her. "We sat and talked till two-thirty. He says it's the hardest thing about the season, trying to unwind."

"You helped him unwind?"

"When I left he was so wound down that he went to sleep on the divan in the front room."

"Full of icing?"

"Hammacher isn't going to like that," Sally said. "He's a mean man. He isn't playing Cookie. Ollie says Cookie is dying to play. He carries those three gloves around with him and he has a bat in his hands in the dugout all the time but Hammacher only uses him to pinch-hit against southpaws. I don't think that's fair, do you?"

"You look after Ollie and I'll look after Cookie."

"Do you think he liked you, Treesha? What did you do?"

"We sat in the park and waited till it was time for him to go in."

"Till three o'clock?"

"It was way past that."

"And the Métro shut and the busses not running. What did you do? How did you get home?"

"Cookie got me a cab."

"He paid for it?"

"Yes," I said.

"What about tonight?"

I said, "I'll come all right, but it's going to be cold in right field."

"Then bring your roller skates and keep warm."

We weren't going to see the guys again until the final days of the season when the divisional championship would be settled. It would probably be decided while the club was on the road. When Ollie and Cookie came home everything would be changed. So the final night of the Pirates' series we brought our roller skates to the stadium in over-the-shoulder bags and put them on during the pre-game announcements. We started skating all over the corridors behind the 300-level seats. There was hardly anybody in the park; the attendance always drops off in the second week of September. Especially for mid-week games. There might have been 10,000 people which looks like nothing in the stadium. We kept ourselves cheerful and warm on skates. We had boots in the team colours; my wheels were bright red and hers were blue. We had little short white skirts. We looked like backup singers in a disco act.

The hardest part was skating up the ramps towards the upper levels. We had to bust our buns to make the climb and could only do it by skating from one side of the ramp to the other instead of sailing straight up. Coming down was something else. We had a big crowd watching us by the start of the fourth inning. The team was losing; half the guys in our section came back inside out of the wind to watch us skate. We got them started cheering and betting while we were digging for the top of the ramp.

"My money's on the little red wheels; who's taking the blue ones?"

Sally took my hand when we turned and started down. We knew without talking about it what we were going to do. We started at the 700 level and whooshed down, cutting to one side and then the other like we'd been doing it all our lives. Coming off the first ramp we joined both hands and whirled around and around. Then we pushed off down the next ramp, first on one leg, then on the other. When we came to the very bottom, we started to scamper around the parking area, chasing each other in and out between the concrete pillars. There were chilly fans lined up along the ramps clapping their hands and cheering. We finished up by skidding to a stop, hips together and arms in the air. And then we bowed. Nobody watching the game action. The ushers were laughing right along with the rest of the guys and the team won their game and left in a hurry to catch their charter to Philadelphia.

They had a bad two weeks on the road. The only good thing about the trip was that Cookie got to play in most of the games; his bat got hot and Hammacher decided to overlook his defensive deficiencies at second base to keep him in the batting order. He was collecting a couple of hits in every game. It started to seem like he might wind up with as many as 250 at-bats on the year; that would give him some leverage at contract time. Cookie has always been able to hit but he isn't a power hitter so he isn't a good bet as a DH in the American League. If he had just a bit more power he'd almost be a star. But there it is. You have to learn to accept your natural limitations.

The whole of the last six days of the season we skated our little rear ends off. Honest to God, I lost seven pounds zipping and zapping up and down the ramps and the passageways but we couldn't get the guys to notice us. Cookie wasn't in the bullpen for the last games. He sat in the dugout next to Hammacher, clutching a bat, or he was in the field. I know he isn't a great second baseman. I realize that. Once he went after a short fly ball that Ollie should have taken. They collided and Cookie hurt his shoulder. We missed the accident. We were in under the stands skating around and teasing the guys when we heard the roar and then the silence. When we skated back outside Cookie was just getting up, still hanging on to the ball. When he trotted back to his position, the crowd gave him the biggest cheer he ever got in his major-league career. On the very next play he booted a ground ball.

On the last day they still had a chance to tie for the lead if they could get to Carlton. Hah! Who gets to Carlton in that situation? Hammacher went with the percentages the whole afternoon; he didn't start Cookie. They got locked in a one-run ball game and couldn't do a thing at the plate. Ollie looked at a called third strike for the final out of the game and the season.

It was awful. Neither of us cried. We picked up our over-the-shoulder bags and pushed through the crowds. The fans made way for us but didn't say anything or lay any bets. We skated in circles for hours and they all went away. At last Ollie and Cookie came out of the sealed door for the fuchsia Cadillac and didn't even look at us as we twirled around them. Cookie said to Ollie, "Damn, I sure the man gonna start me today. I sure!"

They got in the car and drove to sunny California.

THE ANSWER
Fielding Dawson

After John R. Tunis
—for Helen Maldovan

He took his stance under the lights. The machine shot the ball, he swung, and smacked a double into the net.

On the next mechanical pitch he hit a single up what would be the middle.

He missed the next pitch, and cursed.

"Enjoy taking out your aggressions?" she asked, from outside the cage.

"We've been through this before," he said, perspiring.

"If you hit this well during the games," she said, knowing she was making him angry—he was in a slump—"you wouldn't need this."

"I don't need it, I want it."

He hit the next pitch down the nowhere line, which would have gone deep into the left field corner, and had a man been on first the run would have scored. It would have been a double, and if the left fielder had made one false move, a triple.

His base-running style was like that. He rounded first as he rounded second around third: the next base always in his eye and mind, with home the big one ever waiting. He was a natural, hardboiled, fast-handed, first rate pro, and he hit the next pitch to an invisible shortstop for a sure out.

He met the next pitch direct, and sent it into what would have been left center for a classic two base hit. She said,

"That was the best yet."

He agreed, dug in, and hit the next and last machine pitch into the air nowhere, and had there been a center fielder, it would have been an easy out.

"Do you want to hit some more?" she asked.

"No," he said. "I'm sick of you."

"Would you love me if I was a tennis star?"

"I'd hate your Goddamned guts no matter what you were."

"But—"

"Don't give me that but shit. We've been through this. I can't help it. I hit .298 last year and you know what I hit the year before, so you know how I feel. This is my third year and my third slump. They've been good to me so far, as they were last year and the year before. I'll get back somehow. Leave me alone.

She was coy. "I didn't know you could talk so much."

He walked out of the cage, holding his bat, and they walked toward the car.

She was being cruel, and she knew it. A guy in a slump in the baseball circus is a guy gone crazy, and a ballplayer so talented as her husband in this slump made life impossible. It was the same with pitchers on a long losing streak, their wives went through hell, so, she told herself, she should know better. But she too was angry, because it was, all of it, unfair, even though she married into it, and her battle against her self-pity was overwhelming. She wasn't, in truth, introspective, nor was he, but each had an at-bottom sensibility, and together they had their smarts. This was their world, a major league reality, and the odds against him being a star were incomprehensible, too remote for them to think of, and in such demanding draining competition, they did their best to take the games one by one, yet in this slump even his remote starship faded. The grim statistics made actuality crackle.

All he knew by heart and nature, and developed discipline, was baseball, and as they both knew, as the team knew, as ballplayers know, even though he was a dependable, fast-handed, fast thinking second baseman, he would be finished, if he was lucky, in so few years that the children, Nick six and Becky seven, young as they were, were already showing stress signs.

At twenty-seven, she was twenty-eight, he—or they—had been in the majors for two years. This was his third. It had taken him four years, after college—a B.A. in Business Administration.

Two years ago he had come within a handful of votes of making Rookie of the Year, and the reason he didn't wasn't reported in all the papers, but anybody who knew baseball knew his year's end .296 batting average had come from .251 in the second week in August, and helped bring his team into 4th place from 7th, finishing, in a tight race, six and a half games out.

Then, in July of last year he had gone into a five week slump, and was, he felt, responsible for his team's losing second place, although he had gotten hot—again in August, and from a .235 average, ended hitting .298. Fifth in the RBI column, seventh in hits.

Second in doubles. These second year statistics were impressive, but the papers had their usual fun. A hot weather hitter. Lucky he didn't make Rookie of the Year because he'd be where the guy who did make it was—hitting .170, etc., yet this second baseman, his wife and their children were bitter, frustrated, confused and helpless. They read the papers every day, and in this, his third year, they read about him. Last year he had gone almost crazy, became more superstitious, choked up an inch on his bat, shortened his stance, and kept remembering what Clemente had said—"All I want is a clean base hit"—that beery July, that became the August and September champagne days, singles stretched into doubles, stealing third, and the daring race to home on shallow outfield flies, as the crowd went wild.

But this season—this was the first week of June, and the anxiety at home was dreadful. She was so neutralized by her involvement in his slump it was difficult for her to separate her feelings—his slump and confusion as against the real tasks at hand. She didn't know what to do, nor did he, and the children were as if stunned by parental self-control over fury and conflict, and in the face of it, in the family as a whole, a pattern of violence was beginning to form.

That night, after they'd driven away from the suburban batting cage, they drove in silence, reflecting in a scarlet gloom. It had been a night game, and with men on first and second, two down, bottom of the ninth, he had looked at the third strike, and they lost it by one.

He was, he felt, in a trance, or suspension. He seemed fated, and in the literal storm of irrationality he didn't know what to do. In the locker room he had fought hard, but then had wept, changed clothes without showering and left the stadium. The other ballplayers wore masks of unconcern, for they might be next. Except Jake, their catcher, who watched with concern as his second baseman changed clothes, then walked out.

The team's wives, who had sat with his wife, comforted her, for she too had wept. Those wives knew. You bet they knew. The team knew, the owners, the reporters—everybody inside knew, although the knowing was irrelevant, because the situation was impossible. From out of nowhere Fate had made a gesture, and one man's life became a nightmare. He'd had one hit in his last seventeen games, and that a blooper. He was hitting .229.

Jake was coming out of a brief slump, thank God, but to the man who followed Jake in the batting order— Jake hit 4th—it was doomsday, and with Jake on first, and their center fielder on second, he had taken that third strike. The manager had shaken up the batting order as it was, and this could not go on.

What is it? he asked, as he drove.

And the fans, those wonderful fans, who had cheered, and cheered, and cheered to make the stadium rock had, on that third strike booed, and booed some more before they all went home.

Meanwhile the papers were having fun, one columnist saying, regarding the second baseman's slump, August was looking like the discovery of DNA as seen from the 16th Century. Others said other things (bench him).

His wife sat beside him in the car, tightlipped, hurt, and in such fury and chaos she looked like a smooth but hollow white statue, her pretty face drawn and ashen.

He couldn't get the image of himself taking that third strike out of his mind. He had as if seen the pitch from a distant place, and the ball, taking its graceful sliding curve down over the outside corner, on the knees, seemed an alien object. But *why?* he asked. *Why?* That wasn't me. I *never* take the third one. Never! What is it?

He felt he was floating, and within himself he was terrified. After tonight's game—.226, his team was in fourth place, percentage points from fifth, four games out of third, six from second, and nine from first. True, he had turned over an unassisted double play which had, it appeared, saved the game, but they needed his bat—life needs blood.

"Let me drive," she said.

He pulled over, stopped the car, and they changed places.

"Why don't you see the team shrink again?" she asked. She despised shrinks. They took him away from her.

"It won't work," he murmured. "It's up to me. Me alone. I've got to do it. There aren't answers because the questions fuck them up. I'm going crazy—*why* is it? Why? I'm a *good* hitter!"

She wiped her eyes and drove with care, God how unfair it was. Twenty-seven years old—so young, yet so sophisticated it became a paradox—all unfair! *And so brutal.* He hung his head, and slumped forward, like a boy.

Every single thing they did, had, knew, felt, wanted, and needed—or owned, owed, loved and avoided or took for granted—was on his shoulders. Their world was up to him, and his guilt, anxiety, sense of helplessness, frustration, fear, confusion and fury threw their world into frenzy. The word *hit* had implications the children were beginning to act out.

When he had taken that third strike, her heart had stopped.

She pulled into the parking lot of an all night diner, braked, cut the engine, turned to him and said,

"What's it going to be, August or Business Administration? I want an answer."

"I don't know," he mumbled. "I'm in a dream."

"Well," she said, keeping control. "I'm not, although what I'm witnessing, and feeling, seems like it, *I* am not in a dream, nor are our children."

But—as he put his arms on the dash and his head on his arms—in a flash of higher consciousness, she saw him, and in him, a terrible vision of a broken boy, close to the edge, who might go over, helpless. She stared at him, and suddenly—

Fight him. Fight him!

"Get out of the car," she said. "Come on, get out of the car."

He looked at her in disbelief.

"Get *out* of the car," she repeated, opening her door, and getting out. He was startled, and baffled, but he got out, and they walked around until they faced each other in the beam of headlights.

In fear, fury, and a morality mix, she gathered her strength—

"If you don't hit me first I'm going to hit you."

She counted out loud to three, and slapped him, surprising him as he took a couple of steps backward, but she followed, counted to three again, and with flashing eyes and clenched fist in an overhand swing socked him square in the teeth. His lip split, and began to bleed—he backed away, hands out, still surprised, and confused as she advanced again counting to three, and swung. But he caught her arm and they stood, locked, but she struggled, and bit his left forearm with all her power, he cried out, released her, ducked under her right swing and in quick rage and his eyes blazing pasted her cheek with a left jab and her jaw with a hard right cross. She stumbled backwards, and fell, but when he picked her up she hit him in the eye and he delivered a shot from his shoulder which sent her reeling, and she fell—down, and almost out.

He bent over her, as she lay on the asphalt parking lot. He smiled an angry smile, his lips and teeth bloody, and dripping on her cheek, he asked,

"Want some more?"

"No." She tilted her head to avoid his blood and to spit out her own, saying, "But thanks anyway, you bastard."

Her upper lip was split and bleeding, and the tip of her left eyetooth was somewhere on the asphalt. He helped her up. She put her arm around him, and as they walked, she asked if he would drive, as she didn't feel very well.

He helped her into the car, walked around, got in the driver's seat, they wiped each other's blood off, with his handkerchief, and Kleenex from the glove compartment, blotting blood from their clothes, and as she held his hanky to her mouth and they pulled out onto the highway again, she said,

"Jesus. I didn't know you could hit like that."

In the innocent pun dawning, they began to laugh, but when the pun turned into irony, they laughed harder.

"I'm pulling over," he laughed. "I can't drive!"

The car angled onto the shoulder of the highway, and they sat in the front seat laughing out of control, bleeding anew, until they were exhausted, and he drove home, thanked and paid the astonished babysitter, and after washing up, applying iodine, bandaids and ice packs, they sat at the kitchen table and each drank a cold beer through straws, looking at each other. They held hands across the table. Then went to bed and fell asleep in an embrace, wiped out, but before he went altogether unconscious, he realized his bloodstream had changed. His body felt fluid and warm.

She had a smile on her face. His sleep was pure, and deep.

The next day was predictable.

He knelt in the on-deck circle, in the bottom of their first, and watched Jake slash a single into right, advancing their third baseman to third. One out, one run was in. The man in the on-deck circle rose to his feet, took a couple of swings, tossed the ring-weight away, walked to the plate—not glancing at his wife in the stands. Their dentist had sanded her eyetooth down, her upper lip was swollen and bandaged. The other wives were embarrassed, staring out at the field, and the game under the lights, not seeing much of either, nor not quite knowing what to say. She was a fright, in her hope.

What was in his mind, or in himself, he didn't know, or care about, but with a black eye, split lip, bruised cheekbone, aching right hand, and left forearm bright with teethmarks—which the team enjoyed no end—he dug in the box motioning to the umpire to allow it, which the ump acknowledged, himself a little startled, watching that battered ballplayer dig in, take a couple of swings, and as the umpire nodded to the pitcher, as from a vast and remote section of the galaxy, an alien force invaded the batter, and as the pitcher, glancing at the men on base, went into the stretch, the man he saw at the plate seemed a different man, whose eyes glowed, with tiny looping nuclear crystals at center, something demonic in that bruised face, something lethal in that batter's stance, something not quite explainable, but yet quite clear, for what followed in the rest of the game, as well as that season, I mean what that man did with that bat, and his glove, made an exact transition to the glory of July in the next year, as the record books tell us. Jake again started for the National League All-Star team. His buddy was number two choice at second (Joe Morgan started).

Number two stood in the dugout, face a mask, he felt the thrill, relaxed and confident—.302 batting average last year—watching a blonde rock star walk to the microphone at home plate, and begin to sing the Star Spangled Banner. Jake stood on the steps of the dugout, catcher's gear on, ballcap held over his heart. The song rose, he looked at his feet, not seeing anything, but beginning to hear the ballpark turn in on the jewel of itself, suspended between fifty thousand people and himself, that song, and as it went toward crescendo, space narrowed to a margin he knew by heart, a margin which gave him peace of mind, and in a cresting crashing wave of sound the anthem was over. The park winked back to its stoic limits. The game was on.

In the fifth inning he hit for Morgan, lined deep into left center for an out, and in the next inning, the sixth, score tied two all, with one out, the fastest base runner in the American League reached first on a bunt, and on the second pitch to the right-handed hitter, the runner broke for second, the batter swung to protect his runner and Jake in one fluid motion followed the swing of the bat with a single throw to the perfect running action of his second baseman, the sweeping tag was made, the runner was out, and as the fans cheered, the second baseman, professional face without expression, snapped the ball to his shortstop who zipped it to their third baseman, and thus the ball returned to the pitcher. The second baseman resumed his position, wanting, above all things, that the ball be hit to him. His wife was in the stands, sitting beside Jake's wife, both women happy, and pretty, their children beside them.

"They're sensational."

"They are," the second baseman's wife agreed. "Jake's a genius. He knew that guy was going."

"So did your husband," Jake's wife smiled, and the two women gazed at each other, their eyes warm, as the hitter sent a lazy fly ball high above the brilliant green grass of the field, the small white sphere reached the peak of its arc, and below a deep blue and black moonlit sky, fell for the third out into the waiting glove of the National League's left fielder as millions round the world watched, either on satellite or domestic television, or saw it in their ear's eye over radio, bringing childhood's vividness back again, or making childhood in fact that much more vivid. It went to American businessmen and GIs by TV or radio everywhere in the world—to certain interested parties in England—it swept through Mexico, Puerto Rico and to Fidel Castro himself, as well as Hawaii, Australia, the Philippines, to Korea, Alaska, to the baseball island of Japan, and to all guys and women of all races at bars across the U.S. and Canada, to speeding trains, to planes midflight, and to astronauts among the stars—a small, old woman in a rocking chair, bright eyes glued to the TV screen as Jake walked to bat in the living room of her small, clean woodframe house on the outskirts of Sweetwater, Oklahoma, as she whispered *Come on Jake, come on boy,* and rubbed her hands as she smiled.

OCTOBER 1, 1961
George Bowering

Do you remember those death threats Roger Maris was getting in August and September of 1961? There he was, wearing the Babe's pinstripes, and he wasnt even Mickey Mantle. At least Mickey Mantle was a Yankee from the word go. Maris was a Cleveland Indian first, of all things, and he was never going to hit .300. Mantle was chasing Maris all summer, and one thing was for certain: as a couple they were going to knock off Ruth and Gehrig.

But Mantle didnt get any death threats.

Even I got some death threats. One of them is coming true right here on this foldaway couch.

Do you remember those death threats Roger Maris was getting? Did you think they were all from fans of the Babe? Old timers who didnt want anyone to get 61 home runs, even with the schedule expanded to 162 games?

For those who dont know what I am talking about, here are the bare details, though why I should bother, I dont know. Babe Ruth's record of sixty home runs in 1927 was the favorite myth in baseball. Ty Cobb's lifetime batting average of .367 was harder to do. Joe DiMaggio's 56-game hitting streak is not likely to be topped, as they say. But Babe Ruth's sixty dingers gave the biggest galoots in the game a yearly target to assault. A few guys had got into the fifties. Trivialists liked to point out that the second-best total was Ruth's 59 in 1921.

Then along came 1961. It was as if the last two digits called for some kind of disrespect toward the Bambino. Two things happened in 1961 to break a lot of hearts, or at least to leave the sour taste of ambiguity in baseball fans' mouths.

In 1961 the American League of baseball added two teams. Until then each team played 154 games a season, 22 against each of the other seven teams. In 1961 they would have to play 162 games, 18 against each of their nine opponents.

In 1961, Roger Maris and Mickey Mantle staged a home run race that had every newspaper in the western hemisphere providing a graph on the front page every playing day. By mid-August it was clear that Roger Maris at least was going to hit more than sixty home runs. The commissioner of baseball said that if Maris didnt have 61 by the 154th game, the Babe's record was still there. After 154 games Maris had 59 homers. In the last eight games he got two more. They put an asterisk after the number wherever it was reprinted.

But those 61 homers were still there. And as the years went by the asterisk disappeared, along with other records by the Babe, such as his 711 lifetime homers. Sixty-one years after Maris's meretricious heroics the asterisk was not even remembered. And for sixty-one years no other big leaguer was ever able to hit more than sixty homers, no matter how many games there were to a season. I know. I was born in 1961, and I was in the stadium in Toronto on the October day when Coral Godard hit his sixty-first homer.

That was seven games from the end of the season. In those seven games big hairy Godard marched to the plate thirty-three times. He struck out twenty times. He was walked once. He was hit with a pitch once, a wonderful piece of ironic bravery by a rookie left-hander who had gone to Godard's high school ten years after the hairy person more or less graduated. Once he got the ball on the fat part of the bat, but this was to center field in the plastic Miami ball park, and it was pulled down on the Cubaturf warning track.

In his last time at bat in the last game, when the divisional results had been settled for three days, the large first baseman hit a foul ball that passed the pole at mid-height and probably reached the Gulf Stream. On the following pitch he swung his lamino-club so hard that idlers in both dugouts involuntarily flinched. But he caught only the top third of the ball. The Miami infield dawdled and posed and lobbed a man out. The season was over, and so was the pursuit.

Coral Godard had sixty-one poppers, just like Roger Maris. He had no asterisk. The Toronto sportwriters started what they supposed would be a traditional journalistic remark, noting that Godard had achieved the highest total in the twenty-first century.

The total would do a lot for Godard's already inflated salary. But the pelf was offset by the remarks he would hear all winter and well into the following season. People felt that they had to comment upon that last week, with those thirty-three trips to the platter. At least Roger got two long balls in his last week, they would point out, and he had nothing but an old fashioned bat made from a mountain tree.

A typical bad day would be May second in Cleveland. Standing three meters off the bag at first, Godard had acquired the skill of singling out sentences and near-sentences from the thin roar of the usual light assemblage of Indians fans. If you were there and had his ability, this is some of what you might have heard:

"You couldnt carry Roger Maris's jockstrap, ya bum!"

"He cant carry his own jockstrap!"

"Yer a choke artist, ya big hairy creepoid!"

"Roger woulda hit a hundred homers if he was alive now!"

"He woulda hit seventy-five when he was seventy-five, ya jerkoff!"

"Belle montre et peu de rapport!"

"Shaddup, Frenchie!"

"Hey, Coral, yer sister…" (*etc.*)

You will have noted that abuse from the grandstand did not evolve much as major league baseball stepped across the century line for the second time.

Godard, and even most of the sportswriters in the American League thought the razzing and threats would begin to fade away as the season proceeded into the hot months, especially if he had, say twenty homers in June. But on June twentieth in Baltimore someone left a dead cat with a pinstriped baseball uniform at the door of his hotel room. There was a number three on the back of the little uniform. In Detroit later that week Morgana IV, the kissing bandit, ran out to first base in the home half and kicked the great hairy first baseman in the slats.

In August Coral had seven home runs and twenty-five runs batted in. The Jays' psychologist advised Grand Cayman Island, where the team's spring training facility could be set up for rest and recuperation. Coral was opposed to the idea. Then in Kansas City someone took a shot at him. He left for the Caribbean the next morning. The paper sent me down with him. I thought I would stay for a few days, file a couple stories about how the big fellow was filling his days, and coincidentally pick up a few rays. I had not imagined how hot it gets on Grand Cayman in August. I decided to leave after three days. So did Coral.

As we were on the same plane, I thought I would play my hunch, and go wherever he was going. He took a connector flight from Atlanta to St. Louis. St. Louis hasnt been in the American League since 1953. This was getting pretty interesting, especially because it was obvious that I was going to follow him everywhere I could. First he tried to shake me, but when he found me sitting on his lap in a taxi, he just laughed, and then sighed and then said

"The season cant get any worse than this," and away we went.

To see a voodoo queen. To see a Washington University physics professor. Maybe not quite a professor. Sort of a graduate assistant. She was gorgeous, a St. Louis honey blonde, but you dont want to hear about that. It certainly didnt seem to matter to Coral Godard, not at first.

Now I am not a science reporter, and I dont expect that 21st Century physics is going to make much sense to a fuddy-duddy reader in the twentieth century (remember, I used to live there), so I will not spend a hundred pages on the plans and specs of the Deutero-Tempus machine, patent pending. In fact, I still cant believe that's what that lady graduate assistant called it. I think she was razzing me with a midwest sense of humor. Who knows? She said she was from *East* St.

Louis, and you might know what they are like over there.

How did Coral know about Lorraine Knight? Hey, how did your favorite NFL lineman know about Dr. Needle? If there is something illegal but helpful, your professional athlete will hear about it. If there is a new gadget on any university campus on the continent, there will be two people wanting to know what it is capable of: the contract lawyer from the Pentagon, and a veteran ballplayer who needs an edge.

I think Lorraine had a liking for a man with curly black hair on his back. Either that or she had a romantic notion about the relationship between science and the human heart. She thought the Pentagon and most of the Scientific Community was a little short in the heart. Whatever the case, she said that the Deutero-Tempus could put a human being back into any year in the last hundred and ten. She was working on longer range stuff, while there were hardly any professors at Washington University who would even believe a decade. Most of those physics professors didnt even have straight hair on the tops of their heads.

I stuck with Coral as much as I could, but there were times over the following week when I lost track of him *and* Lorraine Knight. She was apparently a lot nicer to him than the fans in either Cleveland or Toronto. She told me later that she faced a tough conflict when Godard volunteered to be her first sixty-two year voyager.

You see, she had to explain to her ballplayer that time-travel is so far a one-way trip.

I say this despite the strange logic of narrating this tale in the past tense about events that will not happen until another fifty-nine years have transpired.

Be that as it may.

In the old movies people like Danny Kaye were always zipping back to more scenic times, and then zooming back home in the present. But put your head to this: if you are going to send me back to Chicago in 1882, for instance, you just have to send me back over the tracks the world has made since then. But how are you going to send me into the future? There arent any tracks.

That is not the real scientific explanation, but it is close as you can get in a journalist's language.

"She says she wants me to take a short trip first," Coral told me in the bar at the Mark Twain Hilton.

We sports writers are often cast in the role of straight men. That might explain why so many of us evolve smart-ass writing styles.

"What does that mean?" I asked.

"She says I should go back one year. Then I could look her up and we could get together and have some fun for a year before I head out."

"Head out?" I asked.

"That's the technical language for going back through space in the Duteous Tempo," he said. A lot of ball players couldnt have got that far without saying "you know" at least once.

"One," I said, "That is not quite the right name for the gizmo. Two. There isnt any technical language for all that yet. Cripes!"

That's what I said. Cripes. In the twenty-first century.

"Be that as it may. I told her I thought she was a very nice person as well as a great scientist, but."

"But?" I asked.

"But I have to get back to 1961. Before the end of the season."

"What are you going to do that for?" I asked. "You cant come back, you know."

"I know. I think I can handle living in the 1960s. As long as I stay away from my family. I think I could even manage to handle living in Toronto in the seventies and eighties. But."

"But," I said.

"But the main reason is I have to do Something about Roger Maris."

"Tell me about Something."

"I think I might let him get sixty. Maybe fifty-nine."

Have you ever read any novels about time travel? They always bring up this basic problem: what if the time traveller does something to mess up history? What if the gink from the future sees the lamp beside the cow and takes it away, and there's no great Chicago fire? I wrote a story about that a long time ago when I was still wondering what kind of writer I was going to be. I had a historian from Northwestern University go back and torch Mrs O'Malley's barn after all. He felt terrible about all the suffering he caused, but there are certain higher principles, which means greater dangers. He went back to his job a hundred years later at Northwestern. I didnt know real space travel would have to be one-way.

To tell you the truth, there were times I wished I were inventing this story instead of covering it.

One morning I went over to Frankenstein Knight's condo and they werent there. So I went to the laboratory and he wasnt there. But she was. There was a scent of eucalyptus in the air, used to be my favorite smell.

"Gone?" I enquired.

"Gone," she said. Her demeanor was ambiguous as you can get. She was deprived of Coral but she had sent Godard along the tracks.

"How do you know he didnt go to 1927?" I asked.

"Check the encyclopedia," she said.

I went back to Toronto and tried to re-enter normal life, if talking to naked men in a dressing room after they've been getting all sweaty playing a boy's game in front of thousands of people eating junk food can be called normal life. I guess you might call me and my colleagues the historians of popular life. I shared a desktop at the Toronto Star instead of Northwestern University.

Yes, you know what I was thinking. But I needed some time to think about it. I figured I had all season anyway. I could even cover the Jays if they made it into the late-Fall Classic. Coral Godard might be following Roger Maris around the league in 1961, but if I was going to go back I could go whenever I wanted to. Time was something we didnt know everything about, but I knew that much. If you are going to travel to Minneapolis, you can get there from Vancouver or Miami or Keokuk. If you are going to September 1961, you can get there from today or next Tuesday or a year from now.

Yep, I had time pretty well figured out. Then I woke up one night on a littered floor, surrounded by lockers, and I couldnt remember how I got there. A doctor who usually looked at the bare bodies of much younger men told me something I hadnt thought of regarding how much time I had.

"If you're one of those newspaper guys who have a novel in the desk drawer, get busy on it," he said.

I like a guy with that attitude. Reminds me of the guy I thought I would make of myself.

So you know why I went back to St. Louis.

"Why havent you sprung your success on the world?" I asked.

There was still a part of me that thought she had Coral hidden away in her bedroom closet, or in a shallow grave on the banks of the Mississippi. I thought maybe Coral had decided to live somewhere up a river in Paraguay, with some refugee nembutal dealers.

And I know this much about science: whenever there is a landmark invention or discovery, there are usually hundreds of people involved. Whenever the Nobel prizes in physics or medicine are announced, they name several guys in white coats at Berkeley and Manchester. Whenever it is a single maverick you have to be a little suspicious.

On the other hand, she told me, there were those two men who did nuclear fusion in a pot of heavy water at room temperature.

"I still dont know whether he is there in 1961," she said. "The message he was going to send hasnt arrived. He might have been spread out and sent all over the time map, for all I know."

I, of course, transferred that notion to myself. I could not imagine my molecules sprayed all over the last half of the twentieth century.

"What was the sign?"

"He was going to jump out on the field and greet Roger Maris when he hit his sixtieth whatchamacallit," she said.

That's what he told *her*, but I thought I knew a little better.

"Send me to spring training, 1961," I said. "I'll send you a sign. I've been thinking about this: if I arrive safely in 1961, I'll talk to somebody in the printing trade who needs a few dollars. That's the year Allen Ginsberg's *Kaddish and other poems* came out. Lot of people still think it's his best book."

"I know less about old poetry than I know about baseball," she said, with a little patronizing impatience.

"Take my word for it. If I make it, you can have a look at page 38 of the first edition of *Kaddish*. If the second line still says 'or will we find Zoroastrian temples flowering on Neptune?' I didnt make it. If it says 'be' instead of 'we,' that will be the misprint I paid for.

"Why did it have to be something about ancient poetry?"

"I didnt think I could influence Khrushchev about the Berlin wall."

"Why would you want to go back there when you cant return?"

"A guy in expensive shoes told me I'm not going to see the 2023 season, anyway. So I figured I would like to watch Mantle and Maris slug it out. And I want to get reacquainted with baseball on natural grass."

Here is something we should all know about scientists. They deal with objects and forces and energies they tell us are objectively observable, though one of their own tribe told us a century ago that that was a myth. But in the middle of all this impersonalism they are as vain as opera singers and novelists. You can get them in their vanity.

So I played that card. I loaded myself down with little valuable things I could trade for the local currency, and miss Svengali Knight turned the dial.

Later, or should I say earlier? Anyway, on the day that Maris hit number 33 off Bill Monbouquette in Yankee Stadium, I had this thought: if I could talk her into sending me after the large hairy one, somebody else could talk her into sending him after me. The hit man always looks over his shoulder for *his* hit man.

Of course you people would never know the full ramification of these pursuits. If a contract killing occurs you see it as a newspaper crime with an unknown motive. Then you are stuck with the new history. As far as you are concerned, if I failed in my quest Roger Maris never did hit his sixty-first.

If that is the case, I just had to leave this letter, to let you know that at one time he did. Maybe it never got into your *Official Encyclopedia of Baseball,* A. S. Barnes & Co., 1970, but it could have if I had succeeded. (Is this foreshadowing or back-shadowing?)

Of course you will be justified in disbelieving all this. Roger Maris got an asterisk for *tying* Ruth, you can say.

Unless you are reading this in 2022, and thinking this confirms where I went when I disappeared.

A blast from the past, I suppose you might say. A present meant for the future.

September 27, 1961 in New York City. Who would want to be anywhere else, any other time? It was certainly a baseball writer's dream to be there. I guess I was the only person in town for whom the dream was edged with a bone-scraping nightmare. I dont know whether Roger Maris got any sleep last night, and I dont know where Coral Godard spent the night, but I can report to you that I sat up all night smoking cigarettes because in September of 1961 you could not get in New York City what I was accustomed to employ to get through a bad night.

The night before, Baltimore's young Johnny Fisher had offered Maris a fastball at the knees, and Maris had shown his appreciation with a high drive that curled around the right field foul pole for his sixtieth homer. I saw this from a seat I had bought the rights to from a gent in the parking lot. It felt rather nice to be in the paying seats instead of the press box. But I could not sit back and relax, glug beer, joke with my neighbors, the special grace of the baseball park. I was scanning the crowd for Godard. I didnt see him till the home run. Ruthian clout, I caught myself saying in my head.

Most of the crowd of sixty-two thousand people yelled their heads off, delirious that they were here to see this historic dinger. A few thousand of the older fans booed or remained seated, getting out their asterisks during the ten minutes it took to get the game started again. I stood up, mainly so that I could see. As Maris circled the bases, the Yankees in their milky white pinstripes rushed out to greet him. Some of them did. It would be interesting to look back at whatever photographs there are, to see which Yankees were still in the dugout. John Blanchard was out there first because he had been the on-deck hitter. Yogi Berra was there. Hector Lopez was there with his enormous toothy smile. He jumped on Maris and demanded to be carried to the dugout, but he was pulled off by Whitey Ford.

Coral Godard was there. Or almost there. All at once we thousands could see a new dark blue blazer among the pinstripes. Then we could see a number of New York's Finest in leather jackets, converging on the suit and leaving the field for the ball players. I dont know exactly what Coral had planned for that moment, but I was grateful for the foresight of the people who run the House that Ruth Built.

In all the noise and turmoil I was out of my seat and headed for the exit. I figured I wouldnt run into much traffic headed that way, and I banked on the cops' deciding they just had to get that hairy and over-excited fan outside the stadium rather than cuffing him and hauling him to the slams. Yes. I found Coral out-side section 12, trying to rub a mark off the toe of a brand new loafer.

"Was that just the signal, or did you have more in mind?" I asked.

"If I'da had a gun they wouldnt have just left me here, would they?"

"Dont play dumb, Godard. You could kill a gorilla with your bare but furry hands. If they still have gorillas in 1961."

He looked at me hard, under the shadow of his single head-wide eyebrow. He emanated protein. He was strength personified, or maybe beastified. I wasnt afraid of him. But I was getting confused about history.

"I gotta stop him," he said at last, having reached as complex a conclusion as we were likely to see.

"Okay," I said. "Let me ride with you again."

"You try and stop me, and you'll wind up in the same basement," he advised.

I had to start thinking on my feet, and while sitting in the cab. I had to think about how to stop this creep from killing Roger Maris, and I had to think about the ramifications regarding time and space, which simple people in the twentieth century thought were aspects of each other. In the world of physics Albert Einstein had been the Bambino, but someone was going to come along and hit sixty-one in that league, too. I was thinking as fast as I could, and I was not about to take the time to think about how Coral Godard managed to get the address of Roger Maris's apartment. I will only say that a guy who can find Houdini Knight's laboratory in St. Louis should be able to find an outfielder's abode.

I thought and I thought. Coral didnt interrupt me: he was trying to think too, I guess. When we got out of the cab on that darkened corner in Greenville, Coral was going to kill the home run leader of the American League. But by the time he was banging on the front door with his fist or his head—I forget which—we had a deal. This is the sentence with which I ended my persuasive argument:

"There's more than one kind of time travel."

Which meant this: there were three letters in a green metal box in the office of an editor of the New York *News,* or was it the New York *Times?*, written by your humble servant, who had the advantage of knowing which New York newspapers would still exist in 2021. One letter instructed a sequence of editors on what to do with the other two letters. The other two letters were addressed to the president of Washington University in St. Louis and to the commissioner of baseball. Those letters are there right now. They are part of the reason for my writing this story.

In other words I got it through Coral's well-armored cranium that his great venture would come to nothing if it was proven that he had been alone in breaking Ruth's record only due to an act of homicide. He would, I said, receive the asterisk that would have gone to Maris.

You can see the problems in tense created by the combination of narrative, speech, and time-travel.

Roger did not look like a front-page athlete. He did not even look like the Roger who had slapped homers all through spring training. He had lost a lot of hair, and his skin had gone grey. There was some kind of colorful disorder spreading on the skin of his lower arms. He stooped. He seemed unable to lift the long revolver he was carrying when he came to the door of his green-sided bungalow. It was three in the morning. Roger Maris was not going to sign an autograph.

Coral reacted to the armament by rushing his predecessor, driving him against all the furniture in the living room. Luckily there was no one else in the house, or if there had been they had departed by the back door or window at the first sign of athleticism.

Coral banged Roger several times. He socked him once on the nose and once on each eye.

"Why the deuce are you doing this, man?" might be a paraphrase of the only question Roger could get out. But his words did stop the knuckle man from the future.

"He doesnt want you to hit sixty-one home runs," I said.

"He's got company," said Maris, between energetic gasps. "That's why I'm living in this nowhere dump."

He opened the door a little wider and spit some blood mixed with sputum and saliva outside.

Then he agreed to the deal. This deal, like all realistic pacts, would disappoint all three of us a bit, but make the times we were living in habitable.

The hard part was going to be persuading the New York Yankees. The second hardest part was going to be fooling or placating the home plate umpires. The surprisingly easy part was going to be making Coral Godard look like Roger Maris. He wasnt that much bigger, maybe a little more muscular around the chest and shoulders. A lot of the difference faded when we shaved a kilogram of hair off his arms and the middle of his long eyebrow.

Anyway, it worked, more or less, or you wouldnt need this story now. You might remember that there were suspicious stories at the time, but they were chalked up to the circus atmosphere of the homer hunt. The ball player the reporters saw after the game was Roger Maris, a man with two black eyes. The outfielder the Bronx beer swillers saw in the wide green was Roger Maris, an oddly bent figure in pinstripes. Yogi Berra and Mickey Mantle and Bobby Richardson ducked interviews all that week. Coral Godard was a twentieth century major league purloined letter.

He went to the plate at Yankee Stadium twenty-three times over the next four and a half games. Although it was illegal according to the rules of baseball, he was wearing the same number on his back as that on the back of his teammate in the dark tunnel behind the dugout. Have a look at pictures of Bill "Moose" Skowron during those tense nights: his facial expression can not be attributed to the pennant race. There wasnt any pennant race. Bill really thought he could solve Maris's dilemma by socking the interloper in the front of the head. Organized baseball, or at least a local contingent of it, kept the wrappers on him. It's only for five nights at the most, Bill, they said.

Coral struck out and grounded out and lined to the first baseman. He could not reach the Orioles pitchers and then he could not handle the Red Sox pitchers. Once he got within fifteen feet of the warning track in center field, no mean feat at Yankee Stadium. Roger Maris stood in the dark tunnel, smoking Chesterfield cigarettes and wishing he were in the game offensively. On the plus side you might say that it was a good thing that Coral didnt reach base very often. There was no guarantee that a Boston infielder might not spill the baked beans.

But thank goodness, as millions of unknowing fans said, for Tracy Stallard, a name that will live forever in the annals of the game. On October 1, 1961, the last day of the season, Tracy finally dealt Coral Maris a knee-high fastball, and the shorn one lifted it magisterially into the upper deck of the next borough. Babe Ruth had hit his sixtieth on the last day of the 1927 season, off Washington's left-hander Tom Zachary, right here at Yankee Stadium. Coral rounded the bases, got jumped on by twenty-eight people in Yankee uniforms, including one with the duplicate number on his back, as you can ascertain by looking at a photograph in *Sport Pictorial*, and then left big-league baseball for forty-five years.

He was not, as he told me in athletese, completely satisfied. He would be condemned, through some portion of the twenty-first century, to sharing the major league home run record, but at least he will have been the only person ever to have hit a sixty-first home run.

"Who knows? Maybe you would have hit sixty-*three* home runs if you had stayed around for the 2023 season?" I said. I admit that I was sporting a grin that showed just the tips of my teeth.

He stared at me with the rudimentary beginnings of emotion on his face. He hadnt thought of that.

After he left that game, I was hoping that Maris would pop number sixty-two in his last at-bat. But he grounded to second on a pitch he should have taken for ball four. Aint that always the way?

The Yankees won the world series easily, in five games over the Cincinnati Reds. Maris hit a homer in the third game. I watched it on a rudimentary black and white television. I dont think Coral was interested. Then, as always happens when the world series is over, a winter loomed, and the reality of the workplace reasserted itself. As I did not have a workplace I had to find myself some fake I.D. and hit the concrete. It didnt take as long as I had feared. I landed a sports page job in White Plains, mainly horse races and track meets. I didnt tell them about the little visitor inside my middle regions. But it's a couple years later now, and they are going to learn. I havent been able to get out of this foldaway couch for seven days.

So here I am completing the last part of the deal, the part Roger wasnt told about. Coral wanted me to tell the whole story. I am supposed to consign it to a time capsule at the *News*. Coral got the idea from me, of course. His idea was that the time capsule is to be opened the day after he disappears from the Blue Jays in 2022. Well, it appears that I was able to get the story down, but I dont know about the time capsule. Maybe the person who finds this will seal it and deliver it to the *News*.

Coral said to tell every detail and make it realistic. He said that way history would eventually get it right. People would know that Roger Maris never hit a sixty-first homer. All I had to do was tell the story and dont leave any loose ends.

BALL TWO
Jerry Klinkowitz

Costy Pedraza's first pitch has been low and outside, almost past the catcher, forcing him to lunge head-first toward the base line and start this first inning with a snootful of dirt. He swings back on his heels and pumps his mitt upward, urging Costy to keep the slider from breaking too soon, then snaps the ball back to him on the mound.

Billy Harmon, who's playing second this game, wanders over to the bag between pitches and motions to Eddie at short. Eddie's English isn't much, but still better than Costy's, and so he's the guy who translates minor-league plays and instructions from the manager. Eddie's from Panama, though, and since Costy is only eight weeks off the plane from the Dominican their Spanish can get mixed up, meaning utterly different things.

One wet afternoon when Eddie suggested taking their raincoats to the park Costy thought he was talking about rubber diapers. Another time Eddie saw Costy talking with a pretty young woman near the dugout and walked over to compliment her hairdo. But Eddie's *pelo* was not at all what the word meant to Costy, who almost decked him right there. So Eddie's wound up thinking that this new kid is a little bit bananas, and vice versa.

But the little bit of English Billy and Eddie share—evolved as roommates through spring training and the first weeks of A-ball—keeps the middle infield free of ambiguities and fistfights. Billy has caught the pitcher's signal to them, a shrug of the left shoulder, which means he'll wait until the catcher calls for a fastball, so any grounder will surely go Eddie's side of the bag. "Your ball, man," Billy says with his glove shielding his lips. "You bet," Eddie answers, his favorite American phrase, which handles just about anything.

As Costy paws the mound and the infield gets back into position, the benchwarmers pick their topic for the day. The madly erratic clubhouse shower that scalded one of them and nearly froze another has them thinking about water, and after a bit of grumbling Buddy Knox, the reserve infielder whose beer gut is growing with each day's lack of play, starts the second-string outfield on their pet obsession: discovering the headwaters of the Mississippi.

The Mighty Mississip' is a big item in their lives this year. Two of the clubs they play in Iowa are river towns, and for road games in Wisconsin and Illinois they cross it every trip. Lynn Parson, whose California hipness finds everything about the Midwest cutesy quaint, has been telling the bench how he and Rafael Quinones traced it to its source during three days of rainouts at Eau Claire last summer.

Out in the bull pen the long-reliever, two middle men, and the reserve catcher are—like the pitching coach who's joined them—just slouching and staring as if their game hasn't begun. The players sit quietly and Mack isn't thinking about anything at all. Costy paws while all the action's in the dugout.

"It started that first day we'd planned on Eau Galle," Lynn recalls. "Yeah, you said the reservoir was full of walleyes," Buddy adds, and for a moment there's some thought about Wisconsin game fish. Their rivals in Madison, after all, are called the Muskies, and the fans have a fish cheer and everything. But now Lynn reminds them that the Eau Galle looked mean that day. "Storms?" the new bat boy asks. "Nope, bunch of boys in campers acting like the place was locals only," Lynn scoffs. "So Rafael and I took our little All-Americas tour to the river and just headed on up. When we found Lake Wabedo Raffy phoned to be sure the game's called off and we fished all night."

"Fish stories!" Billy spits across the dugout as he says it and notes that Pedraza is shaking off a lot of signs. Some game, if this is only his second pitch. Mack spots the delay from the bull pen and leans out from the bench to see if the manager wants his help. But Carl is motionless on the dugout step, just resting on his knee and staring like the others toward the field.

Lynn fills the gap as Costy fidgets and Carl stares. "Hey, these good folks at Wabedo felt bad we didn't get a walleye strike, so next day they send us further north." "Still raining?" Buddy asks and Lynn says sure, they decided to chance it and see how the Mississippi looked north of Reginald. "I hear you can step right across it, there," Carl turns around to say, surprising everyone that he's been listening, but Lynn protests to all of them: "No way, kids, all the way through Sainer it's still a good twenty-feet wide and faster than a demon." Carl turns back, remembering those long-distance calls from a half-day's drive away. "We rained out again, Skip?" What could he have told Kansas City if they'd called—a left-fielder and star shortstop were two days A.W.O.L., looking for a place they could straddle the Mississippi River?

The catcher goes back to one finger—fastball—and this time Costy nods okay. What's this, he can't read numbers? The catcher's flashed it to him twice before, but now he gets the message—this shrewd Dominican is confusing the batter, making him think all sorts of exotic pitches and locations, when in fact it's going to be the straight one down Main, okay!

Costy fingers the ball and leans back in his stretch. Billy glances over to check that Eddie's in position, but Eddie's not with it at all—he's mooning over toward the dugout where Carl's perched on the top step, trying to ignore the jockeys behind him. Billy wants to yell a "Hey, man!" but Costy's spooked enough from that first bad pitch. What on earth is Eddie up to? There's his little *niña*—the cute young shagger who's been flirting with him ever since his fence-hopper in batting practice nipped her ankle. She's in the first-row box over the dugout, where kids don't belong anyway and certainly not when they're shagging. "Hey man, *trouble*," Billy wants to yell, but he doesn't have the words and what a can of worms, what a crazy Latin mess to get into. Maybe one of the older Spanish players—Quinones if he comes back down from Chattanooga—can straighten Eddie out. Mason City, Iowa, sure isn't Panama, or anyplace else but Iowa for that matter.

"Quinones, my man Raf-a-el!" Lynn is musing. "Wanted me to play winter ball in Colombia, said we'd get to Venezuela, meet his wife and kids." "Yeah, but what about the river?" Buddy prompts, now obsessed himself. "How far up did you guys get, did you ever see it get, like, real small?" He wants an answer—every third day this story gets started and then Lynn is called in to pinch hit or reserve, or following some other action just gets bored with it and changes subjects.

Lynn doesn't answer, as he's joined Carl in puzzling over Pedraza's actions on the mound. Costy's dropped his arm and has stepped off the rubber, staring toward Jim Smith the catcher as if he's in a daze. Smitty has called to Carl and is shrugging his shoulders, asking if he should check with Costy on the mound. "Sanmarda!" Carl calls to his shortstop, "Sanmarda, *vete*"—one of the few Spanish words he knows, as he gestures Eddie over toward the pitcher. "Settle him down, hey?" "You bet!" Eddie thinks to himself as he trots in toward Costy.

"Mi amigo, mi compadre," Costy is thinking happily as Eddie joins him on the mound, with Billy and other infielders looking on suspiciously from their positions. But then Eddie greets him with the words Costy would use to summon a waiter or correct a servant, and his grin changes to a pucker, ready to spit. "What's the problem?" Costy says to break the tension, meaning it friendly enough but Eddie takes it to mean his own problem.

"I got no problems, man, it's you that's not pitching."

"I am too pitching, why don't you play shortstop like these Yankees pay you to?"

"I can't catch what they don't hit what you don't throw, baby!" Eddie says, again meaning it friendly, doing his best to put the funny words his teammates use into Spanish slang. But he's answered with a thick spray of tobacco juice across his uniform top.

¿"Niño? ¿Niño?" Costy is screaming. Eddie's looking down at his shirt, wondering what he's said, and is knocked clean off his feet by Costy's swift shove.

Costy is now bellowing insults and kicking at poor Eddie, who's struggling in the dust to find his feet. He's halfway up, finding unsure balance on the mound's steep slope, when Pedraza knees him in the chin and sends him head-over-heels toward the plate.

By this time Carl is out there, pinning Costy's arms from behind, while Jim blocks off Eddie, who's standing again but somewhat tipsy from the two quick blows. Both benches have emptied, but no one else is fighting—just the American players turning toward their Latin colleagues to ask what on earth is going on. "Shortstop called him a kid," the Angels' batter is telling the ump. "Down in the Dominican you'd say that to your own child, but for any other kid, not related, you know, it means brat, a dirty kid in the streets, you know." "No, I didn't know that," the umpire says, not really listening, as he wonders how to discipline this mess.

He walks toward Carl, who's released Costy on the mound. Not having the least idea what to say, he simply takes a schoolmarmish traffic-cop attitude and prepares to stare the manager down. "Don't look at me," Carl protests, "I don't understand these Latinos any better than you do." The ump is still silent. "Now don't go tossing anybody," Carl warns, anticipating an argument, "my boys didn't touch the other team, this is all my business, not yours." "Are they staying in?" the ump asks. Carl looks around to see that Eddie is still a bit woozy and bleeding from the mouth. "Shortstop's coming out," he decides, "pitcher stays in." The ump looks skeptical. "Hey, we played a doubleheader last night, I don't *have* anybody else!" Carl pleads, and the ump lets him off. But as he turns back to the plate he gives Carl a stern warning: "When I crew your game, *do not* play those bozos together, got me?"

As he passes the mound, Carl has three words for his pitcher. "Pedraza—hundred dollars!" He points as if to underscore, then stalks back to the bench. Costy looks about helplessly and settles on first baseman Andy Thompson, Spanish-speaking from home and college. Andy answers his mute question in clear, grammar-book language: "He's fined you one hundred dollars, Costy. Now behave!"

The players finally clear, but not until Lynn and the Angels' third baseman have finished up their chat. "Hear your showers are out, man," the infielder has said, and Lynn is giving him the whole rundown on how old Mack came running out naked through the clubhouse, scalded and steaming like a lobster. "Old Mack?" the Angel twists his head, "That's awesome! Bet he'll get it fixed, those old guys don't put up with none of this shabby A-ball stuff."

Lynn starts in on the great shower-leak story as the two teams brush past each other toward their dugouts. "We looked for it all last year, figured there had to be an absolute source, something real small-like, you know," he's telling the Angel as Buddy and the bench jockeys pass by.

"So where'd you find it?" the third baseman asks, as Buddy and the others stop to hear Lynn's answer.

"In the hot-water tap for the sink, you never would believe it!" Lynn explains as he slaps his rival with his glove and trots back to the bench.

Buddy is transfixed by wonder and disbelief. "Hey Skip," he calls as he approaches Carl, "Parson finally told us where's the source!"

"The source?" Carl asks, not following and not caring.

"Of the Mississippi, of the river!" Buddy exclaims. "It's in some kitchen sink, some leaky faucet!"

Carl just stares, writing off this senseless line to the general lunacy that has prevailed since Costy's first pitch. He's thrown a few tosses to get loose again, and Escobar's in at short. The ump pulls down his mask and calls for play, squatting behind the plate. Smitty signals a fastball and it comes in high, a mile out of the strike zone.